KT-465-902

6/9/23

WITHDRAWN

Get **more** out of libraries

Please return or renew this item by the last date shown.
You can renew online at www.hants.gov.uk/library
Or by phoning **0300 555 1387**

Hampshire
County Council

C015926846

THE SEPIA SIREN KILLER

Prior to World War II, black actors were restricted to minor roles in mainstream films — though there was a 'black' Hollywood that created films with all-black casts for exhibition to black audiences. When a cache of long-lost films is discovered by cinema researchers, the aged director Edward 'Speedy' MacReedy appears to reclaim his place in film history. But insurance investigator Hobart Lindsey and homicide officer Marvia Plum soon find themselves enmeshed in a frightening web of arson and murder with its roots deep in the tragic events of a past era . . .

RICHARD A. LUPOFF

THE SEPIA SIREN KILLER

Complete and Unabridged

LINFORD
Leicester

First published in Great Britain

First Linford Edition
published 2016

A catalogue record for this book is available
from the British Library.

ISBN 978–1–4448–2952–5

1

The corpse was still warm when Hobart Lindsey arrived. The fire engines were gone, the familiar yellow tapes were up, and someone had produced a couple of giant fans to blow the toxic fumes away. That way, everybody in town could get a little bit sick, instead of a few people getting very sick.

The Pacific Film Archive was in turmoil. Fire had broken out in a combination office/screening room where a graduate student was screening ancient footage on a similarly ancient Movieola. Now the student was dead and the room was scorched. Blobs of fire-retardant foam hung like tan soap suds from furniture and fixtures.

A Berkeley police officer stopped Lindsey before he could get past the yellow tapes. He showed his International Surety credentials. The officer remained adamant. Then a uniformed sergeant laid her hand on the officer's shoulder and said, 'It's okay, let him in.'

A fat man in a white shirt, a striped tie flying over his shoulder, seemed everywhere at once. He wrung his hands, ran his fingers through his hair, tried to talk to everyone in sight.

The police officer shrugged and motioned Lindsey into the chaotic scene. Lindsey said, 'Marvia. I was scanning KlameNet at the office and this thing came over. Talk about prompt!'

Sergeant Marvia Plum indicated the fat man. 'That's Tony Roland. He's in charge here. Soon as he found this out, he summoned the firefighters; soon as they found the body, they summoned us. He must have an emergency procedure that included calling the insurance people.'

The staff had cleared the Film Archive and its host institution, the University Art Museum. Students and workers and street people milled around outside the yellow tapes. One wild-eyed, bearded individual was waving his arms, making an impassioned speech.

Lindsey said, 'What happened? The computer flash didn't really tell me anything.' Before Marvia could answer, he peered around. 'I'm surprised Elmer Mueller isn't here. He's supposed to take the claim.'

A team of uniformed men, one in police blues, the other in firefighter's togs, brushed past. The policeman exchanged a few words with Marvia. Then she said to Lindsey, 'Young exchange student, Italian, doing her work. Somehow the fire broke out. Come on and have a look.'

Lindsey gagged.

'That's just the stink,' Marvia said. She took Lindsey by the hand and led him to the Movieola. The young woman slumped over it didn't look dead. 'This place is full of toxics. Most modern buildings are full of them. The furniture's the worst. Burn a chair and you get poison gas. Not to mention the film itself, in a place like this.'

Lindsey looked around. What the staff of the film archive hadn't coated with foam, the firefighters' hoses had drenched with water. 'It's a mess, but I don't see much actual fire damage.'

'There wasn't much. Just enough to

send up the gases that killed her.'

'You say she was an exchange student?' Lindsey was able to look at the young woman's face now. Dark hair, rich and lustrous, chopped short. Soft features, smooth olive skin. She had to be in her early twenties.

Tony Roland, the fat man, came careening by. Marvia stopped him. 'You'd better talk to Mr. Lindsey. He's from International Surety.'

Roland stuck out his hand and mumbled something polite. His eyes didn't look focused.

Lindsey handed him a business card and Roland looked at it briefly before stuffing it in his pocket. Lindsey asked, 'Who was she?' He indicated the body. He couldn't get used to seeing dead people, even after all his years in the insurance business.

'She worked for me. I mean, I was coordinating her project. She came from Italy. She spoke English, though. A lovely — a lovely — ' Big tears rolled down his face. He patted his pockets, obviously looking for a handkerchief. Lindsey found his own handkerchief and handed it to the man.

'Keep it,' Lindsey said.

Roland blew his nose then stuffed the handkerchief in his pocket. 'Thanks.'

'About the girl . . . '

'University of Bologna. Has her master's. Working on a doctorate.'

Lindsey had his pocket organizer and his gold International Surety pen in his hand. KlameNet and Elmer Mueller should really deal with this. Lindsey was part of SPUDS, Special Projects Unit/ Detached Service. Corporate troubleshooters. But Mueller was absent from the scene, probably in Emeryville looking after his real estate investments.

'What's her name?' Lindsey asked.

'Annabella Buonaventura.' Roland spelled it for Lindsey. 'Your company is our insurance carrier. I don't know if we're responsible. What if her family sue us? You'll pay for the damage, but will you stand by us if they sue?'

Lindsey frowned. 'That's up to Legal. Were you negligent? This is a modern building. Don't you have sprinklers?'

Roland pointed at the ceiling. It showed modern, minimalist, bare-pipes construction. There were fire-sprinklers overhead but no evidence that they had been activated.

Sergeant Marvia Plum called to the police-and-fire duo. They responded. 'What about the sprinklers?'

The police officer, another sergeant, said, 'We've checked them out. They should have gone. Take a look.' He hopped on a desk.

Marvia followed. She said, 'Come on, Bart.'

Grunting, he climbed onto the crowded desk. The sergeant pointed at the nearest sprinkler. 'See that? Putty. Somebody gimmicked the sprinklers so they wouldn't let go when the fire started. Could have been a lot worse.'

They clambered down. Lindsey said, 'That makes it murder. Even if it wasn't intentional, if it was caused by an arson fire then it's felony murder.'

Marvia said, 'That's why I'm here. Why are you here?'

'I.S. will pay, even if it was arson. I don't see contributory negligence. Any ideas who did it?'

Outside the archive's glass doors, most of the curiosity-seekers had gone on their way. The orator was still at it, preaching to an audience of three. One of them lost interest and wandered away. The orator cranked up his passion. The remaining two looked at each other and headed toward Telegraph Avenue, holding hands.

Lindsey jotted what notes he could. He managed to get Anthony Roland to stand still for a few minutes and talk about the damage. Lindsey said he'd talk to Elmer Mueller. Processing the claim was Mueller's job. International Surety would send out a contract estimator. The Film Archive could send in their own estimate on repair costs and other losses.

'I'll have to inventory the film,' said Roland. 'I don't know everything Annabella was working on. Some of our holdings are unique. How can we put a value on them?'

Lindsey tried to sound sympathetic. He'd dealt with rarities before, collectibles, irreplaceable treasures. No matter how hard it might be for people to put a price on a lost item, they always wound up taking the check. 'Everything should be described in your policy. There should be a value listed for each item.'

The coroner's squad arrived. They took photos and measurements and samples and the body and left.

Lindsey wanted to talk with Marvia, but this was obviously not the moment to talk with her about personal matters. He touched her hand and promised to call her.

2

You wouldn't call it a great party. Ms. Wilbur wore a dress to the office for the first time in Lindsey's recollection. A couple of women from the costume jewelry distributor across the hall had chipped in to buy her a corsage.

In fact, the party had a distinctly floral theme. Harden at Regional had sent a small display and Ms. Johanssen at National had sent a slightly larger one. The morning's *Oakland Tribune* was spread on a desk to protect valuable company property from any water that dripped from the flowers. Both displays bore friendly handwritten messages congratulating Ms. Wilbur on her retirement and wishing her great happiness in the future. And Elmer Mueller, the Walnut Creek branch manager, had sprung for sandwiches and punch.

It was all according to the International Surety Operations Manual. Lindsey ought to know that. He'd worked for International

Surety for his entire professional life. Lindsey had sat in the very chair Elmer Mueller now occupied before he'd strayed from the true path of the OpsMan. In the course of so doing, he had trod on a few sensitive toes and got himself kicked upstairs to the Special Projects Unit/Detached Service. If SPUDS was the graveyard of International Surety careers, then Desmond Richelieu, its chief, was the company's in-house undertaker. Desmond Richelieu sat in his tower office in Denver and sent out the word. *Demote. Suspend. Terminate.*

It was not a good thing to be invited to a meeting with Desmond Richelieu, yet Lindsey had survived several such. Maybe Richelieu considered him too small a gadfly to bother swatting. Or maybe he liked having somebody around who could break the rules when he felt that a higher good was involved. It was a funny way to do business, and no one had ever accused Richelieu of having a sense of humor.

Somehow, Lindsey had hung onto his job.

Conversation was desultory. Lindsey let his eye drift to the *Oakland Tribune* peeking out from under the flowers. The local news section was visible; it featured a photograph of a blocky, modernistic building and a headline about the fire at the Pacific Film Archive. Lindsey slid the page out from under the flowers and read the story. Most of it he knew. Less than twenty-four hours had passed, and the fire was jostling a dozen other stories for space. Another day and it would disappear.

But in Berkeley, the Anti-Imperialist Front for the Liberation of People's Park had issued a manifesto claiming responsibility for the fire and threatening 'More Deaths, More Destructin Until Justis Is Serve.' The Central Coordinator of the Front, one Dylan 'Che' Guevara, had appeared at police headquarters to demand that the Pacific Film Archive and its host institution, the University Art Museum, be converted into rent-free permanent residences for the poor, to be financed and maintained by the city.

Lindsey wondered if Guevara was the wild-eyed orator of the previous afternoon. But Guevara denied that the Front was responsible for the fire. 'We can spell better than that,' he said.

Anthony Roland, manager of research projects for the archive, condemned the attack as cowardly. 'Besides,' Roland was quoted as saying, 'the archive has nothing to do with People's Park. I was gassed in '68 and I'm all for the park. Why would they attack us?'

The body of the dead researcher would be returned to her family in Milan, Italy for burial. Condolences would be forwarded to the parents via the Italian consulate in San Francisco.

So Roland had calmed down enough to talk to a reporter. That was something.

Lindsey ran his eye over a few other stories. The most interesting from an insurance viewpoint was the latest in a series of industrial burglaries. The favorite target nowadays was computer components. Somebody had hit a warehouse in Fremont and driven away with a load of top-of-the-line processor chips worth half a million dollars. The loot was literally worth more than its weight in gold. There was no end to human ingenuity when it came to finding ways to make a crooked buck.

With a sigh, Lindsey slid the page back under the floral arrangement. One of Ms. Wilbur's friends from the jewelry distributor had brought a portable stereo and the music, something by Barry Manilow out of Neil Diamond, very nearly drowned out the timid tapping at the door.

A visitor's silhouette was visible against the frosted panel. Ms. Wilbur had been chatting with her female friends while Lindsey and Elmer Mueller, cordial enemies, maintained a stony silence. Lindsey moved first, relieved to have an excuse to escape from the loathsome Mueller.

For an instant Lindsey thought the visitor was a child delivering an envelope. His mind flashed to Whitey Benedict, a 1940s actor who'd made a career of delivering telegrams, flowers, and department store packages in scores of black-and-white movies.

The visitor was a wizened little man. He might once have stood five-six but now he looked a good six inches shorter. He wore a threadbare black suit, a frayed white dress shirt and a narrow black necktie. He held a business-size envelope in front of him, extended toward Lindsey.

He said, 'I want the Global National Guarantee Life Company.'

Lindsey said, 'I'm sorry, but this is International Surety.'

'I can read. I've been at the library for weeks. Ever since it happened.'

'I'm sorry, sir.' There was something in the man's eyes that held Lindsey's attention. They were almost as dark as his black, wrinkled skin, except for the milky pools of half-formed cataracts. Lindsey said, 'Can you see?'

'Well enough.'

'Please, come in,' Lindsey invited. 'Maybe we can help you. This is the International Surety Corporation. I've never heard of that company you said.'

The little man held the envelope so Lindsey could see the return address. There was a corporate logo in ink that might once have been a vivid green but was now a faded yellowish olive; the name of the company was spelled out in old-fashioned typography.

Lindsey tried to take the envelope but the little man clutched his end. Lindsey tilted his head and looked at the two-cent postage stamp and the faded cancellation mark. The letter had been mailed in Los Angeles, California on January 31, 1931.

Elmer Mueller came over. 'What's this all about?'

The little man started to ask his question again, but Mueller cut him off. 'No personal visitors at this office. We process claims here. You got personal business, take it up with your insurance agent.'

The man said, 'But, I couldn't find — '

Mueller grabbed the envelope. It came loose from the man's fingers. Mueller was turning the envelope over, eyeing it with casual curiosity. The man made a sound that was half a whimper and half a moan.

Lindsey angrily took Mueller's wrist in his fingers and dug into the veins. With his other hand he lifted the envelope and returned it to the little man. He said, 'You'd better keep this in your pocket.' He put his arm around the man's shoulders and guided him into the office.

He felt as light and as dry as an empty corn husk. Lindsey guided him to a leather couch that stood against the office wall. He asked the man if he'd like a drink or a snack and received the reply, 'Thank you, sir, I would.'

Lindsey watched the little man while he gathered a sandwich and a cup of punch for him. If Mueller moved on him again, Lindsey was prepared to tackle him. But Mueller only glowered.

The man took the paper plate gratefully, and picked up a sandwich and chewed it slowly. Lindsey wondered if he had any teeth. He took a sip of the punch, then looked at Lindsey and said, 'I trust there is no intoxicant in this?'

Lindsey smiled. 'No, sir.' He pulled over a computer chair and faced the old man. 'Now, sir, what was this about Global National, uh — '

'Guarantee Life,' the old man corrected him. 'I tried to locate the company through the pages of the telephone directory, but they were not listed. I called directory assistance but they were unable to assist me.' He spoke as if he had just enough

16

strength to move the air over his vocal cords. 'And then I thought I might learn something from the library. A very helpful young lady assisted me. And here I am.'

Lindsey said, 'You might have tried the State Insurance Commissioner in Sacramento.'

Elmer Mueller's rough voice said, 'Maybe he still ought to. He knows we don't take visitors here. You know it too. What, since you're a big shot out of Denver, you too good to follow the rules like the rest of us?'

Lindsey said, 'Elmer, I'm just trying to help this man.' He dropped his voice. 'Look at him. He must be ninety years old. What do you want to do?'

'I want to call Security and have the geezer gently but firmly removed from the premises. What if he dies in our office?'

A woman's hand separated Lindsey and Mueller. 'Break it up, boys.' Ms. Wilbur squatted in front of the old man. 'Are you all right, sir? What's your name?'

The old man peered at Ms. Wilbur. 'My name is Edward Joseph MacReedy.' He turned from Ms. Wilbur to address Lindsey again.

'The librarian suggested contacting the Insurance Commissioner, but there was no record in Sacramento of the Global National Guarantee Life Company.'

Ms. Wilbur said surprisingly, '*I* remember them.'

For once Lindsey and Mueller harmonized. 'You do?'

'You wouldn't recall old Mr. Woodstreet, who was here when I started. He retired thirty years ago. And he was an old man. Dead now, I'm sure. He used to talk about the old days. I mean the old days for *him*. The 1920s, '30s.'

Mueller said, 'Spare me, please. What's that got to do with this one?' He gestured toward the old man.

'Mr. Woodstreet used to talk about the Depression, about the companies that went belly up. International Surety wasn't International Surety then.'

Mueller said, 'Don't tell me *this* company was Global whatever, National Guarantee Life.'

'Not quite.' Ms. Wilbur took Mr. MacReedy's paper plate and cup from him and set them on a desk. The old man had dozed off and was wheezing gently in his sleep. She said, 'International Surety used to be just Surety Insurance. They took over half a dozen failing companies back in the '30s. The old Global National Guarantee got tangled up in two or three mergers and takeovers and finally disappeared into Surety Insurance.'

Mueller grunted. 'So you mean this is our policy?'

Ms. Wilbur said, 'I'm not sure. Maybe it's up to Legal. Mr. Woodstreet used to love to talk about Global National. He got a kick out of Global National Guarantee because it was such a tiny company. They used to sell life policies door to door. Send agents around to collect the premiums, fifty cents a week, twenty-five cents a week, even a nickel a week. They worked mostly in Negro neighborhoods. Pardon me, I grew up speaking the English language and I'm accustomed to speaking it the way I learned.'

Mueller said, 'So you think this fossil has a claim on us? Let's see what he's got.' He reached toward MacReedy's jacket, but before he got any further Ms.

Wilbur had gently opened the old man's jacket and extracted the envelope.

She said, 'I'll take a look at this.'

Mueller said, 'No you won't. You're retired. You have no job here any more.'

'I still work here for — ' She paused and turned to look at the digital clock. ' — another hour and a half. I might as well stay useful.'

She made her way to her desk and clicked away at the computer keyboard, Lindsey and Mueller standing behind her. Ms. Wilbur turned around, grinning at them. She still held Mr. MacReedy's envelope, its contents now extracted and carefully unfolded along age-yellowed crease lines. 'There it is, boys. A perfect match.'

Lindsey leaned forward, comparing the glowing letters on the computer screen with the faded writing on the pages. The letters on the screen were green. The ink on the policy had long since turned to brown.

Ms. Wilbur said, 'Look. Face amount is the same on the policy and the screen. It's a joint policy, made out to Edward Joseph MacReedy and Nola Elizabeth Rownes

MacReedy. Upon death of either party, the surviving party is to receive full payment of benefits. Of course, look here.' She pointed to the screen. 'Policy was all paid off by 1934. It's a whole life policy. Been drawing compound interest ever since. Look here, the cash surrender value exceeded the face value by '36. They should have paid it out back then, but this doesn't show that they did. Shows the policy still in force.'

'Huh. What's it worth now?' Lindsey asked.

Ms. Wilbur clicked away until the computer screen showed a new figure. 'Based on an average annual interest rate of four-point-five percent, International Surety owes Mr. MacReedy $400.19.'

Mueller growled, 'For God's sake, pay the old guy his money and get him out of here. Give him the twenty-five bucks out of petty cash. Or cut him a check for four hundred and nineteen lousy cents. How the hell they could play around like that beats me.'

Lindsey said, 'Money went a lot further during the Depression. Even so, it's an awfully small policy.' He studied the papers in Ms. Wilbur's hand. 'I mean, a $25 whole life insurance policy.'

Ms. Wilbur said, 'It's too bad you never knew Mr. Woodstreet. He'd tell you that back in the Depression you could hold a first-class funeral for $25. That's what they took the policies for, you know. People had a hard, sad life. A good send-off to the other side was important. Some of the policies they issued were for even less than that.'

Mueller said, 'Well, we can put it in through KlameNet. If National doesn't issue a check, what the hell, we can take it out of the coffee money. You'll chip in, won't you, Lindsey?'

Lindsey said, 'You're getting too far ahead. There's something odd about this.'

Mueller rocked back on his heels and exhaled. 'Don't tell me you want to pull this one, put it into SPUDS.'

'I don't know.'

'Sheesh, I don't see how this company stays in business. Hire a flake like you, turn you loose on every kind of fruitcake case you want to play with. You're like a baby. Anything shiny, anything different, it grabs your attention.'

Lindsey said, 'Now, Elmer, that isn't fair. I've saved the company a lot of money on those odd cases — something like three quarters of a million dollars.'

'Yeah. And that B-17 that disappeared from the airport, I suppose you covered yourself with glory on that one, too.'

'That was a tragic case. And it did cost the company, I'll admit that. But when there's a legitimate claim, it's our duty to pay.'

Mueller exhaled. 'Exactly my point.' He patted Lindsey on the shoulder. 'We owe the little man $25. If he didn't cash in his policy when it matured, that's his problem. We don't owe him four hundred. Let's pay the twenty-five and get on with our business. We have no reason to poke around in some ancient policy.' He reached for his wallet. 'Hell, if nobody else will pay, I'll personally pony up the $25.'

Lindsey heard a dry, rustling sound from behind him. He turned. Mr. MacReedy was struggling to stand up, feeling his pockets frantically. 'My papers,' he said, 'where are my papers?'

Ms. Wilbur hurried to him and helped him stand. She said, 'Here's everything, Mr. MacReedy. Not to worry. We were just checking our computer records against your policy. Everything seems to be in order.'

She folded the policy and stuffed it back into the old envelope, then helped Mr. MacReedy place the envelope carefully in his inside jacket pocket.

Mueller said, 'You're placing your claim based on that life policy, Mr. MacReedy?'

MacReedy nodded. He appeared to be afraid of Mueller.

Mueller said, 'We'll need a death certificate for the insured and a birth certificate or other identification proving that you are the legal beneficiary of the policy.'

MacReedy said, 'My wife died three weeks ago last Tuesday. She was buried three days later.'

Ms. Wilbur said, 'Who paid for the funeral, Mr. MacReedy? I thought that was what you needed this money for.'

'No, the center paid for the funeral. We lived together at the Paul Robeson

Benevolent Retirement Center for the past twenty years, since our last child died. We had grandchildren, but they've all gone on to lives of their own. They don't know us anymore. They lost track of us. But the center buries its members.'

Mueller said, 'Do you have the death certificate?'

'It's in my room at the center. We had two rooms, but after my wife died I had to give up one of the rooms. It's a rule.'

Lindsey looked around. Ms. Wilbur's friends from the costume jewelry firm had made their exit. Ms. Wilbur hovered behind Mueller, who said, 'You'll have to file the death certificate and your own ID and then we can pay the claim. Do you understand that?'

'Yes.'

'How did you come out here, Mr. MacReedy?' Ms. Wilbur asked. 'I know the Robeson Memorial. My house is in north Oakland. It's no trouble to swing through Berkeley on my way home.'

MacReedy lifted his head proudly. 'I traveled here by the rapid transit train. I use it regularly.'

'Well, I'm leaving here in just a few minutes.' She gathered the two floral displays. 'I'll be happy to give you a ride home, Mr. MacReedy. And I'll be happy to see these beautiful flowers at the center. I don't need them in my house.'

'That's very kind of you. What did you say your name was?'

'You may call me Mathilde.'

MacReedy could walk unassisted, but Lindsey used the excuse of helping the old man to the garage. It got him out of Elmer Mueller's presence. He could hardly believe that Ms. Wilbur was retired. She was his friend, had taught him the ropes of International Surety, had alerted him to more than one case of corporate back-stabbing. Now Mueller would bring in an office manager of his own choosing. Lindsey wasn't formally assigned to the Walnut Creek office any longer; he just got desk space and computer support there. SPUDS was autonomous within the company and he could rent an office of his own if he chose. It was just him and Ducky Richelieu; he didn't answer to Mueller or to Harden or even to Ms. Johanssen anymore.

Maybe he'd rent an unobtrusive space somewhere, make it his secret headquarters, keep a set of tights in the closet, rush out to solve cases like a cartoon superhero. Insurance Man. Or maybe Captain Claims. Huh, that had a ring to it. Hobart Lindsey, Captain Claims. He smiled.

But how could he handle it without Ms. Wilbur? He watched her Toyota pull out of the garage, Mr. MacReedy's tiny form silhouetted in the passenger seat. Then he climbed into his Hyundai and followed the Toyota into the street. He stayed with the Toyota as far as the freeway on-ramp, then continued past it and headed home.

Mother had got there ahead of him. She looked tired from her day's work, too tired even to change from her office clothes. But she had tied her apron over them and was making dinner for herself and him anyway. It was her week to cook and she wasn't going to let him take over. He put his arm around her shoulders and kissed her cheek.

'You have a message on the answering machine,' she said. 'I played it back; I thought it might be for me. But it was for you. A woman named Aurora.'

SPUDS business, thought Lindsey. Aurora Delano had been in his training class in Denver, then been assigned to the New Orleans office. She'd worked with him on a case in Louisiana. If it wasn't a screamer — he checked the tape, and it wasn't — he'd call her back in the morning.

After dinner they were just settling into the living room when the phone burbled. The first words Lindsey heard were, 'You'd better get over here, Bart.'

He recognized Ms. Wilbur's voice. 'Over where?'

'Over to the Robeson Center. You know it? Near the old Deaf School in Berkeley?'

'I can find it. Is it Mr. MacReedy?'

'You're so smart.'

Lindsey rubbed his forehead. 'Wait a minute. You're retired.'

She said, 'Bart, get your little hiney over here. I don't want Mueller to get his hands on this.'

★ ★ ★

Gravel crunched beneath the Hyundai's tires as Lindsey pulled into the parking lot in front of a gothic building. Judging by its looks, the Robeson Center had been constructed in the 1880s and had withstood the storms, fires and earthquakes of a century and more.

The cold air hit Lindsey as he climbed from his car. The contrast with the car's cozy warmth shocked him awake. That, and the fire engine that stood in front of the Robeson Center, a lurid warning light revolving on its cab. The crew of firefighters must be somewhere else, because only one person had stayed with the heavy truck.

3

Whatever Ms. Wilbur didn't want Elmer Mueller to get his hands on, it didn't make the broadcast news. Lindsey kept the car radio tuned to an all-news station on his way from Walnut Creek to Berkeley. Reactions to the Berkeley museum fire had degenerated into the usual exchange of name-calling between University of California officials and People's Park advocates. The People's Park faction charged that the Anti-Imperialist Front was a phony organization set up by the university, and that the fire had been set by the UC Police Force to embarrass the legitimate claimants to the land. After that came something about the Coast Guard and the Immigration and Naturalization Service stopping a Chinese freighter full of illegal immigrants.

Lindsey jogged past Ms. Wilbur's Toyota, a Berkeley fire chief's car and a police cruiser. He climbed the front steps, crossed the portico and pushed open heavy doors. They were stained a dark mahogany, with large cut-glass ovals in each. Inside the Robeson Center the air was dry and thin. The shabby decor looked as if it had been patterned after a hotel in a Depression-era film. A dark-skinned man in a suit and tie stood behind a reception counter. A rectangular badge identified him as Oliver Hendry.

Lindsey asked for Ms. Wilbur.

Hendry smiled a desk-clerk smile. 'You mean the lady who came to see Mr. MacReedy? She's with him in the coffee lounge.' He tipped his head, indicating a doorway that opened off the lobby.

Lindsey found Ms. Wilbur and Mr. MacReedy sitting at a Formica-topped table. There were cups of coffee in front of them, obviously untouched. Ms. Wilbur spotted Lindsey and gestured him to the table. Without preamble, she said, 'Somebody tried to burn out Mr. MacReedy.'

'When?'

'This afternoon. At least whoever did it isn't a killer. He waited for Mr. MacReedy to leave. He must have done it while Mr. MacReedy was with us in Walnut Creek.'

Lindsey looked at the old man. He lifted his coffee cup to his lips and then lowered it to its saucer again, its contents untouched.

'They tried to put it out with fire extinguishers. Then they called 911 and the fire truck got here in a couple of minutes and doused the flames. Didn't seem to do much real harm, except burn up Mr. MacReedy's possessions.'

'How can you be so sure it was arson?' Lindsey had pulled a chair from the next table. 'Maybe it was just an accident. Somebody smoking or starting a fire in the fireplace or using a heater.'

Ms. Wilbur shook her head. 'The investigators are here already. A fire lieutenant, Vince D'Onofrio, and a police arson squad sergeant, Olaf Stromback.'

Lindsey pulled out his pocket organizer and jotted down the names. 'They still here? I saw their cars outside.'

'They're in Mr. MacReedy's room. Come on, you want to see this.' She patted Mr. MacReedy's shoulder. 'You'll be all right here. Mr. Hendry can see you. He'll get you anything you need.'

Mr. MacReedy lifted milky eyes. 'I don't need anything, but thank you all the same.' He lifted the coffee cup to his lips once more, then lowered it.

The little man's room was at the end of a ground-floor corridor. Lindsey could detect the smell of fresh ashes and cold watered embers before he got there. The door frame showed a few areas of charring, and smoke had discolored the ceiling just outside the door, but those were the only signs of fire.

Inside the room everything was different. The air stank. The walls and ceiling were black. The single bed had been badly burned, large sections of water-soaked black showing on the mattress and pillow. An old wooden dresser, a sofa, a ladder-backed chair and a four-drawer filing cabinet were all wrecked, all beyond hope of repair. Worst of all were the remains of a couple of corrugated cardboard file boxes, which were barely recognizable. There was no fireplace, no visible space heater, not even a television set to start the fire.

So much for Ms. MacReedy's death certificate and Mr. MacReedy's claim. Well, he could get a duplicate death certificate easily enough.

D'Onofrio and Stromback were talking in undertones when Lindsey and Ms. Wilbur arrived. Lindsey could tell them apart by their uniforms. They'd brought in a small, folding metal ladder and set it up. D'Onofrio had laid a notebook on one of the rungs. He was leaning on the ladder with one elbow. He said, 'Who's this?'

Lindsey handed International Surety business cards to both men. 'Insurance,' he said. D'Onofrio and Stromback both looked at the cards, then slipped them into their pockets.

Lindsey said, 'Ms. Wilbur says it was arson but I want to know what you think.'

Stromback said, 'No question. See these marks?' He pointed to some black smudges near the doorway. 'Look at the feathering. Somebody threw an accelerant in here and tossed a match in after it. Even found the match. Must have done a good job — looks as if he only needed the one.' He pulled an evidence bag out of his pocket and showed it to Lindsey. The cellophane baggie contained an ordinary paper match. A cardboard information tag identified the location and circumstances of the great discovery, and carried Stromback's scrawling signature. Fat chance of ever discovering the origins of a charred match.

D'Onofrio said, 'You smell that? You smell that stuff?'

Lindsey said he did.

'It's gasoline. Perpetrator soaked the bed, the filing cabinet there, these cardboard boxes. Then he laid a trail back to the door. Then he threw in a final shot of the stuff, tossed in a match, and closed the door behind him.'

'Must have wanted the fire to do its job before anybody even knew about it.' That was Stromback. 'Would have been a lot worse if he'd left the door open, or if he'd thrown something through the window on his way out. Could have got a nice cross-draft. Really made a nice fire. As it was, the oxygen got depleted pretty fast.

Didn't save this room but it saved the building.'

Lindsey frowned. 'We're near the university, aren't we? Do you think this was connected to that fire at the art museum?'

D'Onofrio turned his face to the ceiling. 'I don't know about politics. They're all crazy, for my two cents. But I saw the report on that fire. Didn't look like this one. Don't go seeing patterns just because there were two fires.' He had a green pen in his hand and pointed it at a fire sprinkler.

Lindsey hadn't even noticed them before this. 'How come the sprinklers didn't open and douse the fire?'

'See for yourself.' D'Onofrio took Lindsey by the elbow and guided him to the folding ladder. Lindsey climbed a couple of rungs. Near the ceiling the stench of gasoline and burned paper and fabric was stronger. 'Look at that sprinkler.'

Lindsey spotted it at once. 'Somebody plugged it.' He craned his neck for a better look. 'May I touch it?'

Stromback yelped, 'Don't! That's evidence. Mustn't touch.'

'Okay.' Lindsey climbed another rung.

He was just inches from the sprinkler. 'Looks like some kind of fast-drying putty. He climbed up here and plugged the sprinkler? Look, there are two of these in this room.'

'Got 'em both.'

'Was this ladder here?'

Stromback said, 'Nope. Borrowed it from housekeeping. Whoever set the fire was very tall — or more likely he dragged something under each sprinkler when he plugged it. Maybe the bed.'

'In other words, it could be anybody.'

Stromback looked up at Lindsey. 'We'll figure it out. We'll get him.'

Lindsey climbed back to floor level. 'I hope you do. The sprinklers at the museum were plugged, too.'

'Very observant.' Stromback grinned.

'Then there is a pattern, isn't there?' Lindsey pursued.

'Fair enough. I wouldn't call that conclusive, but we'll analyze the putty and see if it's the same. If it is, that could mean a lot. Do you carry the fire insurance on this building, Mister, ah . . . ' Stromback fished the business card from his pocket and read it. 'Cost a couple grand to fix this room up, but nobody's going to touch it 'til my gang gets in and takes photos and samples. Including the putty in the sprinklers. But what about my question, Mr. Lindsey?'

'No, I'm not here about the fire. Mr. MacReedy's wife died recently and my company is processing a death benefit in the case.'

'Then what's your interest in the fire?'

Ms. Wilbur had stayed outside in the hallway, breathing cleaner air. Through the open doorway she said, 'That depends on the reason for the arson, don't you think, Sergeant Stromback?'

Stromback rubbed the back of his neck. 'Little bit hard to follow you, Miz, ah . . . ' He fumbled in his pocket and brought out another card. He must have received this one before Lindsey arrived at the Robeson Center. 'Ms. Wilbur. If, let me see . . . ' He consulted the card again. 'If International Surety doesn't have to pay for the fire damage, why do they care about this at all?'

Ms. Wilbur said, 'Mr. MacReedy was in

Walnut Creek visiting our office when the arsonist struck. Did the criminal simply wait until Mr. MacReedy was out of the center, or was there some connection with International Surety? Do you think he might come after us next?' She shot a glance at Lindsey. He didn't give her away.

'You'd better alert Walnut Creek PD, Olaf,' D'Onofrio put in. 'Ms. Wilbur might have something there, and if our bozo turns up with his faithful Zippo they want to be ready for him.'

With a nod, Stromback ushered Lindsey from the room. When the room was cleared, Stromback sealed the door and hung a yellow plastic tape across it. 'My gang should be here any minute. Meanwhile, want to talk to that fellow at the reception desk.'

D'Onofrio and Stromback, Lindsey and Ms. Wilbur traipsed back to the lobby. Lindsey caught a glance of Mr. MacReedy still sitting with his permanent cup of coffee. It must be ice cold by now.

Stromback stood questioning Oliver Hendry. Lindsey studied the desk clerk.

At first glance he had appeared brisk and natty. Now, Lindsey realized, a layer of fatigue lay draped on the man. Hendry spoke and gestured. Lindsey couldn't make out his words, but the meaning was clear. People came and went at the Robeson Center. They were understaffed and overworked, and why would anybody want to sneak in here, where the residents were all borderline charity cases? What was there to steal?

Moving together, Lindsey and Ms. Wilbur sat with Mr. MacReedy. Ms. Wilbur asked, 'Did the officers question you, Mr. MacReedy?' He nodded. 'Do you have any idea why anyone would want to burn up your room?' He shook his head sadly, and she put her hand on his. 'Will the center give you another room? Will you be all right? Do you have any money or belongings anywhere?'

'You know, we were together for sixty years,' the old man said.

Ms. Wilbur stroked his hand. He turned his opaque gaze on her and said, 'I was much older than my wife. I never thought I would have to bury her. I used to say, 'Don't mourn when I die. You'll have many years to live; don't waste them in mourning.' I didn't think she would die first. She used to get angry with me and say, 'Don't you dare talk about dying. Don't you dare die on me.' She could be mean, yes. But no one told me not to mourn. No one warned me.'

Lindsey saw Lt. D'Onofrio leave Hendry at the desk and head for the exit. Sgt. Stromback strode away from the desk and approached Lindsey and the others. He said, 'My gang are here. They'll take care of the evidence. Then, ah, Hendry there says he'll have housekeeping clean up the mess in Mister, uh, Mr. MacReedy's room. And he says he'll have another room for Mr. MacReedy to use. I called McKinley, and they're going to send a patrolman out to stay here overnight in case the bozo comes back, which he won't. And, oh yeah, Mr. Lindsey — I called Walnut Creek PD, and they're going to keep an eye on your house and your office. Got anything out there the bozo might want, do you think?'

'I don't think so,' Lindsey replied.

Stromback turned to MacReedy. 'You'll be all right, sir. Really sorry for all of this. Really. You'll be all right.' He shook the old man's hand and walked a few paces away. 'You call me if you need me. Any of you.' He came back and handed them each a card. Then he left.

4

The voice on Lindsey's telephone when he picked it up was Ms. Wilbur's. 'Now that you don't have to punch a clock anymore, what time do you roll out, Hobart?'

He rubbed his eyes and blinked at the clock. 'What's the matter? Ms. Wilbur, aren't you retired?'

'Sure I'm retired. How's your own calendar, Hobart?'

'A ton of routine stuff. Why?'

'I'm at the Robeson Center. I'm still not satisfied with Mr. MacReedy's situation.'

'KlameNet can handle it. You know that Mueller's full of bullstuff.'

'Bullstuff, hey? I thought you were going to say a naughty word for once.'

Lindsey had his feet in his slippers. 'What are you doing at the center? Is MacReedy all right?'

'I think you ought to come over to

43

Berkeley again. We'll talk about it when you get here.' She waited for his grunt of assent, then broke the connection.

He drank coffee and ate toast with Mother, who had already been up. After breakfast he dropped her at the bus stop, then drove back to Berkeley. It was definitely an advantage, having the freedom that went with his assignment to SPUDS, but at the same time it frequently left him at loose ends. Was he earning his salary? Was he contributing to the company? Was Desmond Richelieu watching, ready to pounce at Lindsey's first misstep?

The commuter traffic was heavy. The news on the car radio was dominated by reports of an earthquake in Japan and a massacre in the Balkans. At length the station switched to a syndicated Hollywood update. Arturo Madrid, one-time matinee idol and latter-day character actor, was to receive a lifetime achievement award on the occasion of his eighty-fifth birthday and sixty-fifth anniversary in films. The ceremony would be carried live on cable and excerpted for network television.

Local news coverage was slim, consisting mainly of a sidebar to the Arturo Madrid story, playing up an Oakland angle. Surprisingly for Hollywood, the powers-that-be had decided to hold the climactic ceremonies of the Madrid honors at the Oakland Paramount. Local politicians were falling over each other to get onto the program with the great actor. Other than that, there was little out of the ordinary. Not a word about the fire at the Robeson Center.

The morning was bright and in it the Robeson Center looked far better than it had the previous evening. For the first time Lindsey saw a carved oval plaque mounted above the main entrance. It was shaped like a giant cameo brooch. The face was heavy-boned, the lips broad, the nose flat. It was Paul Robeson, all right. He turned up occasionally on TV in movies made in the 1930s.

Ms. Wilbur and Mr. MacReedy were sitting beneath a Corinthian pillar on a round, cushioned seat. Ms. Wilbur wore a casual outfit. Her gray hair was pinned up. Mr. MacReedy wore a threadbare blue suit and a black tie, probably the same ones he'd worn the day before. Apparently he'd been able to borrow a fresh shirt, anyway.

Today a woman stood behind the reception desk. She sported a rectangular badge that identified her as LaVonda Hendry. Lindsey wondered if she and Oliver ever saw each other except when changing shifts.

A Berkeley police officer nodded to Lindsey. Well, police HQ on McKinley Avenue had taken Sgt. Stromback seriously, at least.

Ms. Wilbur stood up and drew Lindsey out of earshot of the others. 'A little test, Bart. Why would somebody wait for Mr. MacReedy to leave, then burn out his room? Five points for the correct answer.'

'He has an enemy?'

Ms. Wilbur looked exasperated. 'Two points for that. But why wait for him to leave? If somebody wanted to harm him, wouldn't it make more sense to start the fire when he was in the room?'

'He would have called for help. He

would have seen the arsonist. And maybe whoever it was didn't have that much against him, didn't want to risk his death in the fire. He just wanted to destroy MacReedy's property.'

'You think there was some particular property the arsonist wanted to destroy?'

'I wouldn't know.'

'Suppose Mr. MacReedy had something, or the arsonist *thought* he had something, that the arsonist wanted destroyed. He might have stolen the . . . whatever, and destroyed it at his leisure. But then the theft would maybe have been detected. And that would draw attention to the object of the robbery — exactly what the criminal wanted to avoid. Do you follow me?'

Lindsey frowned. 'I follow you right into some nutty old movie. You ever see the Hildegarde Withers pictures? *The Penguin Pool Murder, Murder on a Honeymoon . . .*'

'You're being nasty.'

'Look, Ms. Wilbur, I thought you were going to stay home and play housewife once you retired from International Surety. You never said you were going to become a sleuth.'

47

'I'm not. I'm just concerned about Mr. MacReedy and I'm concerned about this fire.'

'There are professionals working on the case. There's a cop right over there,' Lindsey said.

'I talked to him.'

'And what did he tell you? Were the arson investigators here? Don't you trust Sergeant Stromback?'

'I'm sure that Sergeant Stromback is doing a fine job, Bart. In fact, the officer didn't want to tell me anything, but I managed to worm a couple of facts out of him. They found some scrapes in the lower hallway and several spots where the arsonist apparently spilled gasoline. That must be how he got in and out of the building, and he could have sent the whole place up in flames if he'd wanted to.'

'Good that he didn't.'

'Don't you see, that proves he *targeted* Mr. MacReedy.'

Lindsey turned back toward MacReedy. The old man sat patiently on the round sofa, his hands folded in his lap. A few other residents drifted through the lobby.

They were all old and they were all black. From time to time an ancient individual would stop and exchange a few words with MacReedy. They all touched him, all either shook his hand or kissed him on his cheek. He acknowledged each with a nod.

Lindsey said, 'MacReedy looks okay. Let's take a walk and talk about this thing.'

The heavy doors swung shut behind them. They descended the old steps from the portico. A wheelchair ramp had been added beside the steps. Canyon Road ran through the hills between the University of California campus and the old deaf and blind school, now taken over by the university as a conference center. Surely UC would love to pick up the strip of land that separated the two campuses. If the Anti-Imperialist Front was a catspaw of university schemers, and if the league had started the fire at the art museum, it might be equally interested in getting the Robeson Center to close down and make way for the university's land acquisition program.

Lindsey and Ms. Wilbur were on the

Robeson Center's unkempt lawn. Lindsey said, 'Look, Ms. Wilbur — '

'You may call me Mathilde.'

'Mathilde, do you have anything solid to go on? Did Mr. MacReedy tell you anything you can use to figure this out? Because if not, I think the police are going to send you packing. You and me both. Why are we playing cops and robbers? Or cops and arsonists?'

'Because Mr. Hendry told me something that your Sgt. Stromback was apparently too dense to think of, so he didn't even ask.'

'All right,' Lindsey sighed, 'what did you find out?'

'Mr. Hendry told me that there are storage rooms under the Robeson Center. The building was originally a mansion. It was built as a *pied à terre* by a millionaire vintner from Sonoma County. There are huge cellars dug into the rock, where the owner kept his private stock.'

'Which of course is long gone.'

'Of course. Once the old guy died, his heirs couldn't wait to sell off his wine collection and invest in something more lucrative.'

'And?'

'And the Robeson people — they've operated the building as a retirement home for forty years. They divided the main cellar into storage areas. There are dividers, chain-link fences, and locks. Every resident has the use of a storage room. It's too grim down there to use the cellar for anything else, and they don't have the money to spruce it up. So they store their belongings down there to keep from getting the sleeping rooms too cluttered.'

'Swell,' Lindsey said. 'Good detective work. But I still don't see where you're going with it.'

'Hobart, how are you ever going to get along without me? Whatever the arsonist wanted to destroy — maybe he didn't get it. Maybe it's in Mr. MacReedy's storage area in the cellar. And if the arsonist knows about the cellar — if that's how he got in and out, of course he must know — he's likely to *come back*. In any case, we need to get in there and find the thing first.'

Lindsey grimaced.

Mathilde Wilbur said, 'Besides, have you noticed that Mr. MacReedy looks a little bit familiar?'

'No.'

'And I thought you were such a movie maven! There was a TV feature about MacReedy on the evening news a few months ago. He's a retired movie director, and his wife was once a movie star. She was called the Sepia Siren. Made movies in the 1930s and '40s. Some reporter discovered they were still around and they did a nice little story on them for the local station.'

Lindsey shook his head. 'I missed that one. If it was just on the local news, it must have run while I was in Denver talking to Richelieu.'

'Oh yes, dear Ducky Richelieu. Well, it was a cute story. I recognized Mr. MacReedy. Must have been just a few weeks before poor Mrs. MacReedy died. So sad.' She squared her shoulders. 'Well, to business. We still have those storage lockers to investigate.'

'You want to bypass the police and go searching in this cellar, right? For something we don't know we're looking for?'

'That is correct.'

'Well, frankly, I think this is absolutely insane. Not to mention dangerous.'

'All right. I am still going down there and have a look-see.'

Lindsey ground his teeth.

★   ★   ★

MacReedy had a key to his personal storage area in the cellar. They led him away from his place on the circular couch and the friends who still came by to offer condolences. The Berkeley police officer had apparently taken a moment's leave for a pit stop, and Lindsey didn't want to get into an extended dialog with him.

The cellar was reached by a staircase in the back of the Robeson Center. Lindsey fumbled for a light switch. The temperature dropped with each step as they descended into the old, carved rock. The only lights were dim incandescent bulbs. If Lindsey had had more notice he would have brought some flashlights.

MacReedy's storage area was roughly fifty feet from the foot of the staircase. The little man handed his key to Lindsey, and Lindsey turned the key in a surprisingly heavy padlock. If a thief wanted to break into the storage room, he would do better to bring a pair of heavy wire-cutters and clip the metal links themselves.

The room contained two more filing cabinets like the one that had been destroyed in MacReedy's room upstairs. There was a trunk and a standing wardrobe. Lindsey ran his hand down the side of one of the cabinets. Beneath a thick layer of dust, the burnished wood felt like silk. He'd seen reproductions of old wooden filing cabinets selling for hundreds of dollars. These originals would be worth a fortune to an antique dealer. The wardrobe might bring even more.

He turned to MacReedy. 'What's in these?'

MacReedy hesitated. 'It's been so long,' he said at last. 'I haven't been down here since — I think, since we moved into the center. Since Lola Mae and I . . . '

Lindsey examined the filing cabinets, the wardrobe and the trunk. The cabinets were secured with locking rods, the locking rods with padlocks. But these, unlike the lock to the room, were combination locks. And the trunk was secured by straps and latches; they could be opened, but not without a struggle.

But the wardrobe had no lock. He decided to tackle that first and asked MacReedy if it was all right to open it. Again, MacReedy stood silently before answering. It was as if the old man slipped away into the past each time he was left to himself.

'Surely,' MacReedy said. 'I would like to look at the old things once again, myself.'

Lindsey worked the wardrobe's ornate cast metal handles. The tarnished handles were stiff, but they yielded to pressure. The wardrobe's hinges were equally stiff, but they must have been oiled long ago, and with enough pressure they worked silently.

Inside the wardrobe were clothes that Lindsey hadn't seen except as costumes in period pictures. On one side were rigid-looking men's suits, an ancient broad-brimmed fedora, a heavy bowler hat, even an ivory-headed ebony walking stick. On the other, women's clothing: flapper dresses, cloche hats, beaded purses.

Ms. Wilbur said, 'But this is wonderful.'

Then the lights flicked out.

Lindsey thought, *I've really fallen into a movie.*

He heard slow footsteps approaching.

Lionel Atwill. Dwight Frye. Conrad Veidt.

He heard fumbling, brushing, scraping noises from both sides. A light skittered across the room. He could see Ms. Wilbur swinging a beam in circles. She'd brought a flashlight in her purse. He thought, *Why didn't I think to ask her?*

Ms. Wilbur's light glinted off metal. Mr. MacReedy, all ninety years and ninety pounds of him, stood *en garde*. The metal was a thin, graceful blade, blue-black and deadly. The walking stick was a sword-cane. Whatever was coming for them, Mr. MacReedy was ready.

Ms. Wilbur swung her light away from

MacReedy. She pointed through the cage-like room divider. The light flashed across a face. Lindsey caught a glimpse of startled eyes. The suggestion of a wispy mustache. And something odd about the top of the head, as if the intruder was wearing a small hat cocked over one ear.

Then a second thin beam of light reflected from dust motes. Someone trotted away. Soft-soled shoes shushed up the staircase. A door slammed.

5

Officer Mike Ng ('Pronounce it Eng, that's all, like there's an invisible *E* on the front') seemed to control his anger with a major act of will. 'Sir,' he said, 'and ma'am, what you did was very dangerous. Very irresponsible. I'm here to protect Mr. MacReedy. You thought it was clever to spirit him away when I was called away for a moment. And then you come scampering back like scared children.'

Lindsey said, 'We were only looking at some things.' He felt like a schoolboy called into the principal's office.

Ms. Wilbur said, 'Never mind that, Officer. There was a prowler down there in the cellar. He doused the lights down there and he was coming for us. It was just lucky that I had a flashlight and that Mr. MacReedy had a weapon. Who knows what might have happened if we hadn't turned the tables.'

Ng was still short of breath from trying

to chase down the intruder. The fugitive had got out the back exit of the Robeson Center, setting off an alarm as he went. From there he had proceeded on foot. There was no trail to follow, not in this environment. If he headed west, toward the bay, he had reached Telegraph Avenue by now and blended with the street people there. Or stopped first at People's Park and disappeared among the homeless crazies, the drug dealers and common thugs who had driven out the flower children of an earlier age.

Mike Ng led them into the coffee lounge. Lindsey felt aged eyes tracking them across the lobby. In the lounge they took a table. Ng took out his notebook and said, 'All right, he's gone. We can't seal off the rear of the center, that's a fire regulation. I've called in and they're going to assign a second officer.'

'For how long?' Lindsey asked.

Ng shrugged. 'You know we're short of personnel. It's all the budget. Mr. MacReedy, is there anyplace else you could go and feel safe? Relatives, maybe?'

'I have nowhere else,' the little man

replied. 'No one else. I had Lola Mae and the center. Now I have only the center.'

Ng nodded. 'I suppose we could take you into protective custody, but I don't think that would be such a great idea.'

Mathilde Wilbur shook her head. 'Not at his age, Mr. Ng. That would be a very bad idea.'

Ng said, 'Now, let's go over this once more.' After they described the contents of the wardrobe in the cellar, he asked MacReedy what was in the trunk and the filing cabinets.

'Just souvenirs. The wardrobe held our personal clothing. The trunk contained a few costumes and props. The filing cabinets are old records, scripts, and stills. I used to be in movies, but that was long ago. Lola and I had been retired for many years.'

'Yes, but before that you were in the industry.'

MacReedy's face brightened slightly with a faraway smile. 'We made films.'

Lindsey turned to Ng. 'This has to be connected to the art museum case. I saw it in the Oakland *Trib*. At your party,

Mathilde. It was on the desk. It must have been on TV.'

'I don't know the case, sir,' said Ng.

'That Italian exchange student was killed. Anna — Annabella Buonaventura, that's her name.'

'That's a homicide case, then.'

Lindsey managed to contain himself. 'That's exactly what I'm saying. You have two fires. This girl is killed in one of them. There's no apparent connection between the two; you'd think it was a coincidence. Just two fires in the same town, a day or two apart. So what?'

MacReedy had gone back into the past to be with his dead wife. There was something odd about his dead wife. Lindsey would have to remember that; try to figure out what was strange about MacReedy's dead wife.

'Look.' Lindsey waved his hands. 'The Buonaventura fire was at the University Art Museum. But it wasn't at the main museum, it was at the Pacific Film Archive. That's part of the museum, right? Or shares the building, right?'

Nobody disagreed.

'Then Mr. MacReedy's room is burned out, and then there's an attempt on his belongings in the storage cellar. And why? Because he's a retired filmmaker.'

A second Berkeley police officer arrived. This one was a woman, tall and thin. The two officers spoke briefly, then the newcomer left the group. 'She's going to check out the premises, then post herself where she can see the cellar and the back door at all times.' Ng looked at Lindsey skeptically. 'That's pretty flimsy, Mr. Lindsey.'

Lindsey squirmed in his seat. 'But it all adds up. How can you deny the connection?'

The coffee lounge was filling. Lindsey checked his watch. It was noon. 'We do not have separate dining facilities,' MacReedy said. 'This is our dining room as well.'

Ng said, 'I'll stay with you during the meal, sir, if you don't mind. And then what are your plans for the afternoon?'

MacReedy pondered, then said, 'I think I would like to take a little nap.'

★   ★   ★

Lindsey talked Ms. Wilbur into going home for lunch. For himself he bought a sandwich at a fast-food joint, then drove back to Walnut Creek. He still had a desk in the International Surety office, and he wanted to tackle his accumulated paperwork.

A tall, slim newcomer had settled in at Ms. Wilbur's desk and was clicking away at the computer when Lindsey arrived. She looked away from the computer screen and said, 'Yes, may I help you?'

'I'm Hobart Lindsey. I used to be manager here. I work out of Denver now. You do know about SPUDS, don't you?'

She shook her head. She wore her honey-blonde hair back in a modified ponytail that made her look more fifteen than twenty-five. 'You don't mean potatoes.'

He shook his head. 'Never mind. You'll learn. That's my desk over there. I have some work to do today.' His desk had been covered to a depth of two feet with cartons, binders of computer printouts and miscellaneous small kipple.

'The old woman's things,' the girl

explained. 'You might as well put everything on the floor. It's going in the garbage anyway.'

Lindsey cleared an area to work in. 'My name is Hobart Lindsey,' he told her.

'You already told me that.'

'And your name is — ?' He was being patient.

'Oh. Kari Fielding. Spelled K-A-R-I, rhymes with starry. I'm office manager now. I'll handle your requisitions and phone bills. Please submit all requests in writing and please don't interrupt me again when I'm working at the computer.' She turned away.

Lindsey thought, *Maybe I'll rent office space somewhere after all.*

By mid-afternoon he was able to calm down and lose himself in paperwork. Then it hit him. The name listed as 'wife' in MacReedy's insurance policy was Nola. He started browsing through computer files, trying to find the MacReedy policy and pull it up on his computer screen as Ms. Wilbur had done.

After ten minutes with no result, he picked up the phone and dialed an

Oakland number. Ms. Wilbur answered. Lindsey told her he was looking for the MacReedy policy in International Surety's computer net. She told him the path to follow and offered to wait on the line while he tried it.

It worked, and there it was. Co-beneficiaries, Edward Joseph MacReedy, d-o-b 2/29/04, and Nola Elizabeth Rownes MacReedy, d-o-b 5/11/18.

Nola Elizabeth Rownes MacReedy. Why had the old man referred to his wife as Lola? Was it a pet name, or had MacReedy had more than one wife? Had Nola MacReedy divorced her husband, or died years before he showed up at the International Surety office? Or was his mind merely wandering, perhaps to a one-time girlfriend, a childhood playmate?

Lindsey made a notation in his pocket organizer and another on the computer file. He'd have to get a look at Mrs. MacReedy's death certificate as soon as Mr. MacReedy obtained a duplicate from the county. He wanted to see the name on it, the date of birth — and the cause of death. If necessary he'd call Vital Records on Fallon Street in Oakland himself. Maybe they were set up to fax the information to him by now.

He called home and heard his own voice invite him to leave a message. He told Mother that he might not be home for dinner, and not to wait. She was still at work, the best thing that had ever happened to her. Maybe if she'd had a job forty years ago she would never had got as crazy as she had.

He phoned Marvia Plum at Berkeley Police Headquarters. She was glad to hear from him but she sounded harried. She said, 'Is this business or personal, Bart? I'm really up to here in horse-stuff.'

'Both. How about dinner then, your place or yours?'

'Okay. Let yourself in. Whenever.'

★　★　★

She met him at the door, dressed in civvies. He got a long kiss. 'Was I brusque, Bart? I didn't mean it.'

'No. How's your appetite?'

'I'm ravenous.'

'You ever tried Vietnamese? I know a great place in Oakland. Down on Jefferson.'

It was called Le Cheval. The neighborhood would have frightened Chuck Norris and an army of Kung Fu masters but the food was amazing. They kept the talk personal during the meal, which was interrupted by a series of pops from Jefferson. They'd driven from Oxford Street in Marvia's 1965 Mustang and left it across the street from Le Cheval.

Marvia ran to the window. Lindsey stood behind her. Three Oakland police cruisers were flashing their bar-lights in front of a grocery store at the corner of Jefferson and Fourteenth.

After a minute Lindsey and Marvia Plum returned to their table. Lindsey said, 'As long as the Mustang is safe.'

'I hope nobody bothers Lt. High at home about this. He was starting to look a little peaked, last time I saw him. You know he's still trying to recruit me away from Berkeley? If I ever left, Dorothy Yamura would have a fit.'

Lindsey sipped his drink. 'I haven't

seen Jamie lately. Everything all right?'

'Jamie's fine. He likes his school, he's doing his homework, he's getting ready for baseball season.'

'What are you worried about? Not your ex again, is it?'

'No.' Marvia lowered her face into her hands. When she looked up again there were tears on her cheeks. 'It's my dad. He isn't doing so well. You know he's got a time bomb in his lungs, waiting to explode.'

'I know.'

She looked into his eyes. 'Well, the bomb is exploding. Dad belongs in the hospital and he won't go. One day he refuses to admit that he's even sick. Another day he says he's dying and there's nothing the doctors can do for him so he might as well stay home.'

Lindsey nodded. He'd known that Marvia's father had pulmonary asbestosis and that it would someday kill him, but he'd always imagined that day as a remote future time, never as the present. Marvia was clutching his hand. He put the other on top of hers. 'Maybe he's right, and there's nothing the doctors can do. What about your mom?'

'She's okay. She hasn't quit work or anything. Dad can still get around the house a little, and Jamie's only home for about an hour before Mom gets home. Once he is gone, who's going to take care of Jamie? Mom still has to support herself; there wasn't *that* much money from the company. And I can't afford to quit my job.'

'How about Jamie's dad?'

'Maybe. I don't know. He sends me a note once in a while. On his new wife's office stationery, *Ferré, Borden, Squires, Ferré, Quaid: Corporate and Estate Law*. James Senior, Mister War Hero, is going great guns. Claudia's father is bankrolling him. The media out there in Texas love him. They've got a big house in Austin and a ranch somewhere in Waythehellout, and he'll probably be in the House of Representatives in a couple of years.'

Lindsey drew a deep breath. 'Have you told Jamie about your dad? Does he understand about death?'

'He does. I mean, he sees the news on

TV. He knows that his granddad has a very serious disease; he has to know what the outcome can be.'

She was crying a little. Lindsey dabbed at the corner of her eye with the corner of his napkin and she managed a small laugh. She said, 'Thanks.'

The subject of marriage had not come up, but Lindsey had got Marvia's ring size and he was going shopping soon.

The waiter brought them Vietnamese coffee. It felt to Lindsey like time to change the subject. Across Jefferson Street the popping sounds had long since stopped, and now the police cruisers were also gone

After his first sip of coffee, Lindsey asked Marvia if she'd worked the art museum case. It might have started as Arson's case, he knew, but once the body of Annabella Buonaventura had been found, it was Homicide's.

6

The morning sun woke them and Marvia clicked on the TV. An all-news channel was doing a fluff-piece on the forthcoming Arturo Madrid retrospective. An all-movie channel was planning an Arturo Madrid festival, a solid week of his films. The news channel settled for a montage of film clips. Arturo Madrid engaged in a sword fight with Basil Rathbone. Locked in a passionate embrace with Greta Garbo. Sharing a foxhole with John Garfield. In top hat and tails, a brilliant grin showing off acres of teeth, hoofing with Betty Grable. In a rare comedy role, lurching toward the camera in Karloff-type Frankenstein makeup, growling inarticulately, then menacing a pop-eyed Willie Best.

Madrid, in the film clips, changed little with the passing decades. His heavy mustache and great shock of hair gradually faded from black to salt-and-pepper and finally to snowy white. Crow's feet appeared at the corners of his eyes, and deep lines at the sides of his mouth. But his broad shoulders and proud carriage never varied, from 1934's *Werewolf of Wall Street* to 1945's *Submarine Commando* to 1972's *Vienna, My Vienna.*

Lindsey clicked to a local station. They were in the middle of a regional news roundup. A reporter stood in front of the restored Art Deco Paramount Theater in downtown Oakland. 'This is the famous movie palace where Arturo Madrid's pictures showed in past decades, and where the great star will be feted by his colleagues and admirers.'

After the camera panned over the theater's glowing neon marquee, it followed the reporter into the lobby, pausing to show off the plush decor and statuary of a more splendid era. 'Arturo Madrid was born in Oakland,' the reporter resumed. 'Descended from Spanish settlers who were among the first families of old California, Mr. Madrid began his career in 1911 as a child star in vaudeville. He performed at the old Moulin Rouge Theater just a few blocks from this point. He made his earliest films in various Northern California cities, including a stint with the Pan-Pacific International Film studios in Niles, before moving on to Hollywood fame. We'll look forward to welcoming him back to the Bay Area. This is Geraldine Gonzalez at the Oakland Paramount . . .'

If I see one more piece on Arturo Madrid, Lindsey thought, *I'm going to switch to the home shopping network and never come back.*

Marvia emerged from the shower bundled in a heavy robe, a towel wrapped around her short-cropped hair. 'I'm sorry, Bart. It was my Dad. And Jamie. And James Senior and that bitch out in Texas. I don't know what to do.'

He stood up and put his arms around her. 'I'll stick with you, you know that. Whatever happens.'

'I'll make coffee.' As she measured out Jamaican beans, she asked him, 'Were you interested in the Buonaventura case? Did I get that right, last night?'

'Yes.'

While the coffee dripped she said, 'You know I can't discuss cases with a civilian.

Not without a proper reason.'

Lindsey made a quick nod. Remote in hand, he clicked the TV set to darkness. 'You cop types always cooperate with us insurance types. This something new? You can sleep with me but you can't talk to me?'

'What's the connection? It's tragic that she died, but how come you're involved in this one, Bart? Seriously, I mean.' She filled two mugs and handed him one.

'Maybe it's just a coincidence, Marvia. But I've got a benny with a death claim. An old man who lives at the Robeson Center. His wife just died and he filed a claim with I.S.'

Marvia sat on a wooden chair and waited for him to continue.

'My guy used to be in the movie business. About a million years ago, I guess. I was over there yesterday with Mathilde Wilbur, my old office manager.'

'But what's the point? So this old man files a claim on his wife? And the husband was in the movie racket somewhere around the time of King Charlemagne. And there was a fire at the Pacific Film

Archive and an Italian exchange student is killed. What did your guy's wife die of?'

'I'm going to find out today. I assume natural causes. MacReedy — that's the husband — didn't say.'

'Wasn't it on her death certificate?'

'That's the thing, Marvia. You see, that's the connection. MacReedy had a death certificate, but it was destroyed. There was a fire at the Robeson Center. Just MacReedy's room. And it was an arson fire.'

'Do you remember who was there?'

'Sure. Lieutenant D'Onofrio and Sergeant Stromback. And later officer Mike Ng. They left him to keep an eye on the place and on Mr. MacReedy, but the arsonist came back. Or somebody did. MacReedy and Mathilde and I were in the cellar, looking at some things MacReedy had in storage, and the guy came back. God knows what would have happened, only Ms. Wilbur had a flashlight and Mr. MacReedy had a sword-cane — '

'What else does he have, a blunderbuss? A Roman catapult?'

'Marvia, this is serious. The sword-cane may have been all that saved us. That and

Mathilde's flashlight. The intruder ran away.'

'Yeah. And they sent Olaf Stromback and Mike Ng out there. Those two have a combined IQ that might outwit an earthworm on a good day.'

Lindsey shrugged.

'Okay,' Marvia conceded, 'I'll be serious. There's an arson fire at the Film Archive and Annabella Buonaventura dies. Definitely felony murder. And your guy's wife dies, presumably of natural causes, still to be verified. And then there's an arson fire in the husband's room, and a bungled attempt at a follow-up attack. And he used to be in the movie business.'

'Right.'

'I don't get it. That's not the kind of connection that interests the police. Come on, Bart.'

'Don't you remember what Dorothy Yamura always says about coincidences making her nervous?'

'So you really think these two cases are related.' Marvia walked to the bed and straightened the old Raggedy Ann quilt. She went to the closet and began to put on her sergeant's uniform. 'I'll do this much: I'll make a notation on the Buonaventura case folder. It's my case, you know.'

'I didn't know.' Lindsey smiled. 'Isn't that a coincidence. What would Dorothy think?'

'I haven't been handling it personally, but I'll look into it. And you go ahead and follow up on MacReedy. Jesus, Olaf Stromback and Mike Ng on the same case. I'm surprised they didn't burn the place down themselves, looking for clues. At least Vince D'Onofrio was there — he's got a sizable fraction of a brain.'

'I'll call you later.'

They took two cars to work. Love in the modern world.

*   *   *

Lindsey pulled the Hyundai onto the Robeson Center's gravel parking area. He saluted the ebony carving and entered the lobby.

Mike Ng was already on duty. Lindsey asked him if the building had gone unprotected during the night, but Ng assured him that there were shifts of officers watching for the return of the firebug.

Oliver Hendry was presiding over the reception desk. He recognized Lindsey. 'I saw Mr. MacReedy just a few minutes ago. We've got him settled in a new room, but he's out strolling on the grounds just now. You know, we encourage all our residents to stay active.'

Lindsey said sharply, 'On the grounds? Alone?'

'No, that elderly lady friend of yours is with him.'

Lindsey circled the old building on foot, looking for Ms. Wilbur and MacReedy. When he found them, they were walking carefully, Ms. Wilbur gently steering the old man by the elbow. She appeared to be questioning MacReedy, who answered slowly and briefly.

'Right there,' MacReedy said, pointing to a grassy spot near a lush California blue oak. The tree must have been hundreds of years old.

Ms. Wilbur looked up. 'Hobart. What a surprise.'

He shook MacReedy's hand and

mumbled some commonplace greeting.

Ms. Wilbur said, 'Mr. MacReedy was showing me the grounds. This is where he found poor Mrs. MacReedy.'

Lindsey raised his eyebrows.

'She was on the ground, poor thing. He tried to help her up but she couldn't stand. So he went back for help and they brought out a stretcher and took her to Herrick Hospital.'

'She didn't seem so bad,' MacReedy said. 'I thought she would come home to me. She was really very young. But she took a turn for the worse. She never came home.'

Lindsey asked, 'Did she say anything to you? Did she say how she'd fallen?'

There were tears in the old man's milky eyes. He had been amazingly stolid until now. 'She tried to talk, but I wouldn't listen. I always told her what to do, you see. She was smart and people thought she was fiery, but she liked me to tell her what to do. So I said, 'Don't talk. Don't talk. We'll take care of you. We'll make you all right again.' That's what I told her, you see.'

No one spoke.

'She held onto my hand. I just wanted her to be well. But she got worse at the hospital. And she died. She never came home from the hospital. I visited her every day and she held my hand, but she never told me what happened.'

Lindsey said, 'I want to drive down to Fallon Street and see about a duplicate death certificate. We need it to process Mr. MacReedy's claim.'

Half an hour later they stood in the County Recorder's Office. Lindsey had to pay a small fee for the certificate. Under cause of death it listed *pneumonia/pleurisy*. Under secondary or contributing causes of death, the attending physician had written in *broken hip*. The physician's signature, for once in clear, perfect script, read *Apu Chandra, MD*.

Lindsey drove the others back to the Robeson Center. Standing on the slightly overgrown lawn, he asked if either of them had got a good look at the intruder they had encountered in the storage area.

Mathilde said, 'We went over this with the police, Hobart.'

'Refresh my memory.'

'Well, all I saw was a hulking figure. Probably a man.'

'Black or white? Hair? Clothing?'

'Bart, I just caught a glimpse of him, same as you. He was bundled up in dark clothes; it was dark in the cellar. All I really saw was a vague shape. I saw his eyes in my flashlight. Then he was gone.'

Lindsey nodded. 'How about you, Mr. MacReedy?'

'Good thing the fellow ran away. Good thing for him, that is.'

The old man had spirit, but he was more interested in describing his own actions than the intruder. And with MacReedy's milky eyes, the chances were that he'd seen less than Lindsey or Ms. Wilbur had.

They climbed the old steps and sat on a bench on the veranda. The morning mist had burned off, and the hills and the modern skyscrapers of San Francisco rose from the bay like a child's miniature city.

Lindsey turned toward the others. 'I don't know if there's anything here to pursue. Marvia has her doubts. I haven't talked it over with anybody at International Surety, but I'll have to soon. I don't know how I can justify an investigation.'

Mathilde said, 'I thought you were more of a bulldog than that.'

He laughed. 'Still, what can we do that the police aren't doing? We're not a pair of Agatha Christie characters, you and I, running around the English country side solving amusing little mysteries. The only murder we know about is the Italian student's.'

'Murder still. Didn't you tell me the sprinklers were plugged with putty, just as they were in Mr. MacReedy's room?' Mathilde snorted. 'If you want to quit, you quit. You know perfectly well that there's something wicked going on here. Whether the fire at the archive was connected or not, there have been two attempts to destroy Mr. MacReedy's belongings. He is our client and we are responsible — morally, if not legally. I know your mother, and I know the poor soul has had her problems, but she would never have raised you to abandon a person in need.'

Lindsey smiled. 'All right. I'll stay on the case. Assuming there is one.'

'You do that. And keep me up to date on anything you learn.'

He drove back to Walnut Creek to the International Surety office. As he came through the door Kari Fielding gave him a hostile smile. 'Messages on your voice mail, Mr. Lindsey.' She couldn't contain her smirk.

The first was from SPUDS headquarters in Denver. From Mrs. Blomquist, Ducky Richelieu's secretary. *Call at once, Mr. Richelieu wants to talk to you.* The second was from Aurora Delano in New Orleans. Darn, he'd meant to return her first call and forgot all about it.

But before he returned either call, he dialed Herrick Hospital and asked to speak with Dr. Chandra. Shortly, he heard a voice speaking in the increasingly familiar precise, British-flavored Indian accent. 'How may I be of service to you, sir?'

Lindsey asked if Dr. Chandra had attended Mrs. MacReedy.

'I did. Are you a member of the lady's family, may I ask?'

83

Lindsey identified himself. He explained that he was processing a death claim filed by Mrs. MacReedy's husband. 'Dr. Chandra, what can you tell me about Mrs. MacReedy's death? I've read the death certificate, but what caused the broken hip? And why did she die? People don't die of broken hips, do they?'

'In older persons, brittleness of bones is a very serious problem. They can snap and cause crippling injuries. Once an older person is thus bed-ridden, she may accumulate fluid in the lungs, leading to pneumonia, pleurisy, and so forth. I am afraid that is what happened to Mrs. MacReedy. You might say that she indeed died of a broken hip.'

Lindsey pursed his lips. 'So you don't see anything suspicious, Dr. Chandra?'

'Everything appeared in order to me.'

'What about the original injury? Is there any way to tell what caused the break? Could she have been attacked?'

There was a long silence, then: 'If the break were caused by a blow, that might have abraded the skin. But there was a great deal of trauma inside her pelvic area, resulting from the break. Small blood vessels broken; there was considerable localized internal bleeding. This resulted in such swelling and discoloration, Mr. Lindsey, I fear I did not search for such an abrasion.'

Lindsey thanked Chandra and rang off. Now, he thought, Delano or Richelieu? The tough one first, he decided, and lifted the handset from its base.

7

Mrs. Blomquist put him straight through. Without preliminary, Richelieu's hard-edged voiced said, 'You're up to something crazy. This is a business, Lindsey. What do you have to say for yourself?'

Lindsey hadn't filed any reports with SPUDS on the MacReedy case; he knew he was far out of line. He knew he had a reputation in International Surety for taking bizarre cases, for going against policy, and for coming up smelling like roses. Twice Lindsey had saved I.S. large amounts of money by playing detective when the company had wanted to pay up, close the case, and cut their losses.

Once, he had pursued a case beyond company guidelines, and I.S. had wound up paying for a four-engined World War II bomber that had gone to the bottom of the Pacific Ocean, carrying its pilot with it. Lindsey had very nearly lost his job over that one. He'd had to fly into Denver and confront Richelieu personally. But the corporate PR spin doctors had made a hero of Lindsey, and Richelieu had wound up grudgingly offering congratulations to the man he had very nearly fired.

But this time, Lindsey himself had his doubts about continuing the newest investigation. International Surety's obligation in the MacReedy case went no further than the $400.19 the company owed on the old Global National Guarantee Life policy. If some crazed arsonist was after the old man, it was the job of the police to protect him, not of Hobart Lindsey, Captain Claims.

But he wasn't satisfied with the circumstances of Mrs. MacReedy's death. He wasn't willing to write off the second arson at the Robeson Center, or to think that the intruder in the building's cellar was not connected to the earlier fires. And he wasn't ready to believe that the Annabella Buonaventura case was unconnected to the MacReedy matter. He tried to summarize his feelings for Richelieu, compressing them into the kind of telephone soundbite that the man understood.

But Richelieu remained unpersuaded. 'This isn't International Surety's affair,' he said. 'We're going to cut that benny a check and close the case.'

'Is that the official company position?'

There was a stony silence from the telephone. Lindsey pressed the disconnect and dialed Denver again. Mrs. Blomquist said that Mr. Richelieu had left to keep an appointment.

Lindsey reached for his phone-file to look up Aurora Delano's number. He saw Kari Fielding grinning at him through her long, honey-colored locks. He punched in the number for Aurora's office in New Orleans and waited until she picked up the phone.

'This is Hobart Lindsey — ' he began.

'Returning my call,' she cut him off. 'You remember our little jaunt out to lovely Reserve, Louisiana, when you were down here on that Tuskegee Airmen case?'

'Yes.'

'You remember meeting the fabulous Little Walter Scoggins? You remember how Antoine Leroux's office manager,

Martha Washington, announced that she and Walter were going to be married, only he didn't know it yet?'

'Yes to both.'

'Well, they did it. Martha was right. She and Walter are spliced together now, all nice and legal, complete with license, preacher, and happy honeymoon plans.'

'You didn't call me up to discuss that with me, did you?'

'Look,' she said, 'you remember that Walter was a graduate student at Southern U, doing a doctorate in Black Studies?'

'Vaguely.'

'You're not going to believe this, Hobart, but they were in New Orleans, Walter and Martha were, shopping for their nuptial finery, and I invited them out for lunch.'

Lindsey blew out his breath, waiting for Aurora Delano to get to the point.

'Walter was interested in our computer system because he uses the beasts for his research. So I booted up KlameNet to give him a demo, and I picked a couple of names from our gang in Denver. Your old roomie, Cletus Berry, is working in the Bronx now, lucky man. Then I checked to see if you'd entered any transactions lately, and there was this funny entry for payment on the death of Nola Elizabeth Rownes MacReedy, payable to her husband, Edward Joseph MacReedy, and Walter like to take a fit.'

'He *what*?'

'Walter practically jumped off the floor. He said, 'Are Speedy and Lola still alive?''

Lola!

'I said, 'I don't know what you mean.' And Walter said, 'I need to know about them for my doctorate. They were both involved in the black alternate cinema movement back in the 1930s.''

That caught Lindsey's attention. He said, 'Mr. MacReedy said he used to be in the movie business. He showed me a wardrobe full of clothing from the 1930s. Men's and women's both. And he said that he had a trunk full of old costumes and filing cabinets full of what he called old movie stuff.'

'Well, Walter can hardly contain himself. I think his bride is just a trifle miffed, but she says she supports him in his plan to get that doctorate. All he needs is to complete his thesis, and he seems to think that Edward Joseph MacReedy and Nola Elizabeth Rowan MacReedy can tell him everything he needs to know.'

'Nola isn't going to tell him anything, unless he knows how to summon up ectoplasm. But Edward Joseph is still going strong at ninety. What does Walter want to do, talk to him on the phone?'

'Oh no,' Aurora corrected him. 'The happy couple canceled their original honeymoon plans. Anyway, they're on their way to San Francisco.'

'Right now?'

'They're somewhere over the Grand Canyon even as we speak. They're booked into the honeymoon suite in the Ritz-Carlton in San Francisco. They'll check in there tonight.'

Lindsey whistled. 'I thought this guy was a poor student working his way through grad school.'

'They saved their money. Martha's family paid for the wedding; Little Walter's father, Big Walter, chipped in for their nuptial flight; and they're going to splurge. One night first class, top of the chart, then back to earth.'

'I'll send them a bottle of champagne and phone 'em in the morning.'

'You do that. I promised Walter you'd help him with his research.'

'Sure,' said Lindsey. He placed the handset gently on the cradle.

Scoggins would probably want to spend some time at the Pacific Film Archive. And there was a Black Filmmakers' Hall of Fame in Oakland. But the intriguing part was Scoggins' line — if Aurora Delano had repeated it accurately — about Speedy and Lola.

Speedy MacReedy? It sounded like the kind of nickname a Hollywood type, especially one who operated on the periphery of the film industry, would pick up. And Lola. MacReedy had referred to his dead wife as Lola, even though her name was Nola. And Scoggins, too, had referred to her as Lola, not Nola.

Maybe playing native guide to Walter and Martha wouldn't be such a chore after all. In fact, Lindsey was starting to look forward to it. He stood up and started for the door, whistling.

Kari Fielding looked up at him, an expression of surprise on her features. She brushed her long hair out of her eyes. She wore it in a ponytail as she had when Lindsey first met her, but strands had come loose in a manner that looked anything but accidental.

'You certainly seem happy, Mr. Lindsey. What did Mr. Richelieu have to say?'

'He said they were paying the claim.' Lindsey resumed whistling and walking. On his way out the door he passed Elmer Mueller, just arriving. Even that didn't ruin Lindsey's cheer.

* * *

Lindsey pulled up to the Ritz-Carlton and let the valet park his Hyundai. Walter and Martha were supposed to be waiting in the lobby. He started for the concierge's desk to inquire about them when he felt a tap on his shoulder.

Little Walter Scoggins had played tackle for the Southern University football team.

The *Little* distinguished him from his father, Big Walter Scoggins, but it hardly applied to his massive appearance. Martha stood beside her husband, her dark-coffee skin in contrast his much darker complexion. A nimbus of newlywed happiness surrounded them. Walter was dressed in a bright yellow Hawaiian shirt and thin khaki trousers, while Martha wore a silly hat with an artificial bird on it, a sleeveless silk shirt and knee-length shorts.

Martha said, 'Mr. Lindsey, remember us? From Reserve?'

'I do.' He looked past them. 'Is that your luggage? I hope you brought some warmer clothes than those.'

'We dressed for California,' Scoggins said.

Lindsey repressed a chuckle. 'You must have got your information from the movies.'

'I guess we get a lot of information from the movies,' Scoggins laughed.

'Dangerous.' Lindsey frowned. 'You wind up thinking that John Wayne and Ronnie Reagan won World War II all by themselves.'

'Didn't they?'

'They never got closer to the war zone

than a Hollywood back lot.' He tried to read Scoggins' face. 'You knew that.'

Scoggins grinned.

'All right,' Lindsey changed the subject, 'we'll find you something more appropriate for this frigid clime. Listen, did you have any trouble getting into the restaurant last night, dressed like Hawaiian tourists?'

Martha said, 'We ordered from room service.'

Lindsey drove them off Nob Hill, through downtown San Francisco and across the Bay Bridge. 'If you're doing your research in the East Bay, you might as well stay over there. It'll be a lot more convenient and a lot less expensive, both.'

He checked them into the Durant Hotel just down the street from the Pacific Film Archive.

An hour later Lindsey pulled into the parking area at the Robeson Center. He'd phoned there while the newlyweds purchased warmer clothing and changed into it on the spot. Their lightweight togs were safely stowed in the trunk of the Hyundai. Walter Scoggins had brought a 35-mm camera and a microcassette recorder.

Lindsey had spoken with Officer Ng and with Mathilde Wilbur. Mr. MacReedy was taking a nap. Mike Ng wasn't sure that more visitors were really a good idea, but then he decided it wasn't his job to decide about that, providing they weren't criminals. But Ms. Wilbur was all in favor of Mr. and Mrs. Scoggins visiting. She thought that more visitors would keep MacReedy's spirits up.

Lindsey led the others into the Robeson Center. Oliver Hendry was on duty and signaled Lindsey to the desk. Lindsey introduced the Scogginses. Hendry rang Mr. MacReedy's room, and shortly the old man emerged and made his way into the lobby, Ms. Wilbur at his elbow.

Lindsey made the introductions. Ms. Wilbur looked at her watch. 'It's almost noon. Wouldn't it be a good idea to chat over some food?'

Everyone loved the idea. Lindsey knew he would have to pick up the bill, but would I.S. reimburse the expense? Even if he could somehow get to the bottom of the events, even if he made himself a hero to the local police and media, that might bring him up short with Desmond Richelieu.

He squared his shoulders and asked if Mathilde had any place in mind for food. She said, 'Let's get away from the campus area. You know Barney's over in Rockridge?' No one did. Five in one car made for cramped riding, but they parked on College Avenue in Oakland and found a table in Barney's back room. The ceiling was painted to look like heaven, complete with fluffy clouds and fat, smiling cherubs. The food lived up to the surroundings.

Walter couldn't wait to pump MacReedy for information. Before long, Lindsey and Mathilde and Martha found themselves little more than audience for Scoggins and MacReedy.

'We came all the way from Louisiana to see you, Mr. MacReedy,' Scoggins said. 'And what you did was important. African-Americans have to know their history. Your films showed a whole side of America that hardly anybody knows about. There are a few researchers — Donald Bogle, Gary Null, John Kisch. I've read all their books;

I've corresponded with them.'

MacReedy chewed a fragment of lettuce with slow deliberation. 'Then why do you want to bother me, young man? I made my last film in 1951. You weren't even born then, were you?'

'No, sir.'

'It was another age. The world was different. You wouldn't even know about it.'

'But that's just the point, Mr. MacReedy.' Scoggins had found another arrow to fit to his bow. 'I *want* to know about it. Millions of people want to know about it, or ought to want to know what they're missing. They think it was just Amos 'n' Andy and Carmen Jones and Louise Beavers waiting table for the white folks. They don't know there was another whole world. And you know about it, sir. You were in the center of that world. You made that world. You have to share what you know, please.' He stopped. He'd made his play.

The old man said, 'Do you really care? You know, after I lost my company, H-M-R — '

'Yes. I remember H-M-R Productions.

Didn't they call your movies Hummers? I want to know — '

'Harmony, Melody, Rhythm. That was the name of the company because those are the three component elements of music. Not that terrible pounding they call music today.'

Scoggins was drinking in MacReedy's story. Lindsey thought he should have his tape recorder going. Perhaps later he would. But for now, there was nothing to worry about. Walter Scoggins was going to remember every word that MacReedy spoke.

When they got back to the Robeson Center, MacReedy led Walter Scoggins to his new room. Ms. Wilbur had wanted to accompany them, but then Lindsey would have wanted to be present, too, and they couldn't leave Martha out, and MacReedy balked at the idea of being interviewed in front of an audience. Even an audience of three. So Lindsey and Ms. Wilbur took Martha Scoggins sightseeing while Walter Scoggins and Edward Joseph MacReedy plunged ever further into the past. Now Scoggins had revved up his tape recorder and unsealed a carton of microcassettes.

When the interview ended two days later, Lindsey and Ms. Wilbur planned to join the Scogginses and Mr. MacReedy for a celebratory dinner. Lindsey had invited Marvia Plum to join the group as well. She hesitated, then agreed. 'The Buonaventura case is moving,' she told Lindsey. 'I don't want to get into it with all those civilians, but I'll brief you afterward.'

Scoggins was a fast study and a fast worker. With Ms. Wilbur at his elbow, he sent his tapes out to be transcribed. Then he and his bride spent a few days touring the wine country and the gold country north and east of San Francisco. When they got back he received his transcripts, gave them a quick edit to change the question-and-answer format into a straight narrative, and presented draft copies to Lindsey, Ms. Wilbur, Marvia Plum, and of course Mr. MacReedy.

Lindsey settled into an easy chair and began to read. The easy chair was in Marvia Plum's flat on Oxford Street, and Marvia was there as well. She put on a CD of Erik Satie piano music. Lindsey never ceased to wonder at the breadth of her taste and her willingness to share her pleasures with him.

8

It was all so long ago. I don't know why you want to know this. Colored folks didn't have the advantages then, but we had each other. We stuck together. There were still people around who remembered slavery.

How did I get in the movie business? Well, because the book business wasn't so good. Who wanted to read a book that a colored man wrote, about colored folks? Only other colored folks, and we didn't have good schools, and we didn't have enough money for books. We didn't have enough money for food; how could we buy books?

But I figured, if there was money for gin and moonshine, people still needed entertainment. They made gramophone records for colored folks; called them race records. People had wind-up gramophones; they'd buy those records and play them 'til they wore them out. Gospel songs, dirty blues. If people were willing to buy those records, I figured they'd buy tickets to movies.

You want to know about my life? My childhood? You want to know all about me to put in this thesis book of yours. All right, I'll tell you everything.

My mama taught me music and my papa taught me words. He was a preacher. Oh, Valdosta, Georgia. I was born on the twenty-ninth of February, 1904. Never felt cheated. My mama and papa said I was a special baby, a leap year baby. I only had a regular birthday but once every four years. So other years they always had a party for me on February 28. They'd have a birthday cake and we'd play; they let me stay up late. They'd wait 'til midnight and it was March 1 and just at midnight they'd make a big show, they'd jump up and get excited and say, 'There it goes, now don't miss out, there goes Eddie's birthday.' And they'd give me my presents.

We didn't have much, but they always gave me something. I was an only child. My papa would give me a book, every birthday. My mama always gave me musical things. One year she gave me a trumpet, another a violin. She knew how to play everything. She was choir director in Papa's church. She taught me my music. She hated those dirty blues and she made Papa preach against them, but I never thought his heart was in it.

I wasn't a strong child. Work was hard to find. Mostly, I stayed home and read books or practiced my music. I played violin in the church and became assistant choir director. In 1919 Papa received a call from a church in Minnesota. No, there weren't many colored folks in Minnesota. But there were a few. They wanted a church and my papa received the call. Saint Cloud, Minnesota.

I obtained my high school diploma in 1921. Papa wanted me to follow in his footsteps but I never had the calling. And Papa accepted that, though he regretted it to the day he passed. Mama hoped I would become a great symphony musician, but there was no room for colored folks then, and if I even mentioned playing jazz or blues to her, she had a spell. Calling out, crying, praying.

I could get a job as a porter or a dish washer or a day laborer. There was a car factory in town. The Pan Motor Company. The man who ran it was Samuel C. Pandolfo. I always thought he had a touch of the dinge to him. Well, he said he was a Spaniard or Sicilian or something, but I always thought there was something else there. I wouldn't know, not for sure, but I think so. But all his mechanics and skilled workers were white. I could have got a job sweeping up, but that didn't appeal to me.

I thought, all those colored folks all over the country, the books they have to read are written by white people and they're all about white people, you see? I remember when I was a boy, all those books I read. My papa was a broadminded man. Some preachers' children, all they were allowed to read was the Bible. My papa let me read lots of things.

I remember reading *Treasure Island*. And *Dr. Jekyll and Mr. Hyde*. I loved Stevenson. *Kidnapped*. And dime novels. Nick Carter and Buffalo Bill and Horatio Alger. I must have ruined my eyes reading for hours on end, but I didn't; I had perfect vision until my eyes got milky like they are. Maybe I'll have them done. I'd like to see everything clearly once more before I pass.

Oh, I loved Sherlock Holmes. I couldn't believe it when my papa told me they were made-up stories. And some of the other stories — 'The Lady or the Tiger', that was written by a fellow named Stockton. I kept begging my papa and my mama to tell me which door that fellow chose, who was behind the door he chose, the lady or the tiger, and I never did find out.

Movies. Right. I saw movies. Even in Valdosta. When they showed *Birth of a Nation*, all the colored folks stayed home and locked their doors, those who had locks. That went on for weeks. We had lynchings in those days. It was terrible, terrible.

No, I didn't see *Birth of a Nation* when they first showed it. I was only a boy. That was 1915, I remember. I saw it years later. It was a great movie, sure, but it was a terrible thing. What poison that movie spread; how many people died because of that movie.

Mr. Griffith? I met him once, years later. He always denied that he was a racist. He came to my studio; he wanted to see how I did it. I didn't have the money he did; I didn't have the big stars, I just had colored folk. He didn't stay for long, but he shook my hand. What do you think of that?

I read all these books. I read *Dracula* by the Englishman, Mr. Abraham Stoker. You wouldn't think a preacher would want his child to read such things, but Papa gave me the book himself. I don't know where he got it. I can't imagine why he let me read it. It frightened me.

When Papa passed we lost the church. Mama had to take a job as a domestic. She barely scraped by. She could make more money if she took a job as a live-in, don't you see. And then she wouldn't have to pay rent on a place of her own. But what about me?

That was when I wrote my first book. 1920. I was sixteen. I wrote it in a copybook. It was a Western detective story. Maybe I'll see if I have one. No, I don't think you'd find it anywhere. *Murder on the Bar-20*. That was the name of it. I had a colored detective searching for a criminal who robbed a colored church of its treasury and headed out West to hide out. My detective had to disguise himself as a rustler and hire the criminal into his gang to unmask him. And of course there was a love interest. I decided early on, there should always be a love interest. Well of course it sounds familiar. It was filmed in 1936 and again in 1947. Sure, we changed the name both times, but we kept the story line. I wrote the scripts. I directed it.

There were no publishers in Saint Cloud, Minnesota so I tried Minneapolis and Saint Paul, but no luck. I even bundled up my copybook and sent it to a publisher in Chicago, but they just sent it back. So I went to see Mr. Pandolfo. How did I get in to see him? I just dressed in my finest clothing and took my copybook under my arm and went to the Pan Motor Company. I went to the main office and I told them I came to see Mr. Pandolfo and they sent me in to see him.

That man must have had some African in him. I wish I'd had the courage to ask him, but I didn't and he's dead now, dead for many years. Maybe when I get to heaven I'll walk right up and I'll say, Mr. Pandolfo, are you colored folk? I'll do that after I meet Mr. Stockton and ask him if it was the lady or the tiger behind the door.

He said, 'Sit down, young man.' Just like that. He didn't call me boy. He said, 'What can I do for you, young man?'

I told him, 'I've written a book. It's called *Murder on the Bar-20*. It's about a colored detective out West.' I laid my copybook on his desk. Mr. Pandolfo picked up my copybook and opened it. That was seventy-four years ago, young man.

He read a few paragraphs. I sat in that chair; I didn't move a muscle. I knew that book by heart. I could see him moving his eyes and I was reciting those words to myself, in my mind. You know what, young man? I remember them still. Listen to this.

'The roan's hoof beats drummed like a

rhythm in Buck Colt's ears as he spurred westward, ever westward, into the setting sun. His hogleg pistol lay like a heavy weight against his leg and his sombrero was dark with the sweat of his brow. The roan was spotted, brown and white. It snorted at a rattlesnake that reared up in the trail like the deadly cobra of Cairo.'

I could go on like that. You don't want me to. You want to know other things. Mr. Pandolfo read that entire book while I sat on a leather office chair, waiting for him to say something. He didn't say a word. He closed the copybook one time and marked his place with his finger and just looked at me. Then he looked down again and opened the book and read on. He didn't answer the phone, he didn't talk to his secretary, he didn't stop for food or to go to the bathroom. And I didn't dare move a muscle or make a sound.

When he finished the book, he laid it down on his desk. He had a sheet of glass on top of his desk, and he laid my copybook on it. He said, 'You're a very patient young man. I imagine you want to use the facilities. They are through that doorway.'

So I went and I relieved myself in his bathroom and I flushed the toilet and washed my hands off and dried them on his towel. Yes. We had separate toilet facilities in those days, for black and for white. He let me use his toilet. That meant something.

He said, 'And you wrote this all yourself?'

And I said, 'Yes, sir, every word.'

He said, 'You want to have it published?'

I said, 'Yes, sir.'

'There are printers. There's the newspaper — they do job printing too; they do printing for Pan.'

I knew that. I wasn't going to say anything; I just sat there and nodded a little bit, wearing my best clothes.

He said, 'You want me to pay for it, is that it?'

I said, 'If you'll lend me the money, I'll pay for it myself and pay you back out of profits.'

'Who will buy it?' he wanted to know.

I said, 'There are millions of colored folks who would love to read a good story about a colored detective and a colored murderer and a beautiful colored girl.'

He said, 'I can see that. Will the bookstores take it? For the most part they don't cater to colored trade, do they? How will you sell your book?'

I said, 'If you will include one of your Pan cars in the deal, I will load it up with copies of my book and travel all around the country selling books to colored people in churches and barbecues and even door to door. It won't cost much, and they will want to read this book.'

Well of course he said yes; why do you think I'm telling you this story? It took until the next year to get the book printed and bound, but we did it. And I set out.

No, I did not follow Buck Colt's trail. I had two thousand copies of that book printed. I took as many as I could fit in that old Pan car. It was a good car. No hotels or boarding houses would take colored in those days. We had to find folks who would rent us a spare room by the night — why, colored folks, of course, aren't you listening? But that old Pan car, the seats folded down and made a bed. At that age, I guess I could have slept on a cactus plant.

Buck Colt headed west; I headed east. I sold that book in Chicago, I sold it in Detroit, then I headed south and sold it in Pittsburgh. Whenever I ran out of copies I'd wire back to Saint Cloud and they'd ship another carton to me at the next city. I'd pick them up at the railroad depot.

What an adventure that was. We didn't have highways like today. Just city streets and country roads. Some were dirt. I would find the colored section of a town, buy myself a sandwich or a bowl of chili, and start selling books. Sometimes I would sell one or two, sometimes as many as six. Then I'd move on. Another few blocks or another town or another big city.

When I saw Harlem, I knew I would be a success. I'd sold almost one thousand books by then. I knew I was going to sell everything. I saw the theaters in Harlem. Night clubs and vaudeville and legitimate theaters and movie palaces. I went to a movie in Harlem. There we were — the cashier was colored, the usherettes were colored, the candy butchers were colored, the whole audience was colored folks. But the movie was white.

I thought about that as I sat there watching that movie. It was *The Four Horsemen of the Apocalypse*, directed by Rex Ingram, and starring Rudolph Valentino. No, not that Rex Ingram, this was another Rex Ingram. A ruddy-faced Irishman. The picture was set in Argentina for the most part, with scenes in parts of Europe as well. But all I could think of was, here I am, a colored man, and every person in this audience is colored, and we are watching these white people on the screen. I thought, wouldn't colored folks pay to see a movie about colored folks? You see, I had already proved to myself that there was a market for books by a colored writer about colored life. But if I could make a movie about colored life, why then instead of selling one copy at a time, I could fill a theater with an audience of hundreds.

That night I slept in a real bed. I checked into a colored hotel right there in Harlem, I had a fine dinner in the dining room, and I slept in a comfortable bed with fine, clean linen. But I didn't sleep much, no, sir. Most of the night I lay looking at the ceiling, seeing a silver screen there with colored actors in a colored story. You know the colored folks in *Birth of a Nation* were all whites in blackface? Oh, you knew that already. Well, in the early movies, that's how they did it. It wasn't just Al Jolson; they all did it. No, I wanted an all-colored cast playing an all-colored story. I was going to be rich. No, that was not when I got the name Speedy MacReedy. I used to hate that name, but I don't mind. No, I got the name later.

It was ten years before I made my first movie. 1931. What did I do in between? I kept writing books. After *Murder on the Bar-20* I tried a horror story. I still had that old vampire of Bram Stoker's flapping around in my brain, and then in 1922 I was back in my old home town, Valdosta, Georgia. They didn't have enough colored for us to support a theater of our own, like we had in the big cities. So a few of the theaters had colored sections. They'd let the whites sit downstairs where it was comfiest and we'd have to sit upstairs in the balcony where the hot air accumulated and it was stuffy, but we could see the movies. Other theaters, they'd have a colored night maybe once a week. Thursday, that was maids' night out, so some of the theaters would be reserved for colored on Thursdays.

What was I telling you? Oh, yes, about vampires. I remember this like it was yesterday. This was a Thursday night in Valdosta, Georgia, and I was about out of copies of *Murder on the Bar-20*. I was waiting for the last few cartons and then I was going to head back to Saint Cloud and write another book; I didn't know what it was going to be about. And I went to this theater in Valdosta and they showed *Nosferatu*. A great film. F.W. Murnau, director. Actor named Max Schreck played the vampire. That picture scared me almost as much as reading *Dracula* did. I lay there thinking about vampires and were-wolves and ghosts, I was shaking in my boots except I wasn't wearing any boots. I kept seeing these images, weird faces leering at me.

I kept a copybook all the time back then. Just like the one I wrote *Murder on the Bar-20* in. I kept waking up and scribbling notes in my copybook and falling back asleep. By the next morning I had pages of notes. I went over them and put them in order and I had the sketch for my second book. When I got back to Saint Cloud I rented a room in the colored section. My mama was working as a live-in so she couldn't put me up any more.

I went back over to the Pan Motor Company and had another meeting with Mr. Pandolfo. I'd been sending money back every time I ordered another shipment of books, and you know what? My bills were all paid off. I didn't owe Mr. Pandolfo any more money, and I'd even paid off that Pan automobile.

But I didn't have two dimes to rub together. I had to borrow money to live on while I wrote my second book. And then I had to borrow more money to have it printed. And then I set off on the road again. That book was *The Werewolf of Harlem*. Isn't it something — I got the idea from a vampire book and a vampire movie, but when I wrote my book it came out a werewolf. You see, the werewolf was colored, and he terrorized a colored community. The police in the book were colored; the beautiful girl was colored. I figured colored folks would go for the book, just like they did for *Murder on the Bar-20*. And I was right. Another two thousand books. I sold that book from Maine to Florida, driving around in my Pan automobile, staying in houses when I could, sleeping in the car when I had to.

When I got home to Saint Cloud I had paid off Mr. Samuel C. Pandolfo and I had a little nest egg. But it wasn't much and I still had to live, so when I wrote my third book, *Detectives of Harlem Yard*, I tried out a new scheme. I planned still another book, a real ghost story this time. It was called *The Haunted Skeleton*. The book wasn't even written yet; I just had an idea what I was going to write, but I had my designer in Saint Cloud make up a dust jacket for it. I told him what to put on it. When he printed up *Detectives of Harlem Yard* I had him do the dust jackets for *The Haunted Skeleton*, too. I slipped some onto copies of other books and took them on the road with me.

Whenever a store bought some copies of *Detectives of Harlem Yard* I got them to order *The Haunted Skeleton*. I said it was in production, and when the book came out, instead of waiting for me to come around on my route, they'd get the first copies, shipped straight from the printer. Talk about a great idea. It worked liked crazy. I sold as many skeletons as I did detectives. The scheme was a big success. And after that I just kept one book ahead, selling the next book when I delivered this book. Oh, it was glorious.

I wrote *A Mother's Pain* and I wrote a sequel to that, *A Mother's Joy*. I wrote another Western, then I finally got around to my vampire novel, then I wrote *Return of the Werewolf of Harlem*.

Then came the Depression and I went

broke. No, you young fool, of course that didn't end my career. Why are you here? That was how I got into the movie business.

9

Lindsey lowered his copy of the MacReedy narrative and rubbed his eyes.

Marvia asked, 'What do you think of it?'

Lindsey grinned. 'It's a great little story. Of course Scoggins will have to run more sessions with the old man. He started out to research MacReedy's film-making career and all he has here is Valdosta, Georgia, and Saint Cloud, Minnesota, and writing books. I didn't know that MacReedy wrote books. And driving around as he did . . . what an adventure that must have been.'

Marvia dropped her copy of the manuscript on a reading table and slid onto Lindsey's lap.

'But I don't see anything about the movies yet, except that he used to go to them when he was traveling,' Lindsey said. 'I don't see anything that could connect with the Robeson Center arson, no less the Film Archive fire.'

'We'll have to wait for the next installment of his story, I suppose. If we had more to go on, the police should be questioning MacReedy. But we just don't have the case or the people. Thank heaven for Walter Scoggins.'

Lindsey said, 'I'd better get a move on if I'm going to hit the hay in Walnut Creek.'

'What the heck,' Marvia said into his ear, 'let's be public-spirited and not pollute the atmosphere with automobile exhaust.'

Lindsey called his mother to make sure she was all right. She was.

★　★　★

He was awakened by the telephone. Marvia was already awake and took the call. She listened, spoke, listened, then broke the connection, crawled across Lindsey and headed for the shower. When she came out she said, 'What's your schedule this morning?'

'Nothing that can't wait for afternoon.'

'Okay. Hang with me. You'll enjoy this

and it may be important.'

'What is it?'

'Breakfast at Laffy's. A breakfast that you'll never forget. I guarantee it.'

'I don't know. I think you've got something up your sleeve.'

'If you don't mind, Bart, could we take your Hyundai instead of the Mustang? And try to dress down a little. No coat and tie. And don't shave.'

* * *

Marvia directed him to a seedy section of San Pablo Avenue. They parked at a meter in front of a saloon. The paint was peeling and one window had been cracked, held in place by layers of masking tape. The faded sign over the door had a picture of two ancient biplanes firing machine guns at each other. Above them scrolled the words *Lafayette Escadrille*.

'Laffy's, eh?' Lindsey dropped a coin in the parking meter.

The air inside the saloon hadn't been changed in a long time. He was amazed to see customers propped against the bar this early in the morning. Laffy wore a handlebar mustache and wire-rimmed glasses and an apron tied high over a massive belly.

One of the barflies, a filthy harridan, saw Lindsey and Marvia Plum and crawled off her stool and headed for the back of the saloon. She disappeared down a dingy hallway.

Marvia nodded at Laffy. After a moment she guided Lindsey by one elbow, following the harridan. She stopped at what looked like a maintenance closet, applied a key, and drew him through the doorway.

They sat in an office furnished with a desk and some ratty-looking wooden chairs. Marvia's boss, Lieutenant Dorothy Yamura, sat behind the desk. Like Marvia, she was casually dressed.

There was a fourth person in the room. The female barfly had preceded them into the back room. Her face and hands were streaked with dirt; her hair hung down in strings. There were twigs in it, and Lindsey wondered if there were bugs. Her clothing was filthy and ragged.

Dorothy Yamura said, 'Celia Varela,

Hobart Lindsey. You know Sergeant Plum, of course.'

Lindsey hesitated, then tentatively shook hands with the woman.

'Don't cringe,' Dorothy Yamura told Lindsey. 'Tell him who you are, Celia. Mr. Lindsey is an insurance investigator. He's worked with us several times.'

Celia Varela said, 'I'm a homicide officer. I'm assigned to an investigation in People's Park.'

Yamura said, 'Marvia, I wanted you to hear this because you've been working on the Pacific Film Archive case. And, Mr. Lindsey, I understand you believe there's a connection with the arson incident over at the Robeson Center.'

'That's right.'

'All right. I'm recording this conversation, just for the record. I assume you have no objection.'

'No, of course not.'

Celia Varela cleared her throat. 'First of all, I've been trying to get some information on the Anti-Imperialist Front for the Liberation of People's Park. Basically what we have here is one of the fringe groups. Professional radicals. Their program is fairly specific. No development of People's Park; they want the volleyball and the basketball courts out, the free soup kitchen back, no police interference with popular sovereignty in the park.'

'Meaning no interference with drug dealing,' Yamura said. 'Meaning no use of the park for ordinary citizens except at the risk of their life and safety; meaning safe haven and immune sanctuary for muggers, burglars and shoplifters who set up light housekeeping in the park.' She raised her elegant black eyebrows.

'I'm not sure that I'm supposed to make that judgement, but as far as I've been able to observe, that's what it means.' Celia Varela reached for a cup of coffee on Yamura's desk. 'I'll be thrilled when I can wash off this filth and get rid of the stink. Lt. Yamura, I hope I get something worthwhile out of this assignment.'

Yamura smiled faintly. 'The satisfaction of a job well done in the service of your fellow citizens. Now, what about this fellow who loves to rant?'

'You mean 'Che'? Dylan Guevara — pseudonym of course — sets fires in the park; loves to come to city council meetings and make disruptive speeches. Was involved in spraying stink-chemicals at one meeting. No known connection with the attack on the UC chancellor's house, at least that I can pin down.'

Yamura nodded. 'At least that's something. What about his performance after the Film Archive fire? You think he was connected with the fire? Was the Anti-Imperialist Front responsible?'

'Hard to tell. I think it may have been opportunism. You know, these types will claim responsibility for everything. I'm not so sure that the Front *wasn't* involved, though. I just don't know.'

'Fair enough. Work on that, will you? Any more on Guevara?'

'We all know he leads street demonstrations and marches on Telegraph Avenue. Loves to get on the evening news. Arrested for looting and vandalism on six occasions. One conviction.'

Yamura wanted more than a review of

Dylan Guevara's history. 'Tell me something I don't already know. Sergeant Plum is familiar with the situation. Mr. Lindsey could use some filling in.'

'All right.' Celia Varela slurped her coffee noisily. 'Guevara's real name is Daniel Garfinkel. Born Philadelphia, Pennsylvania. Age 44. Veteran of the Free Speech Movement, original People's Park riots, one-time force in the Peace and Freedom Party, later associated with the Revolutionary Communist Party. Now allegedly non-partisan, anti-Communist, populist.'

'Married? Family or close associates?'

'Not altogether clear. I did some digging into his background. Father a rabbi, mother a psychotherapist. Both apparently still active. Two sisters, both married, both still living in the Philadelphia area. Apparently Daniel married a classmate while attending U of Pennsylvania. Became involved in the student radical movement. His wife ran off to join a religious commune; I haven't been able to track her down after their senior year.'

Yamura said, 'Okay, I know you had the

clerks checking this guy out. For the record, what's the story on the name change?'

'Right. After Garfinkel's wife left him for the cult, he remained at U of P and got a degree in English Lit. Attended grad school briefly at Harvard, then he got a scholarship to attend grad school at Berkeley, enrolled briefly, then dropped out to join the local political community. In his early days he was more of a groupie than anything else. Used to hang around the big-name radicals. At one time he wanted to join the Symbionese Liberation Army. Started making a pest of himself. Played confessor for a while. Claimed he supplied the cyanide bullets for the Marcus Foster assassination. Claimed he knew where Patti Hearst was being kept. Neither checked out.'

Lindsey said, 'This guy sounds like a maniac.'

'When his confessions started flopping, he tried something new. Suicide threats. One time he threatened to jump off the Campanile. Another time he was going to rent an airplane and crash it into the

Lawrence Lab. Or throw himself under a steamroller when they were laying down pavement where he wanted to plant a marijuana garden. He always notified the TV stations and the newspapers. Never followed through on any of his threats, and they stopped sending camera crews.'

Nobody expressed surprise.

Varela continued, 'Garfinkel took the Guevara alias in '71. Chairman and chief spokesman for the Anti-Imperialist Front for the Liberation of People's Park. Used to be quoted frequently in the radical press. KPFA Radio's gone upscale and they won't let him in their lobby let alone in front of a microphone anymore, although some of the more unreconstructed types still quote him once in a while.'

Dorothy Yamura nodded. 'Is Guevara the big cheese of this Anti-Imperialist Front?'

'No way.'

Yamura said, 'I didn't think so. They're too smart and he's too visible. What's really going on?'

'Lieutenant, I've been hanging in that park for months. It's just a good thing that we put together this hag outfit to stop them coming on to me. I managed to get pretty close to Guevara. He appears totally asexual, by the way. He may not be any genius, but he's fairly canny. The Front puts up posters all over the East Bay. They get contributions from a number of sources.'

'Who?'

'Conscience-stricken former radicals for one. A few idealists who think the Front is legitimate, which we know it isn't. And it looks as if some of the local merchants may be paying what amounts to protection money, to keep from getting trashed and looted. I haven't been able to pin that down, but I'm pretty sure of it.'

'How?'

'Che goes into stores and comes out with merchandise. Then that disappears. Every so often he seems to have a lot of cash.'

Yamura leaned back. 'What do you think, Sergeant, Mr. Lindsey? Any comments? Questions?'

Marvia shook her head.

Lindsey said, 'If not Guevara, who is really the brains of this Front?'

Varela looked a question at Dorothy Yamura, who said, 'Mr. Lindsey, you're aware of how very sensitive this information is. You are not to repeat anything you hear in this room, or reveal the existence of this room.'

'I understand.'

'And please don't go bulling ahead of our investigation. You could blow an undercover investigation that's taken years of effort to establish. Celia?'

'It's because I used to work in a print shop. I know a little bit about production and layout; I can run an offset press. And I can do a little desktop publishing work. The Front used to put out its propaganda on little photocopied sheets, crudely hand-written. I bitched about it in the park until somebody said, 'Yeah, well can you do better?' And I said, 'Yes, as a matter of fact I can.' Eventually word got to Che. He'd pretty much ignored me up to that time. But he started calling me Sister, and sharing his cans of chili with me. He doesn't do drugs but he drinks godawful wine, and he shares that with me too. *Yuch*. But it looks as if I'm in the inner circle now.'

She stopped and ran her fingers through her hair. Lindsey wondered what it must be like to live the way she had to live.

'He started bouncing his ideas off me,' Varela said. 'I wrote that flier after the Film Archive fire, by the way. That's going to be Front policy from now on, everything misspelled. Gives us a distinct identity.'

Yamura nodded. 'Go on.'

'Now here's the thing. They're out of the hand-made flier business and into high-tech work, and Che's been taking me up to their headquarters. He's got this amazing old VW van. And the Front headquarters is in a very nice, very upper-middle-class house in Northside. Cedar Street.' Varela gave a number.

'Guevara doesn't own it, does he?'

'I don't think so. A yuppie couple live there. They drift in and out. Che defers to them. He's never introduced me to them, and they always manage to turn away when they see me.'

Yamura grinned. 'No problem to find

out who owns the house.'

'One more important question,' Lindsey put in. 'The second attempt at the Robeson Center — when we encountered that intruder in the old wine cellar. He disappeared, headed west. I think he might have wound up in the park. Any idea who that was?'

Varela said, 'No. I got your description, Mr. Lindsey, but it was so vague; I mean, there must be a couple of hundred people in the Telegraph population . . . '

'Yes.' Lindsey frowned. 'No known arsonists in your circle?'

'Could be, but I don't think so. I mean, Che likes to set bonfires or set trash-barrels on fire. It's just not his style, to sneak around. He loves the spotlight too much.'

'Still . . . '

'Still, yes, it's possible.'

10

Who was the firebug? Was it Dylan Guevara, was it the mysterious well-dressed couple at the house on Cedar Street, or was it some nondescript, possibly itinerant hired hand willing to do anything for the price of his next dose of dope?

Lindsey shook the thoughts away and bounded up the steps of the Robeson Center. Inside, he spotted Officer Mike Ng and Ms. Mathilde Wilbur engaged in intense conversation with Oliver Hendry. MacReedy was nowhere in sight.

Ms. Wilbur gestured Lindsey to join the group. 'Hobart, maybe you can offer some help. Mr. Ng here says the police are going to withdraw their people.'

Ng looked unhappy. 'We'll keep a patrol. We'll keep the nearest cruiser on alert and they'll check by here pretty often.'

'I'm sorry,' Hendry put in. 'That just won't be enough. We have almost a hundred guests in the center, average age eighty-two. These people need some protection, some security. If you can't do better than checking by pretty often, then I'm afraid Mr. MacReedy will have to go. And we'd hate to see that. He's a real favorite around here.'

Ms. Wilbur appealed to Lindsey. 'Hobart, they want to throw that poor man out and he has no place to go. They took his membership money all those years, now they're going to throw him out.'

Hendry scowled. 'We don't *want* to, but you're forcing our hand. You, Mr. Ng. If the police department won't protect us . . . We know he's after Mr. MacReedy, or Mr. MacReedy's belongings anyway, whoever that intruder was. We just don't have the funds to hire a protective service. And we'll make a settlement with Mr. MacReedy. He'll get his money back.'

Lindsey said, 'Where is he?'

Hendry tipped his head. 'In the wine cellar. Mr. and Mrs., ah, Scoggins are with him.'

'And my partner is keeping an eye on the back entrance and on the three of them,' Ng put in. 'I wanted to seal off the rear entrance but Sgt. Stromback had a fit and Lt. D'Onofrio backed him on it. So my partner is keeping an eye out to see that nobody pulls another fast one while they're down in the cellar.'

'Doing what?' Lindsey asked.

'Looking through a lot of old junk, I think.'

Ms. Wilbur said, 'I think that so-called old junk is at the heart of this. I think that thug was trying to destroy something that Mr. MacReedy owns. That's why he went after the room when he was out and that's why he made his second attempt in the cellar. He wasn't after anybody, certainly not Mr. MacReedy. He was after his property.'

'Look, Mr. Hendry,' Lindsey offered, 'if you're afraid the arsonist will try again and you're convinced that he's after MacReedy's belongings, not MacReedy himself . . . ' He spread his hands. 'Then why don't we just move those filing cabinets and the other things, the wardrobe and the trunk — let's get 'em out of here.'

'What if the arsonist doesn't *know* that Mr. MacReedy's things are gone?' Hendry said. 'He sees him still here; he thinks his belongings are still here.'

'Look,' Lindsey persisted, 'suppose we make a big show out of moving Mr. MacReedy's belongings out of here? We have them designated a special collection, he donates them to the UC Library or to the Pacific Film Archive — '

'They had an arson fire, too.'

'Exactly. But they're part of a powerful institution. UC has its own police force. They've already put a special detail at the museum. They can protect those files the way the Robeson Center can't.'

Ms. Wilbur said, 'I'll talk to Scoggins and Mr. MacReedy. He's taken a real shine to Walter. I'll bet he goes for it.'

'We'll try and get it on the news, get it in the papers and on TV,' Lindsey suggested. 'What do you think, Mr. Hendry?'

'I'll have to take it up with the directors, but it sounds good to me. Mr. MacReedy has our sympathy, especially since he lost his wife. We'd love to have him stay. But we can't keep him at the jeopardy of the institution and our other residents.'

'Understood,' Lindsey said. 'Can you hold off a little longer? I'll see if the Film Archive will accept Mr. MacReedy's materials. I'll talk to Tony Roland over there. That is, if Ms. Wilbur and Walter Scoggins can talk MacReedy into it. This might all work out.'

Hendry nodded. 'That sounds good. Officer Ng, can you folks stay on for a few more days?'

Ng said, 'That's up to headquarters, but I don't think they're going to pull us just yet.'

★　★　★

This time they brought a couple of good-sized portable lamps with them. Lindsey was there with Ms. Wilbur, Walter Scoggins and MacReedy. They restarted the tour from square one, the standing wardrobe.

Scoggins radiated excitement. 'Nobody's seen these things for forty years. Some for more like sixty. What a find!' He had rented a video camcorder and moved around MacReedy, capturing the great event.

For the second time, MacReedy showed

off his old stiff-woven suits, the bowlers and fedoras, and his late wife's beaded dresses and cloche hats, and the later garments — the drab longer dresses of the Depression, and the short skirts and picture hats of the 1940s war years.

The trunk yielded costumes with the tear-inducing fumes of camphor. 'Moth balls,' MacReedy said. Out of the trunk came cowboy chaps and boots, plaid shirts and jeans, white laboratory garb and once-white nurse's uniforms, maid's uniforms, butler's livery, a chauffeur's gray costume, a clergyman's collar and a set of military garb.

MacReedy held up a wartime green tunic with tarnished brass buttons. 'I wore that in *Sergeant Jones*. Faced down a whole Japanese platoon. Most of these things were for other people. But once in a while I'd fill in when we were short.'

Scoggins frowned. 'I thought you used all-black casts.'

'Mostly we did. But for *Sergeant Jones* we needed that enemy fighting unit. There were these trucks of Mexican farm workers going past all the time.'

Scoggins held up his hand. 'Mexican farm workers? Where was this?'

'Niles, California. That's where we were. Not an hour from here. That was farm country back then. We stopped 'em and made a deal with the labor boss. We hired farm workers by the day. They were our Jap soldiers. We borrowed some air raid warden helmets and painted 'em up with rising sun insignia and they were our Jap soldiers.'

Scoggins said, 'Now the filing cabinets.'

'There were three,' said MacReedy. 'I had the best things up in my room. They're gone now, burned up.' The old man lifted the heavy padlock on one of the filing cabinets. He twirled the dial. It spun easily. 'I oil these locks regularly, son. Can't have 'em freeze up on me.' The lock popped open with a soft, metallic click. MacReedy grinned. 'Even after sixty years I always remember that combination.'

The top drawer yielded manila folders full of production records, correspondence, memos. Most were written in the same hand. Answering the unasked question, MacReedy said, 'That is my writing.'

'Will you give me exclusive access to all of this?' Scoggins asked eagerly. 'I'd like to be curator of this collection. My gosh, the Edward Joseph MacReedy Black Film Archive!'

MacReedy opened the padlock to the other cabinet. He let Scoggins roll the four drawers out of their wooden casing, one by one. Not production notes this time. The upper drawers contained scripts. The lower two held stacks of round, flat metal canisters.

Scoggins gasped. 'Are those prints of your films?'

MacReedy shook his head. 'No. Just outtakes. I don't know why I even saved them, but I couldn't throw them away.'

'Do you know what's what?' Scoggins fell to his knees, carefully lifting the canisters from the cabinet. 'Nothing is marked.' He put them back into their drawers, then carefully rolled the drawers shut. 'I don't want to open them here. We need to get them to the Film Archive. Let an expert do it in a controlled room

— gloves, the whole scene.'

'All right.' MacReedy seemed pleased.

Lindsey said, 'I'm going to phone that fellow Roland at the Film Archive about this. This looks too good to delay. And too dangerous.' He borrowed Oliver Hendry's telephone and called the Pacific Film Archive.

When Lindsey finished describing MacReedy and what he had, Roland was practically singing. Of course he'd heard of Speedy MacReedy. Of course he knew the story of H-M-R Productions. 'MacReedy is still alive? And he lives in Berkeley?' Roland couldn't believe it.

'There was a feature about him on TV a few weeks ago.'

'I never watch TV. Just film.' Roland paused to wipe his face. 'I could walk over there in ten minutes. This is astounding. And you say he has files, records, scripts . . . and *outtakes*? Mr. Lindsey, I don't think you can imagine what this means.'

'Maybe I can.' Lindsey had dealt with scholars and collectors before. Whether their passion was for forty-year-old comic books or fifty-year-old airplanes or seventy-year-old cars, their minds all worked in similar ways. They felt that human achievement was bound in the artifacts of human creation; that the preservation and ownership of those artifacts kept civilization on the rails of time.

Lindsey told Roland about Walter Scoggins. 'He has a verbal agreement with Mr. MacReedy. Can you work with him? He's just finishing his doctorate at Southern U in Baton Rouge.'

'He can have Annabella's work area. It's all cleaned up now. We'll have to check his credentials, but Southern is a solid institution . . . I'll tell you what, suppose I come over there right now? The Robeson Center on Canyon Road. Who'd have thought, Speedy MacReedy's been there all this time. And they showed him on TV. I might have to buy one. What a bonanza.'

11

Anthony Roland came puffing up the hillside. The pale, flabby flesh of a man who spent his life in darkened rooms studying the images of long-ago worlds, that was Tony Roland. Lindsey met him on the veranda of the Robeson Center.

MacReedy's filing cabinets were locked up and his storage room was secured, and Mike Ng's partner was stationed where he could watch both the Robeson Center's rear exit and the staircase to the wine cellar. Lindsey was fairly confident that MacReedy's materials were safe.

Roland was eager to meet MacReedy, but Ms. Wilbur and Martha Scoggins had escorted him back to his room. They made it known that he needed his rest.

Roland, Lindsey, and Walter Scoggins huddled in the Robeson Center's lobby. Roland ignored Lindsey, pumping Scoggins for information. He wanted to know what outtakes Roland had found in the filing cabinets.

'He wouldn't tell me,' Scoggins said. 'He seemed embarrassed that he'd saved them.'

'But they could be treasures.'

'Tell me.'

'And the scripts — did you get the titles?'

Of those, Scoggins had. He mentioned a few. Roland jumped halfway out of his skin. 'I've only seen a third of those. My God, man, the others — half of *those* are legends, and the rest I've never even heard of.'

Scoggins said, 'Do you think we can cut a deal? Are you authorized to make a commitment for the Film Archive?'

'You bet I am. Come on, I'll get my director. We'll have an informal letter-of-agreement ready to sign today.'

      ★   ★   ★

The University Art Museum fronted on Bancroft Way, facing the main University of California campus. On the opposite side of the building, where the Film Archive had its separate entrance, Lindsey detected no sign of the crowd that had gathered the day of the fire. Dylan 'Che' Guevara was elsewhere, maybe plotting a new broadside with the help of Celia Varela.

On the way to his office, Roland led them past the workroom where Annabella Buonaventura had died. The walls were scrubbed, the ceiling tiles had been replaced, and the floor had been refinished. Behind Roland's desk, a wall-unit showed the spines of an array of tattered reference volumes — the books were there to be used, not to impress visitors. Roland produced a sheet of letterhead and scrawled a couple of paragraphs on it. He shoved the paper at Walter Scoggins. 'There's a rough memo of agreement. That okay with you? I'll have it typed up, then we can do a more formal one later on.'

Scoggins studied the paper. He handed it to Lindsey. 'What do you think, Mr. Lindsey?'

Lindsey scanned the memo. 'Looks okay to me. Do you always do business this way, Mr. Roland?'

'Tony. Only when there's something this wonderful at hand. I can't believe that Speedy MacReedy has been living right under my nose all these years, and I never knew he was here.'

'Too bad you didn't meet him sooner. You could have met his wife. She just died.'

Roland reared up in seat. 'Lola Mae Turner was alive until this year?'

'We haven't got to her yet.' Scoggins took over for Lindsey. 'Apparently she fell and broke her hip. A typical geriatric injury. She never came home from the hospital. At that age, you know, anything can happen.'

Lindsey asked, 'How important is MacReedy? I never heard of him before this whole affair.'

Roland deferred to Scoggins. 'He was the most important producer-director of black independent films.'

'You mean like *Green Pastures* and *Carmen Jones*?'

Scoggins waved a dismissive hand. 'Those pictures came out of the major studios. This was a whole separate film industry. That's what I've been interviewing Mr. MacReedy about. Black crews, black talent, they played to black audiences. Most white people didn't even know these pictures existed.'

'I've got the idea. When was this? How many pictures did they make?'

'Nobody knows. You know, there are people all over the country researching old films. Mr. Roland knows a lot more about that than I do, except for the black films. There must have been hundreds of them. Some still survive, some we know only from posters or reviews in Negro newspapers, some are completely lost.'

'And Mr. MacReedy was part of this industry.' Lindsey leaned forward.

'He wasn't just part of it,' Scoggins said. 'He was the most important single person in it.'

Roland swung around in his chair. He pulled a fat paperbound volume from his shelf and slid the bulky paperback across the desk. Lindsey picked it up and read the entry Roland had opened it at:

★ ★ ★

MacReedy, Edward Joseph. B. 1902, D. 1961? Producer, director, screen writer, actor. A native of Saint Cloud, Minnesota, father a church music director, mother a secretary. MacReedy was the author of several successful novels of Negro life published by the Pan Publishing Program of Saint Cloud. MacReedy's early success as novelist caused independent producer and sometime cameraman Alton Lincoln to approach MacReedy for screen rights to his novels. MacReedy instead offered to write and direct films based on his books. After a tentative beginning, this led to the formation of the H-M-R Film Company. The principals were Lincoln, MacReedy, and William Hargess (q.v.).

H-M-R began production in 1931. Its first release was *Murder on the Bar-20*, based on MacReedy's original story of the same name. MacReedy served as director and even as an extra in several scenes. (He can be seen playing cards in the first reel, and later, drinking whiskey in a saloon.) Male lead was Alonzo X. Nash (q.v.), female lead was child-star Lola Mae Turner (q.v.) as the rancher's daughter, villain was Hargess.

By 1934 H-M-R had released seven feature films with all-Negro casts. In 1934 H-M-R entered into an agreement with Pan-Pacific Intercontinental Film Corp., a white-oriented sub-Poverty Row outfit. Under this agreement, H-M-R and PPIF shared production facilities while preparing similar 'black' and 'white' films on a common set. Even scripts were shared, with appropriate adaptations for black and white audiences. Each version had its own cast, and the films were marketed and released without mention of the co-production.

The first H-M-R/PPIF co-production was *The Werewolf of Harlem* (H-M-R) and *The Werewolf of Wall Street* (PPIF). Production took place at H-M-R Studios in Niles, California, former site of the famous Essanay Company, which abandoned the Niles location in 1916. Shooting of both films was completed on the same day.

The black and white companies were in the midst of a joint wrap party following the last day of shooting when a disastrous fire broke out. Several actors and crew members were killed including Hargess.

The Werewolf of Wall Street, directed by Philip Quince and starring Arturo Madrid as the werewolf, was released to a favorable reception. *The Werewolf of Harlem*, directed by MacReedy and starring Hargess, was never released. All negatives and prints were reportedly destroyed in the fire.

The H-M-R/PPIF partnership was dissolved following this disaster. H-M-R, due to the death of one of its principals as well as one of its leading stock players, followed shortly. PPIF survived into the 1950s.

Already known as 'Speedy' because of his ability to move a film quickly through the production process and into release, Edward Joseph MacReedy formed The MacReedy Grand Film Corporation. MGFC released at least eleven additional films between 1936 and 1948. Most were shot on sets or in functional indoor locations in Los Angeles, Chicago or New York. An outstanding exception was *Sergeant Jones* (1944), the last known production at the Niles facility. Scenes of all-black American fighting units in combat with Japanese marines were filmed on the sites where 'Broncho Billy' Anderson had filmed his

Westerns in 1912 and where Chaplin had made *The Tramp* in 1915.

MGFC's last release was a Western, ironically titled *Last Roundup on the Bar-20*. Turner and Nash reprised their earlier roles, Turner now in full flower in her 'Sepia Siren' persona. The male lead was young Johnson Locksley, who later became a successful lounge singer.

MacReedy alternated between Hollywood and New York, slipping into lesser assignments as assistant director, uncredited script consultant, and bit player, primarily in films directed by William Castle (q.v.). He can be seen in films of the 1950s variously shining shoes, pushing a broom, pumping gasoline and waiting on tables. MacReedy performed a remarkable comic turn opposite midget disk jockey Paul Dale in Castle's *It's a Small World* (1950). He then appeared as a cab driver in *The Fat Man* (1951) and as a Nubian slave in *Serpent of the Nile*, reprising that role in *Slaves of Babylon* (both 1953). He achieved a brief notoriety for his portrayal of a stomach-turning mutilation victim in George Russell's *Blood Price* (1960).

Last known to have visited a television producer in New York in the spring of 1961, MacReedy may have been alive as late as 1965, when 'he' was introduced in the ring at a prize fight in Los Angeles. Unconfirmed rumors suggest that Johnson Locksley posed as MacReedy for unknown reasons. If Locksley needed the publicity, it is hard to understand why he would use MacReedy's name. The controversy has never been resolved.

★   ★   ★

Tony Roland closed the book. 'What do you think?'

Lindsey laughed. 'They got the birth date and birth place wrong. MacReedy was born in Georgia and moved to Minnesota later. They got his parents' occupations wrong. But nothing is way, way off. Just a couple of years off here, just an event or two there.' He grinned. 'And of course he didn't die in 1961. Or 1965. He's alive and well and living in the Paul Robeson Retirement Center.'

Scoggins said, 'That's why my work is

important. Of course, I don't have to take MacReedy's word for everything he says, either. Maybe he changed his birth date to make himself younger. Maybe he's ninety-two, not ninety. Posing as a kid, you know.'

'And the film credits?' Lindsey pursued. 'H-M-R and those other outfits.'

Roland spread his hands. 'That's where we need to do so much more. Annabella Buonaventura was working on that, in her own way. Of course she didn't have the contact with Mr. MacReedy. She was working with film, doing the kind of frame-by-frame analysis that we like to do in this field.'

'My approach is different,' Scoggins said. 'I'm not primarily a film scholar. That's why I want to spend some more time with Mr. MacReedy. One thing I really want to do is get him down to Niles. He said that's just a few miles from here, right?'

Roland's phone rang. He picked it up, looked surprised, and held it toward Lindsey.

Lindsey took the phone. Marvia Plum said, 'We got the ID on the owners of that

Cedar Street house. Martin and Florence Corcoran, solid and respectable as the day is long. They run a computer consulting service out of their house and they dabble in investment-grade real estate, mostly low-end industrial properties. One Beamer, one Mercedes.'

'What are you going to do about that?'

'I'm working something out with Dorothy Yamura and Celia Varela. You want to be our token boy? How soon can you get down to Laffy's?'

Lindsey looked at his watch. 'I left my car up at Robeson; I'll have to climb that hill to get it. How about forty-five minutes to an hour?'

'Don't look conspicuous when you arrive.'

* * *

The Lafayette Escadrille was a different place after dark. The bar-stools were full and there were patrons at most of the tables. Lindsey glanced at the clock behind the back bar; he was almost fifteen minutes early.

The jukebox was playing something old and melancholy. Sad people came to Laffy's to be sad together. Laffy himself presided over the wake for dead hopes. He nodded Lindsey toward the back. Lindsey made his way down the same stale-smelling corridor he'd walked with Marvia Plum. He knocked, then tried the door of the seeming maintenance closet, slipped unobtrusively into the room, and found Celia Varela lying on the floor.

Her face was blue. Her mouth was taped. Her hands and feet were wired together. There was a narrow crease around her neck, the neck swollen above and below it. Her eyes were open.

Lindsey made himself put his hand on her face. It was cold. She wasn't breathing.

He looked at Dorothy Yamura's desk, hoping there was a telephone there. Yes, there was. He reached for it.

The door opened behind him.

12

Dorothy Yamura had a gun and it was pointed straight at Lindsey. 'Just put your hands behind your neck and lace your fingers. Then get down on your knees and keep going until you're flat on your belly. Then keep your hands like that and spread your feet far apart.'

'But I — '

She waved the gun. Lindsey did as he was told. He watched Dorothy Yamura step around him and pick up the telephone. She held her gun in her other hand trained on him.

There were heavy footsteps in the hall and Laffy shouldered massively through the doorway. He said, 'Oh, Jesus.'

Yamura said, 'Check the back exit, will you?' Laffy disappeared, pulling the door shut behind him.

'Every time I think I've found a safe place, I'm wrong,' she said. 'Every time I think I can trust somebody, I'm wrong.

Don't move a muscle.'

The door opened again. Laffy's voice was grim. 'Gone. If there was anybody. Alarm didn't go off, but that's easy enough to disarm. That guy do it?'

'Don't know.' She patted Lindsey down. 'Okay, put your hands in the small of your back. Don't do anything else.'

He felt handcuffs snapped around his wrists.

'Get him into a chair.' Dorothy Yamura began to curse softly. Once Lindsey was in the chair he could see her checking Celia Varela for signs of life, more thorough and skilled than he had been. She kept trying for a long time.

'Bar under control, Laffy?' she asked.

'A few minutes. I ought to get out there.'

Yamura slid into the chair behind the desk. She gave Lindsey a look that could have been made on a lathe. She laid her gun on the desk, picked up the phone, punched at the keypad, murmured into the mouthpiece and laid the handset back on its cradle.

'You want to tell me anything, Mr.

Lindsey? Here, I'll turn on the tape. God damn it, I'd better read you your rights . . . '

Lindsey sat quietly while Lt. Yamura recited the familiar litany. Then he said, 'I didn't do it. She was dead when I came in, and — '

'Do you understand your rights?'

'Yes, I do.'

'Okay. Laffy, you witnessed that. And it's on tape.'

Laffy said, 'I'd better get back outside. I'll get the county coroner to send a squad.' He left the room.

'Do you have a voluntary statement which you wish to make?' Yamura asked Lindsey.

'Marvia . . . Sergeant Plum phoned me. I was up at the Art Museum with Tony Roland and Walter Scoggins.'

'Who's Scoggins?'

'He's a graduate student. From Louisiana. He's doing a doctorate. Since Annabella Buonaventura was killed, Roland was going to get Scoggins the appointment. They were just working out the details. I was there because I . . . '

Yamura waited, frowning.

Lindsey shook his head. 'This is complicated. Uh — I met Scoggins when I was in Louisiana on International Surety business about a year ago. Scoggins just got married. They wanted to come out here on their honeymoon to combine it with his research project.' Lindsey paused. Yamura continued to frown. 'Well, they didn't know anybody out here except Sergeant Plum and myself.'

Yamura nodded. The desk was between her and Lindsey. 'You came here directly from the museum?'

'No. I left my car up at the Robeson Center. Up on Canyon Road. I drove down here; Laffy saw me come in. I came in here and she was . . . ' He used his head to indicate Celia Varela's body.

'What time was that?'

Lindsey recalled looking at the clock behind the bar. 'It was quarter of. I was surprised; I got here early. There wasn't much traffic. Laffy saw me come in. I didn't stop and talk to him but I know he saw me.'

161

'And?'

'And there she was.'

Yamura scowled. 'Quarter of, eh? And I arrived when — two, three minutes later.'

'Yes.'

'And Sergeant Plum invited you to this meeting? All right. She'll be here any minute. She'll verify that.' She fell silent.

Lindsey waited for her to speak. Finally she said, 'Maybe I acted too fast.'

Marvia Plum arrived before the coroner's wagon did. Her shock at the sight of Celia Varela's body was obvious. 'She has a baby,' were Marvia's first words. In response to Lt. Yamura's questions, she verified Lindsey's story.

Yamura said, 'I'm going to take the cuffs off you, Mr. Lindsey. You're not under arrest, but you found the body and you'll have to give a statement. Is that clear?'

'Yes, that's clear.' Lindsey pushed himself to his feet and rubbed his sore wrists. Yamura put away the cuffs and the gun.

The coroner's squad took photos and measurements. The technician in charge asked Yamura, 'You want to check for articles in her pockets?' She nodded, and the technician patted down the body.

Lindsey tried to look away, but he was fascinated. He couldn't help himself. The technician wore surgical gloves. He ran his hands over Celia Varela's body with studied impersonality. Varela was wearing the same filthy layered outfit she'd worn when Lindsey first met her. He thought, *Well, at least they'll wash her and put her in something clean before they bury her.*

The technician ran his gloved fingers inside Celia Varela's boots. They were low mountaineering boots, or had once been. Now they were badly worn and stained with unguessable detritus. Well, maybe not unguessable. The crime lab would surely work on that and see if they could figure out where Celia had been lately.

The technician tapped one of those worn mountain boots. 'Look at the bottom here.'

Everyone looked. Marvia Plum said, 'There's a hole in the bottom. She stuffed it with folded paper. Common enough.'

The technician smiled. 'Clean paper?'

Yamura said, 'Right! She couldn't walk

five steps with that in there without it getting dirty.'

From somewhere, maybe from the same invisible top hat where she kept her gun and handcuffs when she wasn't using them, Yamura produced an evidence bag. 'Let's see.'

The technician carefully removed Celia Varela's mountaineering boot. From the boot he removed a carefully folded sheet of paper. He laid the paper on Yamura's desk and waited for her to unfold it.

Yamura said, 'Sometimes we can lift prints off paper. You open it, you're wearing gloves. Try to touch it by the edges.'

The note was professionally laid out. Somebody was getting really good at desktop publishing. The text was, 'More Deaths, More Destructin Until Justis Is Serv.'

Yamura muttered a string of expletives to herself before addressing the technician again. She said, 'Please remove the remains. I don't suppose there will be any great surprises, but I want a complete autopsy report, and make it top priority. And try to get time of death. This is just — ' She dropped her head into her hands and Lindsey saw her shoulders heave. But she looked up after a moment, dry-eyed and composed. She said, 'I'll call her husband. I know him. I'll handle it myself.'

Marvia said, 'I think it's time to act. What do you think?'

'Let's talk to the self-styled Mr. Guevara,' Yamura answered. 'And let's have a chat with Mr. and Mrs. Corcoran. I want to see what that Cedar Street house looks like.'

'We need a warrant?' asked Marvia.

'Yes, just in case. This note and Celia's own statement about doing layout work in that house.' She looked Lindsey directly in the eye. 'All right, I apologize.'

'Forget it.'

'Can I make it up to you?'

'I want to come along to Cedar Street. I'm involved.'

Marvia shot a look at Lindsey, then back at Yamura. 'He doesn't have to read them any rights. And if they let us in without using the warrant, we might get more.'

Yamura frowned. 'I have to talk with the D.A. about this matter in any case. So I'll ask for an informal reading on letting Mr. Lindsey play catspaw for us. If Angie Tesla says it's okay, then it's okay.'

* ★ ★

They didn't use an official police car. They used a Jaguar sedan with plush upholstery and personal air conditioners for every seat. 'Got it from a crack king,' Dorothy Yamura explained. 'Poor fella's going to see in the new millennium through barred windows, if somebody doesn't off him in the rec yard first. But we had to fight the feds for the car.'

Lindsey was in the back seat. Marvia was driving, Yamura beside her. Marvia pulled to the curb in front of a tall Tudor Revival house. 'That's the number.'

Yamura said, 'Now, Mr. Lindsey, I'm going to go over this once more. You are not a police officer. Don't try any heroics. We're just here for information. We'll serve the search warrant only if the subjects refuse to cooperate voluntarily.

You will go in first, if they are willing to let you in. If there's any trouble, get out of the house and out of danger's way if you can. If you cannot do that, you hit the floor and try to put a wall or a piece of furniture between yourself and any violence or threat of violence. Do we understand each other?'

Lindsey said they did.

Yamura added, 'You weren't in on this, and it's none of your business, but we have backup.'

Lindsey swiveled in his seat. It was early evening, a reddish-brown glow silhouetting the tall buildings of San Francisco across the bay. Half the passing cars had their head lamps lit. There was little foot traffic, but at the far corner Lindsey saw a pair of lovers pause and embrace, then turn and walk back toward the Jaguar. A few cars away, next to the curb, he could make out a couple of silhouettes.

'If we don't need the backup,' Yamura said, 'they'll just wait till we exit the house and leave. Then they'll do the same. If we need help inside, they'll provide it.

Sergeant Plum and I each have a panic button. One jab and they'll know.'

She handed him a plastic rectangle the size of a matchbook. A button the diameter of a dime protruded from the flat surface. 'Just keep this in your pocket. There's a little interlock on the edge. You have to hold that down when you push the button. That's to keep it from sounding by accident. That won't call all the backup. That's just for Sergeant Plum and me.'

She opened the Jaguar's door and stepped out. Marvia and Lindsey did the same. Standing on the Tudor's slate doorstep, Lindsey used the knocker. It was in the form of a cast-iron horse's head. He couldn't make out the sounds coming from inside the house.

Once the door opened, he could. Someone was playing a Bach composition for organ.

Florence Corcoran was tall and willowy. Her platinum-blonde hair was carefully coifed in little dabs that looked like ocean waves. Each wave was separately tipped with darkness. She wore a bronze silk blouse and contrasting tights to her ankles, and a swirling patterned skirt. There were gold-brocade slippers on her feet.

She said, 'Yes?'

Lindsey extended a business card. Florence Corcoran looked at it without touching it. From behind her the music dribbled away to single notes, then went silent. 'I'm from the Special Projects Unit of International Surety,' he told her.

She nodded almost imperceptibly. 'All the way from Denver. But we're not in the market, thank you.' She started to close the door.

'I'm not a salesman.' Lindsey tried his most ingratiating smile. 'I'm setting up a new office. My unit is pretty autonomous. I want to talk about a computer system. We have a corporate system, of course, but this would be a dedicated system, just for our unit. It could hook into the corporate system but it wouldn't be part of it. Do you see?'

Martin Corcoran now stood behind his wife. His hair was a slightly shorter version of hers. He wore a white silk shirt and white trousers, a broad macramé belt and heavy sandals. 'Say, fellow, why don't you just call a computer store? Just look in the yellow pages.'

Lindsey shook his head. 'I heard about Corcoran Systems and I want the best I can get.'

'Heard about us? We don't advertise.'

'I, ah, our New Orleans office. A colleague of mine heard of this need and called me to recommend you. All the way from New Orleans.'

Florence Corcoran said, 'This is after business hours. This is our home.'

Lindsey said, 'I know, this is unconventional, and I hope I haven't interrupted your dinner hour. But if I could just have a few minutes to outline my needs. This could be a very large order. If this works out for my office, Special Projects might very well install your system corporate-wide. I just . . . '

Florence Corcoran stepped back. 'Very well. If you have to see us now . . . '

Lindsey stepped forward. Daniel into the lion's den. The Corcoran house boasted a flagstone vestibule that opened into a large living room. The ceiling was tall, rising to a peak. The half-beam and plaster treatment of the outside of the house was carried into the interior.

Martin Corcoran had stepped around his wife and guest. Lindsey could hear the heavy wooden door close. He started to thank them for their time but never got a syllable out. He felt a heavy impact on the side of his neck, saw the beautiful living room revolve crazily and flash past him, then felt himself crash to the thick pile carpet before everything went black.

13

He felt himself being dragged over the deep carpeting, and then being painfully dragged down a flight of stairs, bumping on each step.

The cellar was purely functional. Bare floor, rough walls. The air felt clammy and thick. Fluorescent light fixtures, a couple of desktop computers and laser printers. A photocopier and a small offset press.

His ears were ringing. What had Martin Corcoran hit him with — a baseball bat? Or maybe just the edge of his hand. Whatever it was, it had been one beautiful shot.

His senses jolted as the Corcorans slammed him unceremoniously into an old high-backed wooden chair. Martin stood over him threateningly while Florence bound his wrists. She'd finished the job before he had enough control to try and move his hands, and by then he realized that his wrists were wired together and that the wire was looped through a wooden slat.

And Celia Varela had been bound with wires and garroted. Something ice-cold crept through Lindsey's belly. He gasped, 'The police know I'm here.'

'Do they really?' Florence Corcoran circled the chair and knelt to wire Lindsey's ankles. Martin backed off half a stride to give her room. Lindsey heaved himself upright and launched himself at Martin.

A corner of the chair, level with Lindsey's eyes, caught Martin in the mouth. Lindsey felt the impact and heard a crunch. Martin Corcoran staggered backwards, collided with the work table holding the computers, and crumpled to the floor.

Lindsey started for the stairway, carrying the wooden chair on his back. He still had the panic button in his pants pocket. He tried to maneuver his hands to reach it but they were wired to the chair and he couldn't swing the chair around.

He managed to reach the second step

before Florence Corcoran grabbed hold of the chair and yanked him back. He tumbled backwards. The chair bounced off Florence, then crashed onto the concrete floor. The wooden back splintered and Lindsey was able to struggle to his feet again, fragments of chair dangling from his wired wrists.

Florence was on him again, clawing at his face with her fingernails. Then she kneed him in the groin and he doubled over.

Martin was on his feet again, his mouth red with blood, his beautiful pale silk shirt stained with red. He grabbed Lindsey by his ears, tugged his head upright and slammed it against a wall. He caught Lindsey on the bounce and threw him against the wall again.

Lindsey landed on his side. He managed to swivel himself so his hands were at his pocket. He could feel the panic button through the cloth of his pants. He squeezed the milled edge and pressed the button itself.

As Martin leaned over him there was a crash from upstairs. Martin snapped upright, startled. Both Corcorans looked alarmed. They bolted for the stairs, scrambling up from the cellar. They disappeared. Lindsey could hear voices. He struggled to his feet and staggered to the staircase.

At the head of the stairs he saw both Corcorans, and Marvia and Lt. Yamura, badges pinned to their vests, guns drawn. He wondered how the police had reacted so quickly to the button and how they'd got the door open. But those questions could wait. He was safe and the Corcorans were caught.

He thought.

Florence Corcoran was saying, 'That's the man. He talked his way in here under false pretenses. He lied to us, and when we ordered him to leave he attacked us. Look at my poor husband. That madman could have killed him. I want him arrested. You'd better search him — who knows what he's got in his pockets?'

Half a dozen plainclothes officers were in the house now, and uniforms were filing in behind them. Lindsey could see the red and blue flashers of police cruisers pulsating outside on Cedar Street.

Lt. Yamura said, 'Mr. Lindsey, are you all right?'

He tried to show his wired wrists. Yamura saw enough. She gestured to a uniformed officer, who began untwisting the wires. It took only seconds. Lindsey muttered 'thanks' and rubbed his wrists.

'I think you'll want to place these folks under arrest, Mr. Lindsey.' Yamura indicated the Corcorans.

'What?' he said.

'It looks to me as if they treated you pretty badly. I think you ought to make a citizen's arrest. I didn't see anything happen, so I can't arrest anyone.'

Lindsey stared at the Corcorans. Their expressions indicated an amalgam of shock and rage. Feeling like an amateur actor, Lindsey pointed at the Corcorans. 'You are both under arrest.'

Florence's face was deathly white. 'All right.' She pointed at Lindsey. 'You are under arrest!'

Yamura nodded. 'Okay. *Everybody* is under arrest now. We'll all ride down to McKinley Avenue and try to sort this out.'

'Wait a minute,' Lindsey protested. 'They were going to — they had me wired to that chair, just like they wired Celia — '

Lt. Yamura held up her hand. 'We have the wire, that's evidence. These people have brought charges against you, Mr. Lindsey, and you have brought charges against them. Technically, all three of you are under arrest. You will all have to come to McKinley.'

The Corcorans glared.

'And in the meanwhile, there is this.' Yamura flashed the search warrant. 'Mr. and Mrs. Corcoran, we have a warrant to search your home for evidence in the felony murder of Annabella Buonaventura and in the murder of Police Officer Celia Varela.'

Florence Corcoran looked as if she was going to explode. 'Get Shea! Martin, get Shea on the phone. He'll show these people a thing or two.' She turned to Lt. Yamura. 'Look at this poor man. This gangster picked up a chair and smashed it into his face. He needs to go to the hospital. And I want my lawyer, Carl

Shea. He specializes in protecting innocent people from the likes of fascist bitches like you!'

Yamura said calmly, 'Are you finished? Of course you can call your attorney. I'm sure you know your Miranda rights but we'll go over them together just for the record.' She stood close to Martin Corcoran, looking at his mouth. 'That really is ugly. I think it would be a good idea to run you by the hospital before we take you to headquarters.'

Corcoran could only grunt.

'I'm going to stay here and supervise the search. Sergeant Plum will return to McKinley Avenue with you.'

'What about our house?' Florence Corcoran yelped. 'Look at that front door — that's going to cost hundreds of dollars to fix. You fascist gangsters better not break anything. I want to stay here. This house is full of valuable possessions. I want my lawyer here while you search.'

Yamura shook her head. 'You can call your lawyer from McKinley.'

Florence kicked savagely, either at Yamura or at the wall. She connected with the wall and squealed.

'I don't want to have to order my people to handcuff you.' Yamura gestured toward the door.

Lindsey rode in the back seat of one cruiser; he saw the Corcorans loaded into the back of another. A uniformed officer drove.

Nothing happened for a couple of hours, until Martin Corcoran arrived, his face bandaged and his jaw wired. Lindsey felt strangely elated.

Even then, the lawyers had to get into the act. Florence Corcoran called Carl Shea. Lindsey called Eric Coffman. Shea was a tiny man with wispy salt-and-pepper hair. He wore an old-fashioned pinstripe suit and a floppy polka-dot bow tie. He smiled, shook everybody's hand, knew everybody in sight. He was a nexus of energy. The portly Coffman was his usual elegant self. Lindsey got a private conference with him and related the events on Cedar Street.

Coffman looked startled. 'You were acting as a police surrogate and you wound up under arrest for that? Well, I wouldn't worry about it. We'll see a DA and probably get everything dropped. You really ought to bring a civil action, though. And be prepared to respond to one. My goodness, you did a job on that fellow's face.'

'You mean he's going to sue me? After what happened?'

'Sure. Everybody's sue-happy these days. Take a poke at a guy and break your knuckles and sue him for damages. It's a disgrace.'

'But — but you're in the business.'

Coffman rubbed his red-brown beard. He said, 'Hmm.' Then he said, 'I see your erstwhile hosts are represented by Carl Shea. Met him coming up the steps. Very smart man. Can make up into down and day into night. Even wrote a couple of pretty amazing books about his wonderful career. This might be fun.'

Lindsey was booked for unlawful entry, attempted fraud, assault and battery against Martin Corcoran. Florence did most of the talking. Martin managed a few syllables, mostly permitting his wife to speak for him. The Corcorans were booked for false imprisonment, assault and battery on Lindsey. All three were released on their own recognizance.

Coffman said, 'Yes, this is definitely going to be fun.'

Marvia Plum was in the dingy room, waiting for the proceeding to end. When it did, she and Coffman and Lindsey moved to a conference room. 'This is ridiculous,' she said. 'Bart, I'm so sorry this happened. We'll get to a sensible DA in the morning and that will be the end of it. You were doing us a favor.'

'I was doing myself a favor. This is all part of the Film Archive and Robeson Center fires. It's getting worse, isn't it?'

She touched him. 'Don't worry about it.' She turned turned toward Coffman. 'How much do you know about this situation?'

'Nothing. I haven't seen you two months. I thought you were getting married. So where's my invitation? Miriam wants to buy a dress. The girls are all excited. They think it'll make Jamie their honorary cousin or something. Fellow Nintendo fanatics, that's what matters to them.'

Marvia drew back. 'I'm sorry. I do love Bart and I did promise to marry him, but — I don't want to talk about it now.' She drew herself up, suddenly all cop. 'Besides, I'm on duty.'

Coffman said, 'Okay, okay. I was just concerned about my friends, that's all. I didn't mean to pry.'

Lindsey asked, 'What about the search?'

'Yeah. Dorothy radioed,' Marvia told him. 'They found Anti-Imperialist Front materials in the house. That's all. Nothing illegal about that; it's all First Amendment stuff. Carl Shea would love to get his mitts on that.'

Lindsey frowned. 'What about the wire? They must have killed Celia Varela. They were going to do the same to me, I know it. They were using the same wire.'

'We're working on that. But it looked like common enough stuff to me. You know what kind of wire that was? Speaker wire. Every stereo fan in town must have some in his house. I have some in mine. We won't get anywhere with that.'

'Don't you think they did it? I mean, after what Celia Varela told you about

Dylan Guevara and the Corcorans?'

'I'm sure they were involved, but did they set those fires? I don't think so. Did they kill Celia? Maybe they did, maybe they didn't.'

Lindsey sighed. 'I thought this case was being wrapped up.'

'It's just getting started.'

He put his head in his hands. 'You try so hard, and you wind up with this.'

'Yeah. Imagine if you were a cop.'

14

Over breakfast, Lindsey told Mother about his encounter with the Corcorans. He minimized the violence and the danger, but he had to include his ride to McKinley Avenue and Eric Coffman's appearance to get him released.

Mother said, 'I always thought you were in a nice safe business. Paying off insurance claims. I never thought you'd be dealing with murderers and gangsters.'

With a grin, Lindsey loaded his fork with scrambled egg. 'Today should be pleasanter. We're off on an expedition. Ms. Wilbur, Mr. MacReedy, the Scogginses and me.'

'What about your friend Marvia?'

'She's on duty, Mother. She can't just take off on a day trip.'

Mother nodded and took a sip of coffee. 'When are you going to marry her?'

'I don't know.' Lindsey took his mother's hand. 'You wouldn't mind, then?

184

Would you want to stay in the house? Would you want to live alone?'

'No.' She shook her head. 'I think I'll sell the house. Move to an apartment. Do you think I'd get enough for this house to buy a condo?'

'Mother, I'm sure you could. If you want to do that, I think it would be wonderful.'

She smiled wistfully. 'I was thinking, I might even — well, never mind.'

They ate awhile, then Lindsey said, 'Walter Scoggins convinced Mr. MacReedy to ride down to Niles for the day. Down near Fremont, in Alameda County. You know, he hasn't been there in half a century. But Tony Roland at the Film Archive says it hasn't changed very much. I think it's going to be fun.'

What he didn't say was that he had his own agenda for the trip. He hoped to find some clue to the fires at the Pacific Film Archive and the Robeson Retirement Center. And Lindsey was suspicious that the death of Nola MacReedy was not an accident. She had died of pneumonia and pleurisy following her unfortunate accident. But had her broken hip really resulted from an accident? In the days that followed, she had never been fully lucid. What would she have said, what would she have told her husband if she had only been able?

★   ★   ★

The trip from Berkeley to Niles was easy enough. Lindsey picked up Walter and Martha Scoggins at the Durant. Mathilde Wilbur and MacReedy were ready for them, waiting in the lobby of the Robeson Center. Ms. Wilbur wore jeans and a UC sweatshirt. She was as amazing as Lindsey's mother was, these days.

They took Ms. Wilbur's Toyota, Walter Scoggins sitting besides Mathilde, his omnipresent camcorder swiveling between the countryside and MacReedy. They drove slowly down Niles Boulevard, then took an underpass and emerged near the old yellow-painted Southern Pacific railroad station. The line had long since been rerouted, but a section of rusting track had been left in situ.

MacReedy climbed the few steps to the

platform and stood looking around. Walter Scoggins knelt in front of him, camcorder whirring.

MacReedy stepped off the platform onto a railroad tie and walked carefully, stepping only on every other tie. He walked ten or fifteen yards, then turned and climbed back onto the platform.

'That was the track we came on. In 1931. The Depression had been on for two years. You know what happened to my old friend Mr. Pandolfo? His company went under back in '22, and you know, they put him jail. Thought he was a crook. Sold too many cars, delivered too few. Well, maybe he *was* a crook, how could I know? All I know is, he got me started. He even gave my mother a job working in his office, you know that? No colored girls in white offices back then, but he let my mother work for him. She studied shorthand and typewriting, and he paid her just the same as he did the white girls.'

He walked back to the platform edge and peered right, then left, as if he thought a steam locomotive might appear out of the past. 'They put Samuel Pandolfo in jail. I kept my publishing business going and I helped him when the others turned their backs. He helped me and I helped him.'

The camcorder whirred.

'They let him out in '26. His cash was all gone; he was an ex-convict. I loaned him money. He returned to Saint Cloud. That was his home.'

Still no train arrived.

'He started up a little health-food restaurant. I guess he was ahead of his time. Didn't do too well back in '26. Poor Samuel tried everything. Real estate. Insurance. Always eked out a living, but the best he ever did was that car company. That was the zenith of his career. My daddy used to talk about that. About the zenith of a man's career. He believed that every man was entitled to a zenith in his life. That applies to women too, you know. My daddy used to say that man includes woman and woman includes man.'

They climbed into the Toyota and drove back through the underpass and parked on Niles Boulevard, then walked up and down on the sidewalk. After a while they found a marker that read *Site of Original Essanay Studio*. The arrow pointed to a vacant lot. Dried yellow grass lay flat in the lot, punctuated by rusting soft-drink cans and fast-food wrappers. A *For Sale* sign listed a realtor's phone number and address.

'I'd like to buy that,' MacReedy said. 'I'd like to own a piece of that land.'

Walter Scoggins panned from the historic marker to the vacant lot and the *For Sale* sign, then back to MacReedy. 'What did Essanay stand for? Did you work with them?'

'They were long gone, son. Everybody 'round here talked about them, though. I guess the Essanay days were the zenith of this town. Now they need signs on the sidewalk to remind 'em of Essanay. And there's nothing to show that H-M-R was ever here. Nothing to show we were here.'

Ms. Wilbur led MacReedy gently to a wooden bench that stood on the sidewalk outside an antique shop. There was a Charlie Chaplin poster in the window. The bench stood in the shade of an awning. Mr. MacReedy found a handker-chief and wiped his face. 'We had to camp in our trailers; wasn't any hotel would take colored, and no colored folk in town to take us in. But the white folks mostly left us alone. We bought groceries and things; gassed up our vehicles. They didn't mind taking our money.'

His eyes looked across the boulevard to the rounded hills of Niles Canyon, where mist was rising into the California sky. 'I remember the day I arrived in this town. First Monday in March, 1931, it was. I got off that Southern Pacific train, coming in from LA. Couldn't buy a Pullman ticket back then; they let me ride with the colored help. I walked away from that railroad station and down the main street of this town, people staring at me every step. I stopped in a little grocery store and bought some cold meat and rolls, and I walked around eating my sand-wiches and looking at things.'

He was living 1931 again. Lindsey felt privileged that MacReedy would share that with him.

'Everybody remembered Essanay. I told

them all that I was Edward George MacReedy, the famous colored novelist and publisher, and I was going into the movie business with my two associates, Mr. Alton 'Specs' Lincoln and Mr. William Hargess. We were the H-M-R Movie Company.'

He took a shallow breath, all that his thin chest would permit. 'One old woman told me all about Essanay. She *was* old, too, She was born 1842. Think about that, children. She was born in Cincinnati, Ohio and her daddy and mama brought her to California when she was a little child, seven years old, the gold rush of '49. She lived ninety years. She died shortly after I met her, never sick a day in her life, just lived ninety years and then passed. That's what I intend to do, but not yet.'

Another pause, another shallow breath. 'Essanay, she told me. That was S-and-A. S was some old businessman in Chicago; his name was George Spoor. Nobody out here knew Spoor, but they all knew his partner, A. — 'Broncho Billy' Anderson. You see that café over there, Broncho

Billy's Pizza Palace? That was him. At least they remember that much.' He pointed at the restaurant. A father was leading two small boys through the swinging doors. The boys wore cowboy outfits.

'He wasn't really Anderson,' MacReedy went on. 'Everybody remembered him; he was a big good-looking cowboy who could hardly sit on a horse. Famous cowboy, couldn't ride worth a damn! You know who he was? He was Max Aronson, that's who he was. Some old Jewish man from Little Rock, Arkansas! And all those white folks who thought he was one of them. I always thought that was rich.

'Townsfolk used to talk about the old Essanay Westerns, you know all those Westerns had the cowboys riding into town on payday.' He nodded. 'We did the same in H-M-R days. All those location shots, chases and ambushes and stagecoach rides, we made up in the canyon. Essanay made their shots up in the canyon, we did the same. You look at some of those old Westerns, you'll see the same hillsides. Same creek, Alameda Creek. We'd have our cowboys ride across that creek. And the shots on main street, the hitching posts. Those are all gone now.' A sad shake of the head. 'Come on, I'm tired of sitting here. Let's walk back.'

Mrs. Wilbur tried to take his elbow again, but he jerked it away. 'No, I don't need any help to walk, young woman. You see that corner? That's where I had my office. We did our own processing. Did all our inside shots in that building. Now it's just a lot for sale.'

He pointed with a bony finger. 'You see that cute little cottage? Essanay, they built a row of those; rented 'em back to their stars. They had big stars. Ben Turpin worked here, Marie Dressler, Edna Purviance. You remember Wallace Beery, great old character actor? He started at Essanay; was a director. I guess he didn't have the knack; got into acting instead.

'And Chaplin. Everybody remembers Chaplin. English boy. He was another Jewish man, maybe that's why he got along with Broncho Billy. They used to go up to Oakland, San Francisco on weekends, stay in the cottages when they were working. Of course we couldn't stay in them in H-M-R days. Not for colored. But they were nice cottages.

'Essanay moved out in 1916, right. And H-M-R came in '31. In between? Nothing, I suppose. Buildings stood vacant. I'll tell you, boy, the main studio was pretty grimy when we moved in. First thing we did, we had to scrub. Old Spoor made Aronson send everything back to Chicago when Essanay closed down out here, but they missed a few things. Some of their old stock, some of it exposed, some of it still pretty fresh, sealed.'

He picked up an invisible film canister and blew the old dust off its metal. 'No, they didn't leave any cameras or dollies or cranes. Besides, Essanay was all silent. H-M-R, we made all talkies. But those white folks, they left behind some things they didn't think were worth shipping back to Chicago.'

A murmured question from Scoggins.

'What did they leave? Some of the old cowboy things. Worn-out chaps and lassoes, that kind of thing. That's all.'

One more sad look around. 'It's all gone now. All right, I guess we can go now. Sure, I have an appetite. I wouldn't mind eating in Broncho Billy's Pizza Palace.'

★ ★ ★

The old man said, 'That was good. Sure, I liked all those posters. Wonderful posters. I didn't see any H-M-R posters. Most whites, they didn't even know H-M-R existed. H-M-R and some other colored producers. Yes, I suppose those old posters are worth some money today. I don't really know, there might be some in the bottom of the trunk. Sure, you can have them. What am I going to do with them?'

In the car he said, 'This is a very comfortable automobile, Ms. Wilbur. Japanese. I wish I could show you my old Pan. Now that was a car.'

They drove up Niles Canyon, past a scene straight out of Norman Rockwell. MacReedy said, 'See those kids swimming? Alonzo X. Nash swam a horse across Alameda Creek right about there. I think that was in *Rustlers of Montana*.

Had the same scene in *Sombreros and Spurs*. We could have re-used the old footage but we shot the scene again. That's called artistic integrity, young fellow. Remember it.'

Scoggins asked the old man how he could keep to that policy and still bring his films in as fast and as inexpensively as he had.

'They called me 'Speedy' MacReedy because I could make a film fast and cheap. But that didn't mean I did shoddy work. We had to keep our costs down, that was all.'

Mathilde Wilbur had a question.

MacReedy chuckled. 'Oh, the girls. The girls, Ms. Wilbur? You think they called me 'Speedy' because I liked the girls and the girls liked me?' He gave a dry, thin laugh. 'That railroad station, where we were today. I remember the day I laid eyes on Lola for the first time. She was just a little girl. She was thirteen years old. Her mama stayed with her, kept an eye on her because she was a beautiful child. And she looked older than thirteen.' No veering this time. This time he was on a clear path of memory. 'But her mama wouldn't let a soul lay hand on her. Mama's name was Bess. We used her for some character scenes. Billed her as Mammy Bess Barber, she was before Louise Beavers, before Hattie McDaniel. But she mainly kept an eye on Lola.'

A camper had pulled off the road, where a party of fishermen were checking out their gear, casting eager eyes at the creek.

MacReedy said, 'But I knew. I knew the minute I laid eyes on that child, I was going to marry her. I waited 'til she was all grown up. We were married when she was sixteen years of age. I was thirty years of age. Lot of people didn't like that, didn't think we'd last. But Mammy Bess approved, and we were married and we stayed married for sixty years — until this year.'

He let Walter Scoggins help him settle into a more comfortable position. Then he pointed into the canyon. 'That was where Chaplin — you know, we had a comic, did wonderful impressions. He studied Charlie, sometimes he imitated him. We used to promote him that way. H-M-R and the other colored companies, we'd advertise our stars that way 'cause everybody knew the white stars. You wouldn't remember Luther Tucker, maybe? The young man does. Well, good for you. He was the Colored Valentino. Handsome son of a gun; you talk about the ladies loving a fellow . . . ' A nod of self-agreement. Then, 'Alonzo Nash, we used to call him the Bronze Francis X. Bushman. And Will Hargess, he was a great makeup artist. Light-complected. Most of our stars were light-complected, very light-complected. Hargess, he was the Charcoal Chaney. Called him for Lon, the old man, not the son. No, I don't know if they ever met. Maybe they did, might have early on.'

Scoggins asked if Will Hargess was still alive. He could use more interviews, more living fossils for his academic museum. But MacReedy disappointed him.

'Oh, he's dead. He died in the fire, end of '34. What a tragedy. That killed H-M-R. Destroyed the building, destroyed our film, killed Will Hargess, killed Mammy Bess, rest her soul. I guess she's watching over her daughter again. I'll go and see them both pretty soon.'

The trail branched again. 'Oh, the fire. Maybe tomorrow, all right? I must confess, I'm feeling a little tired now. I'll be glad to get back to the center and have my nap.'

The old man's eyes began to close but he opened them again. 'Boy, all you do is ask questions. Oh, all right, one more question, and then you turn off that fool thing there and leave me in peace for a little while.'

Scoggins asked his question.

MacReedy said, 'No, I don't have anything from that old Essanay trash anymore. Why would I save that trash?'

And another question, and another answer. 'The one in my wardrobe? That old derby? Oh, I guess so. I guess we just had the same size of head. Yes, that scene from *The Tramp*, where he's walking up the road at the end of the picture, yes, that's right about here, right here in this canyon.'

But Scoggins wouldn't let go. One more try. And the old man answered.

'Yes, it is the same derby, I do know that for sure. Had his name inside in the sweatband so he wouldn't swap it by mistake with Ben Turpin's. You want it too, sonny? I only kept it because we had the same size head. I thought I might get some use out of the thing, but I never did. Sure, you can have it.'

15

Eric Coffman's office was its reassuring, old-fashioned self. The book-lined walls, thick carpeting, and leather furniture gave it the feel of a nineteenth-century country squire's den. Lindsey sat in a brass-studded green leather wing chair, Marvia beside him in a similar chair, waiting for the lawyer's verdict.

'All right,' Coffman began, 'here's what I worked out with Carl Shea. Now, the Corcorans will drop the all their charges against you — fraudulent entry, assault and battery, whatever. And you have to drop all your charges against them. All you have to pay for is Martin Corcoran's medical and dental bills; they're willing to write off the chair you smashed. Everybody just walks away.'

Lindsey could feel his eyes pop. 'You're kidding, Eric. You can't be serious!'

'You're lucky Shea didn't squeeze harder. Your pal Martin Corcoran has some interesting Hollywood connections. He's been working on the big Arturo Madrid fest, doing some computer design for the producers. I think he fancies himself a potential screen star in addition to his other manifest talents, and he could have claimed that you spoiled his pretty face. Believe me, if Corcoran tried that, Shea would demand *mucho dinero* for loss of potential earnings. You should have known better, old pal. You took a dive into a pool of very hot water this time.'

Lindsey didn't know whether to laugh or cry. 'Listen to me. They attacked me, not the other way around. Somebody blindsided me; it must have been Martin.'

Marvia put in, 'Unless it was Dylan Guevara. If you never saw who hit you, you don't know that it was Corcoran. Dylan could have done it and then scooted out of the house while you were in the cellar.'

'Maybe. But I mean, I was trying to escape — I was actually wired to that chair before I ever hit Corcoran. I don't know what they were going to do to me. I think they were going to kill me just the way they killed Celia Varela. They were going to use that same wire. What a horrible way to die.' Lindsey shuddered.

'I believe you,' Marvia assured him. 'Eric believes you, don't you, Eric? Okay. But the fact is, there are no other witnesses. It's just your word and the Corcorans' word. You *were* in their house under phony circumstances.'

'That was Yamura's idea.'

'No debate. Also irrelevant.'

'Look,' Coffman intervened, 'everybody involved in this mess knows damned well that your version is true and their version is a farrago of lies. And if Carl Shea doesn't it's because he doesn't want to. But no court is going to accept what 'everybody knows'. They can only accept evidence. Physical evidence — what do we have? A broken chair, a man with a smashed face, another man with a piece of the chair still wired to his hands. Forensics will surely establish that the chair was the instrument with which the injury was inflicted. Witnesses? Mr. Corcoran saw you harassing Mrs. Corcoran. Mrs. Corcoran saw you battering Mr.

Corcoran. Your goose is cooked, my friend. It's a goddamned crying shame, but you'd better cut your losses and pull back before they decide to get really nasty.'

★ ★ ★

Leaving Coffman's office, Marvia said, 'Dorothy wants to talk to you, Bart. I'm sorry it turned out like this. It was a harebrained scheme. We should have just gone in with the warrant and not got so fancy. I know Dorothy wants to apologize to you, personally. And maybe talk about some other things.'

Lindsey had to change the subject; this was too much to take. 'How's your dad doing, Marvia?'

'Not so well.'

'Have you given any more thought to — longer-term plans?' He knew that the subject of marriage was on hold.

'Jamie's best friend at school, Hakeem White, lives near my parents. Hakeem's mom says Jamie can stay with them for a while. Maybe for a long while. But I'm not really comfortable with that. It would only be a stopgap.'

They halted in front of a coffee shop, entered and slid into a booth. International Surety was a five-minute walk from Coffman's office, and Lindsey had to stop there before they headed back to Berkeley, but first he and Marvia needed a few minutes together. They ordered coffee and left it untouched.

'Corcoran's medical bills aren't going to come out of your pocket, are they? I mean, if they are, we should be able to find some contingency money in the police budget.'

'I don't know. It wasn't exactly International Surety line-of-duty, but I have an umbrella policy. Everybody in the company gets them, to cover contingencies. Especially people assigned to SPUDS. We're expected to get involved in odd cases. And this is about as odd as they get, isn't it?'

Kari Fielding looked up as Lindsey entered the office. He didn't introduce Marvia Plum.

Elmer Mueller was actually in the office for once. 'Come to pick up your voice mail, Hobie?' He noticed Marvia, or seemed to, with surprise. 'Haven't we met?'

'We have.' She sat facing Lindsey while he checked his messages. There was one from Desmond Richelieu in Denver and there was one from Dorothy Yamura in Berkeley. Richelieu wanted a return call *pronto*. Yamura would like to see him at his earliest convenience.

He punched the number for SPUDS in Denver. Mrs. Blomquist put him through to Richelieu, but fast.

It took ten minutes to explain what had happened and to get Richelieu back off the ceiling of his office. When Richelieu had himself back under control, his voice dripped icicles. 'I just want to know, are you working for me or are you working for the police department out there? Because if you're working for them, that's just fine, but I want you off my payroll. I don't pay you to work for Truth, Justice and the American Way. I pay you to work for the International Surety Corporation.'

Lindsey managed to get Richelieu off the line without getting fired on the spot, but he couldn't remember the water temperature being this hot in all the years he'd worked for I.S.

Dorothy Yamura sounded depressed. She knew that Marvia was with him and that they'd been at Coffman's office. She told him that everything possible would be done at her end to clean up the mess, and would he and Marvia please come and see her right away.

The freeway was fairly empty and they cruised into Berkeley with no delays. Marvia was driving. Lindsey tinkered with the radio controls until he picked up a listener-sponsored station with a notorious political slant. A boy-and-girl team in the studio were talking about the death of Celia Varela. The boy-in-studio asked, 'What was this so-called police officer doing in People's Park? That's what we need to find out. She was posing as a homeless person, infiltrating the people's grass roots political organization. She was a spy, that's what she was, don't you agree, Barbie? And we all know the penalty for spies who get caught, don't we? The uniformed fascists who patrol the people's streets are bad enough, but when you add disguise and treachery to the mix, you have to expect dire consequences.'

The girl-in-studio whined, 'Well, Ken, what did you expect? After the things this government has been doing to suppress people's struggles all around the world, everything excused in the name of promoting so-called democracy while actually trampling the democratic rights of those who fight for justice and equity, well, what did you really expect?'

'I guess I had higher hopes, that's all.' The colloquy continued. 'Well, the people had better organize and stand up for their rights. Otherwise, you can bet your bottom dollar that the bulldozers are going to roll again, Barbie; the hired goon squads will be out there with their billy clubs and their helmets, their wooden bullets and their poison gas canisters . . . '

The signal faded as the Mustang sped through the Caldecott Tunnel, emerging on the cooler westerly side of the East Bay hills.

★ ★ ★

Dorothy Yamura was back in her office at McKinley Avenue. She had switched to her dark blue uniform. She stood up when Lindsey entered her office, along with Marvia. 'Thanks for coming in. I wanted to apologize in person for what happened at Cedar Street. You weren't badly hurt, were you?'

'Not really. The wire was pretty tight. Pretty uncomfortable.'

Yamura sat and motioned Lindsey and Marvia to do the same. 'I wasn't too gentle back at Laffy's. But I was very upset. We take it very seriously when an officer gets murdered. I know that every citizen is entitled to equal consideration, but we're family, you know.'

'Understood.'

'And I didn't set you up with the Corcorans. That was a miscalculation and I take responsibility for it.'

'Is that the end of it, then? What about Laffy's? Are you going to close down that operation? Forget about the Anti-Imperialist League? The end of it all, Dylan Guevara goes on ranting, the Corcorans walk, nothing more is going to happen?'

'Oh, no.' Yamura shook her head. 'We're going to resolve this, I promise you that.' She turned in her chair. 'We'll close down the Lafayette Escadrille operation, yes. Not the whole bar, it's a legitimate business. But we can't keep a field office there, there's no more point in that.'

'What about Laffy himself?'

'He's legitimate. Actually, he's a cop too.'

'So where do we go from here?'

'Are you willing to continue, Mr. Lindsey? After two bad experiences?'

'I think that everything ties together, Lieutenant. The two fires, the murders of Annabella Buonaventura and Officer Varela, the death of Nola MacReedy . . . I don't think that broken hip was accidental — '

'That's an elaborate scenario. What's your explanation, Mr. Lindsey?'

'I wish I knew. Edward MacReedy keeps turning up fascinating little gems of film history, but I haven't seen anything there that would connect the fire at Robeson or his wife's death, either one, with the Film Archive fire or the murder of Officer Varela.'

'Okay, give me a call if you think of anything more, if you get anything from MacReedy that you think fits.'

They shook hands. Marvia offered Lindsey a ride back to Oxford Street, to pick up his Hyundai. 'I want to take a little jaunt around Northside anyway, see if there's anything doing at Cedar Street,' she said.

They cruised past the Corcorans' house. There was no visible damage, no yellow police tape, no sign that this was other than a quiet upper-middle-class home on a quiet upper-middle-class street in a Northern California college town.

Marvia swung the Mustang back toward Oxford. When they were a few blocks from her house Lindsey heard the sound of sirens. He knew then. He didn't believe in ESP but he knew what they would find.

The smoke was visible before they turned onto Oxford, and the flames as soon as they did. The fire engines were there and the firefighters were coating the Hyundai with foam. There didn't appear to be any other serious damage, but several cars and nearby houses, the Victorian containing Marvia's flat included, had been hit by chunks of debris or blackened by smoke.

16

'No question about it.' Vince D'Onofrio and Olaf Stromback were in agreement. 'I'm a simple fireman, an old hoser; this boy is a scientist, ain't you, Olaf? But just look at what Olaf found inside your car, Mr. Lindsey.'

Lindsey looked as directed, but he didn't need to see the evidence to believe that his car had been firebombed.

'This was inside the passenger compartment.' Stromback held up a transparent evidence bag. It contained a charred bottle. The blackened wick still protruded from its neck. The label was burned and discolored, but a little of it remained decipherable. There was a picture of a mustachioed man in a black fedora. Above him was a brand name, *Moretti*.

'Some sense of humor.' Marvia had pulled her Mustang to the curb and run to what was left of Lindsey's Hyundai. He was shaking. Marvia added, 'I think they wanted to make sure you got the message. That old fellow on the beer label could pass for the Godfather, couldn't he?' To Stromback she said, 'Any other evidence?'

'Plenty. We'll impound this car and study it, but here's what it looks like to me. They jimmied the door and tossed this Molotov cocktail inside. Then they opened the gas tank cover and stuffed a rag in it and lit it. They weren't taking any chances. When that went, the gas tank went, then the whole car. Nothing here to salvage, I'd say.'

Lindsey surveyed his car. He was able to calm down by assuming his insurance man's objectivity. If he'd been called on to settle this claim there would have been no question. The car was totaled. Just look up its Blue Book value and cut the check.

He asked Stromback if there were fingerprints or any other sign of who had destroyed the car. Stromback held up the evidence bag and studied the smoky bottle. 'Possibly. But it's also likely that they won't belong to the arsonist. More than likely he picked this out of the street, somebody's recycling bin. He was probably careful, and if we find fingerprints they'll belong to some good citizen who happens to like Italian beer.'

Lindsey said, 'I don't know what happens now. Who did this? The Corcorans? My lawyer said I was getting off easy, that Carl Shea could have squeezed me a lot harder than he did. Maybe they're getting their revenge this way. Or maybe warning me to lay off.'

Marvia told him to stand by. 'Olaf, you get Mr. Lindsey's statement, will you? Lieutenant D'Onofrio, who called this thing in? You and Sergeant Stromback exchanging all your info? Stromback, you better talk to the person who phoned in the report. And you'll get a canvass going right away. Are we agreed? It's your case, but I'm interested in this.'

Stromback nodded. 'I've got people out on it already. Call came in on 911, citizen living in, let me see . . . ' He checked his notebook. 'In that pretty Victorian.' He indicated Marvia's house. 'Didn't see anything useful, though. Said she was

215

sitting reading and the room got bright all of a sudden. Then there was a loud sound. 'Not *bang* like an explosion, more like *whoomph*,' is how she described it. So she ran out in the street, saw the car in flames, ran back inside and called for help.'

'She didn't see anybody running away, or hiding behind another car or a tree to watch the excitement?'

'Nope. You're up on classic firebug behavior, though. Didn't see nobody.'

'Look, Olaf, if any of your people turn anything up, will you let me know right away?' Marvia was emphatic. 'Especially if anybody saw Dylan Guevara in the vicinity. You know the guy?'

'Who doesn't? Wears a beret, little wispy mustache, likes to dress in army fatigues. Sure. Sounds like his style.'

Lindsey looked mournfully at the remnants of his car. 'You folks are going to take it in and look for clues?'

Sgt. Stromback nodded. 'I hope you have insurance, sir.'

Lindsey said he did. 'Any need for me to come down to police headquarters?'

'No, we've got what we need. Got the incident report. If your insurance company needs to inspect the remains of the car or to see my paperwork, have 'em contact me directly. You have my number?' He handed Lindsey his card. Lindsey already had one, but he slipped it in his pocket anyway.

Marvia took Lindsey's elbow. 'This is line of duty. Come on in the house. You need a chance to sit down. A drink wouldn't hurt you, either.'

They climbed to her flat and she urged him into an easy chair. He said, 'I guess I'll need another car. Maybe I'll rent something for a few days while I shop. I don't know what I want. That old Hyundai was a good car but I was getting kind of tired of it.'

Marvia handed him a glass of cold water and squatted on her heels in front of his chair. He held the glass shakily in both hands and drank all the water, then she took the glass and set it on the floor.

'Let me call Tyrone.'

'Your brother? Why?'

'He's in the car business. You know he's

always buying battered cars and fixing them up. My Mustang was a junker when he got hold of it, and look at it now. He'll have something interesting for you. And he'll give you a good price. He likes you.'

She punched a number, talked for a while, and smiled. Lindsey could see her smile, and it was like a burst of warmth in his chest. She spoke a few more words, then placed the handset on its cradle.

'Tyrone says he has the perfect car for you. He says you can come by and take it now and give him a temporary note for it. If you like it, he'll sell it to you. If you don't like it, just give it back.'

'What is it?'

'Blue 1965 Volvo 544. Same year as my Mustang. You'll love it. Tyrone has this one fixed up; rebuilt the engine and transmission, spruced up the body and interior. New paint job, put in a modern sound system. Come on, try it.'

Lindsey got to his feet. 'Where is this car?'

'Tyrone moved his garage. It's down past the SP tracks, near the Berkeley Marina.'

Tyrone Plum kissed Marvia, then shook Lindsey's hand. He said, 'My sister the cop. Who'd have thought it?'

'How's Pop?' Marvia asked him. 'You seen him?'

Tyrone looked away. 'Take the car out. Here's the keys. I'll be working on that Studie Hawk if you need me.' He flopped onto a crawler and disappeared under the Studebaker.

'You drive,' Marvia said to Lindsey. 'You're the one going to buy this thing, you be the one to drive it.'

'I guess it wouldn't hurt to drive it around the block.' He slipped the key into the ignition. Marvia climbed in beside him and buckled her seat belt. That had to be new.

After half an hour Marvia managed to get Lindsey to drive back to Tyrone's place of business and climb out of the car long enough to sign some papers.

'You didn't even quibble over the price, Bart.'

'I know your brother.'

Lindsey walked Marvia back to her Mustang. Inside Tyrone's service garage, it was unmolested. As she climbed in, she asked Lindsey what he planned to do next.

'I'm still convinced there's a connection to Nola MacReedy,' he replied. 'Your people are working on the Buonaventura and Varela killings. They wouldn't want me poking into those anyhow.'

'That's for sure.' Marvia turned the ignition key.

'So I'm going to keep working from the other side. Bet you five-to-three we meet in the middle. But one thing puzzles me. If the Corcorans killed Varela, or whoever did it — how did they get her body past Laffy and into the back room at the bar?'

'My best guess is that Celia brought somebody there for a conference. Somebody from People's Park that she thought she could trust. Or — who knows, maybe our pal Dylan Guevara. Celia and Dylan could walk through Laffy's and fit right in. Once they were in the back room, he managed to turn the tables on her. Maybe slugged her when her back was turned.

Had the wire with him all along. Garroted her while she was stunned, and just walked out through the bar.'

Lindsey let his breath out with a hiss. 'Bastard.'

★ ★ ★

Ms. Wilbur looked perfectly at home in a navy blazer and little brass name badge. She looked up and waved as Lindsey came through the doors of the Robeson Center.

'Ms. Wilbur — Mathilde! What are you doing in that outfit?'

'I'm not fit for retirement. Couldn't stand one more morning of waking up and staring at the clock and wondering what I was going to do today. And it looked as if those poor young people, the Hendrys, never got to spend any time together. Young marrieds need time together. I should know. I was one once.'

Lindsey smiled.

'Listen, Hobart, how's this investigation going?' She leaned on the counter and peered around. 'You find the mysterious figure in the cellar yet? You uncover any clues?'

'There have been too many fires. Two that started this thing off, and now somebody's firebombed my car.'

'Oh, my!'

'Indeed. And didn't Mr. MacReedy say that H-M-R came to an end because of a fatal fire in Niles?'

'There couldn't possibly be a connection. They left Niles in the 1930s. The firebug couldn't still be around. If the fire in Niles was the work of a firebug to start with. I've never heard that claim.'

'Maybe it was, maybe it wasn't. I think Mr. MacReedy has the key to this puzzle locked away somewhere. Maybe it's in those files of his. I hope it wasn't destroyed when his room burned. Or maybe it's just in his head . . . something that he knows but doesn't even know that he knows.'

Ms. Wilbur said, 'He is at the Pacific Film Archive with Walter Scoggins and what's-his-name, Tony Roland. Martha Scoggins is on her own, off doing something. You can walk down the hill and find MacReedy and Scoggins and Roland busily huddling over a Movieola, I suppose, admiring the butts on the actresses of 1934.'

'Thanks. You know, I think you know more than you realize, too. Keep working on this. I'll see you later on.' Leaving the Robeson Center, he patted the Volvo affectionately and trotted downhill to the Art Museum.

MacReedy and Scoggins were in Roland's office. The three of them were huddled over Roland's desk. The desk was littered with photographs. Roland had provided oversized magnifiers.

Nobody looked up when Lindsey entered. He said, 'Got anything good?'

Tony Roland rocked back in his padded swivel chair. Wordlessly, he beamed, then gestured with an outstretched hand, indicating the photos on his desk.

Walter Scoggins jumped up. 'I've been so involved, I should have had this running.' He located his camcorder and switched it on.

The photos had obviously been black-and-white glossies at one time, but now they were faded and brown. They showed motion picture crews at work. Their equipment was bulky and old-fashioned. The men wore cowboy hats or cloth Babe Ruth caps with the visors reversed. So much for fashion innovations of the moment.

Lindsey pointed to a young figure in one of the photos. 'Is this you, Mr. MacReedy?'

'Don't look so different, do I? And look, there's my Lola.' He pointed.

'She's beautiful.'

'My bride. Sixteen years old. That was 1934. Some of these pictures are the wrap party. They still call them that, do they?'

Roland said that they did.

'This was a double wrap party. *Werewolf of Harlem* and *Werewolf of Wall Street*. We finished shooting that afternoon. Everybody gathered in the main building. Volstead Act was gone by then, thanks to Franklin Roosevelt.'

Lindsey leaned over the desk. The images in the photos were still sharp, for all that the blacks and whites were browned and faded. Lindsey picked up a magnifier and scanned one photo after another. Some of the shots were obviously party scenes. Modest enough by modern standards, they would surely have been scandalous in 1934. Whites and blacks celebrating together, drinking together, dancing together. The H-M-R cast and crew mingling with the PPIF personnel.

'Mr. MacReedy, who took these shots?' he asked.

'I took most of them. I was quite a shutter-bug back in those days. Had my little folding Kodak.'

'But you're in some of them.'

'Specs took those. Specs Lincoln. He was my partner and my chief cameraman. He took those.'

'And this is Arturo Madrid, is it?'

MacReedy took the picture from Lindsey. 'No.'

'Who is it?'

MacReedy pointed at another figure, a dashing individual wearing a white suit and a planter's hat, even indoors. 'That's Mr. Madrid. Played a Wall Street tycoon in that picture; played it well. You know, he was another Jewish man. From the Bronx, New York. Jews are interesting people, very fine people. I don't go with those who want to set the Jews and the coloreds at each other's throats. His real name was Israel Mannheim, that's what it was.'

'Wait a minute. Let me think about this. Didn't that TV piece on Arturo Madrid say he was born in Oakland? It said he was from a family of the original Spanish settlers.'

MacReedy shook his head. 'I guess you never heard of a studio biography. Easiest thing in the world to say that Mr. Mannheim from the Bronx is Arturo Madrid descended from Spanish settlers in California.'

Lindsey studied the photo. 'If the man in the white suit is Arturo Madrid, then who's this other fellow?'

MacReedy only had to glance at the still to answer that one. 'That's Will Hargess.'

Another set of photos were not party shots. They were motion picture stills — actors and actresses in costume and on set, posing in a scene from the film for publicity. They hadn't been printed up for release. There were no captions on them, or publicity notices attached. They were just glossies.

It wasn't always easy to tell which of the two werewolf pictures a given still came from. Most of the black actors seemed to have been chosen for their light complexions and European-appearing features. But one glossy showed the leads of the two films, in costume, posed for a gag shot. Two werewolves, two terrified ingenues, two heroic young men. Hargess and Madrid. 'That wasn't for release,' MacReedy explained. 'It would have made too many people want to ask too many questions.'

Lindsey looked from one werewolf to the other, and could not tell which was which.

'That was the night we had the fire. It was terrible. Everything was destroyed. It looked as if both films were lost. We didn't have any prints, and the negatives were there in the processing room at the studio. Poor Will Hargess was killed, just burned up. What a good friend he'd been to me; he was never just my partner. That was the end of H-M-R. Somehow Mr.

Quince kept PPIF going for a long while. They even survived the Depression somehow, and the war as well. I think that Senator McCarthy knocked them out; said they were Reds or something. What nonsense. What a tragedy that fire was.'

He looked up, smiling. 'But I got my darling out of there alive. She lost her mother in that fire. She was heartbroken. She was still just a girl, sixteen years old. No more parts for Mammy Bess Barber. No more Specs Lincoln. No more Will Hargess. No more H-M-R.'

His eyes were dry but he found a bandanna in his pocket and dabbed at them anyway. Lindsey wondered if the old man had cried all the tears that he had.

17

Walter Scoggins bored right in. 'What was it like? How did it happen?' Camcorder on shoulder, directional mike pointing. 'What time of night? How did the fire start? Did anyone come to your aid?'

The old man leaned over the desk, studying the pictures. *If this were only a Twilight Zone episode, Lindsey thought, the old man would dissolve into that scene of 1934. He would be a young man again. He would be with his bride again. And we would be sitting here in this stuffy office, looking at the pictures, and there he would be, looking back at us.*

MacReedy sighed and began his story:

★   ★   ★

We didn't wrap until late that afternoon. The double production worked pretty good. We didn't shoot in sequence, you know. We did all the shots in one location or one set, then all the shots in another location or set. If we had a sequence of the werewolf chasing the girl through Central Park — that was good for both movies — we could shoot that sequence up in the canyon. Then if we had a sequence of the good guys chasing the werewolf through the park — that might be an hour later in the picture — we could still shoot it the same day. Pinch Quince really liked my work. Mr. Philip Quince, he was the president of Pan-Pacific Intercontinental. Everybody called him 'Pinch', short for Pinchpenny. He liked me; he was the one first called me 'Speedy' 'cause I could set up a scene and shoot it fast.

The white actors, they wouldn't work for no colored director, of course. They didn't like the idea too much of working with colored at all, but I got together with Quince and we talked it over, then he went and sold the idea to his people. We worked it out together one night over a bottle of bourbon — Prohibition was over then, by '34; not that anybody ever paid too much attention to it in Niles.

Sarita Morgan, Adolfo Gonzalez, Bonnie

St. Paul, Whiskers Tennyson, how we going to get them to go along with this? Old man Whiskers especially. He used to do character parts, comic sidekick parts. You remember Fuzzy Knight, Gabby Hayes? Well, Tennyson was right up there with them. He played the same role that Walter Davies did in our movie. Used to call Walter the Chocolate Chaplin, he was so good. Well, Whiskers Tennyson did this comic relief role in *The Werewolf of Wall Street* and Walter Davies had the same part in *The Werewolf of Harlem*. That man's real name was Alfred Lord Tennyson. No joking. But nobody ever called him anything except Whiskers.

Well Pinch says, 'My people don't want to work for no colored. Especially Whiskers.' See, whites had a funny attitude back then. But what went on after hours . . .

You know Will Hargess, a great fellow. And Sarita Morgan, she was Arturo Madrid's intended. Well, Madrid was kind of a scoundrel, and Sarita meets Will Hargess and he could almost be Arturo Madrid's brother. Just a little bit tan, you see. He was light-complected; could have passed, I think, if he'd a-wanted. Well I don't know what happened, but those two used to disappear at odd times, Sarita and William. And they'd turn up again on the set, and you'd see these looks between them. I don't say that anything actually happened. But there sure were these looks between them.

Oh, about Whiskers Tennyson. He was from South Carolina somewhere. Congaree, that was it. They had some battle there in the Civil War. He was a little boy during the war, you see — what he used to call the War Between the States. He wouldn't never call it the Civil War. His daddy went off to that war and came home without an arm. He was some kind of grand high muck-a-muck in the Knights of the White Camellia, scaring blacks off their land. They done lynchings; they were very bad people. He used to carry little Whiskers — I guess his daddy must have called him Alfred when he was a little boy, just like that Englishman. His daddy used to carry him on night rides, torchlight parades. Wouldn't surprise me if I heard he saw some lynchings when he was a boy, maybe even done some when he was a younger man. Well, he just hated colored. So how was he going to work for a black director?

So we worked it out. I said to Pinch Quince, 'You tell Mr. Tennyson and all the rest of your actors that you're the boss. You're the producer and director of this film. You can even tell 'em that you wrote the script, I don't care so long as you pay me like you promised.' And I had that in writing, too — don't you think I trusted that man to keep his word. 'You tell 'em that you're the boss; tell 'em that I'm just your messenger boy. I'll call them actors 'mister' and 'miss' and I'll even say 'yassuh', 'yassum' if I have to. I'll tell 'em, 'Well, please, you do what that Mr. Quince told me to tell you, please, or you'll get me in trouble with that Mr Quince.' And you tell 'em, 'Specs Lincoln, the cameraman, why, he's just a little helper. Mr. Quince, he hired a real cameraman to come up from LA, and he delayed. So he hired this colored boy from H-M-R just to fill in. Now he's not too smart, he don't really know what he's doing, so you gotta be patient with him and don't holler; he scares easy and he'll just run away.''

But that Alton Lincoln, he was the finest cameraman I ever met. I knew the best of 'em, and Specs Lincoln could have been the best of the best if he'd been a white man. Even so, he made MacReedy Grand what it was. Instead, I'll bet you never even heard of him, did you?

But that was my scheme. I told my scheme to Philip Quince and he says, 'That's a great idea. Don't you say anything to your people about this, and whatever you do, don't say anything to my people. Just sit tight and act respectful if they say anything to you.'

I said I knew how to act respectful. Now don't squirm so, boy. We did what we had to do. I'm alive here today, you been to college, you stay in the best hotels. We did what we had to do; I won't have you condemning us for that.

So we worked that way. Yes, I directed both pictures. Even Tennyson, long as I called him 'sir', he did what I asked. He was a good actor, a professional, even if he called me 'boy', me and Alton.

Arturo Madrid? Sure I directed him. Sure I know about this big foofaraw they're getting up for him. You think I don't have TV? No, they didn't invite me to be in it. Don't know if I'd want to go if they did.

Arturo loved his pleasures. He had a big foreign car down there in Niles. Had a chauffeur drive him up from LA; he didn't want to come on the train. Sent the chauffeur back on the train, and then Arturo drove the car himself. Used to go to Oakland on weekends, stay at the big fancy hotels. Used to take some of the actresses with him. Sarita Morgan was sweet on him. He was a handsome devil — big strapping fellow with all this dark hair and a mustache. They'd go off to San Francisco, come back Monday and make us late. Used to love his liquor, too. He used to get to work late, hung over, sometimes show up drunk.

He had a cottage. You know, Essanay built a whole row of cottages for their people to use. They were still there in

H-M-R days. Still there now, far as I know. Arturo Madrid had one, Sarita Morgan had one, they were next-door neighbors. Parties every night; they loved to party. They had music; they'd hire bands to come down and play, and they'd drink and dance — all the whites did. Half the time the bands were colored, but no colored at the parties of course. Not 'til that last party.

Yes, Israel Mannheim — Arturo Madrid didn't want anybody to know his real name; he hated it when anybody let on they knew — he had the looks and he had this way about him, all the men would have liked to be in his britches and all the women would have liked to get him into theirs. I used to see him watching Lola — that was my wife's screen name, Lola Mae Turner. Sent a chill through me. Made me glad that Lola Mae's mama was there. I think she would have killed that man if he'd laid a hand on her baby. She scared me half to death, and I was Lola Mae's husband.

I'll tell you something, young man, something nobody in this world knows

— nobody who's alive, that is; nobody in this world knows except Mr. Arturo Israel Mannheim Madrid and me, and now you're going to know it. More than once, Arturo Madrid showed up too god-damned drunk to work, and I sent him back to his bungalow to sleep it off at home. You know what I did then? I told Will Hargess to put on some makeup. He had to work on his hair to make it look like Arturo Madrid's hair, like that big pompadour Arturo Madrid always wore. Finally Will made up a wig for himself. That man was a genius. William Hargess was every bit the equal of Lon Chaney, and light-complected to boot. And he doubled for Arturo Madrid, and when we looked at the rushes we couldn't tell the difference. Except Hargess was a better actor.

We finished the films. Everything was in the big studio building left over from Essanay days. We had a band came in from San Francisco. We decorated the building inside; you'd think it was New Year's Eve and the Fourth of July all wrapped up in one.

That was quite a building, that old Essanay building. Old Max Aronson knew what he was doing. The roof was all peaks and valleys, like a little mountain range all of glass, so they could get plenty of sunlight in there. And muslin cloth, what we called light diffusers, hung across under the glass to give a nice even light on the sets. One whole wall was tilted glass, you know; it was set in the frame on an angle, not vertical, to give that nice light inside, and you could tilt it up and down to get rid of the glare.

Everybody was there. Both crews, both casts. H-M-R and Pan-Pacific all together. Everybody came over from the bunga-lows. Pinch Quince, he had a suite at the old Stoll Hotel; he wasn't too cheap to put himself up in a fancy hotel. He went back to the hotel and changed out of his working clothes and got himself all guss-ied up and came back to the studio.

Everybody had a wonderful time. Toasts were drunk to all. Everybody was dressed to the nines. Everybody was dancing. I turned around one time, and there was Arturo Madrid dancing with my wife. I couldn't believe it. She looked a little looped at that. Arturo Madrid was, too — more than a little. And there was William Hargess watching them, and there was Sarita Morgan watching them.

Mammy Bess was watching, and you could tell she was just about at her limit. She give me a look as if to say, 'You are her husband, Edward; it's your duty to do something about this.' I remember that moment like today. I can hear that band playing, see the decorations, smell the chemicals from the lab. The lab was in the same building, you see; everything was under one roof.

I could see Hargess and Sarita Morgan. I could see Whiskers Tennyson, standing by the liquor table smoking a big black cigar, holding a bottle in one hand and a glass in the other. Beside him was Philip Quince, a drink in his hand as well. He was smoking a pipe. Everybody used to smoke in those days. Nobody smokes anymore. Tennyson and Quince were both dressed in fine suits. They looked like a couple of millionaires. Whiskers Tennyson looked at Arturo Madrid and my wife, dancing together, and you could see the hatred in his eyes. He knew Arturo Madrid's real name, of course — everybody on the set did; they just had to pretend not to know. Tennyson hated that Jewish man almost as much as he would have hated a black man.

There we were in the middle of that party, everyone happy and celebrating, and yet at that moment I could tell that we were doomed. There was an evil presence in that studio, and a cloud looming over us, and we were doomed.

That was when I smelled the flames. That's right. The building was mostly of wood; it was full of wooden props and canvas flats. The film stock and the chemicals were going to go up. I knew it was a disaster. We had no fire extinguishers. We could call for fire engines, but they had to come all the way from Oakland. I knew we didn't have a chance. In that one moment, I knew everything.

Those muslin light diffusers started burning. Then the glass panels in the roof started falling in. People were screaming, running around, trying to get out of the building. People started fighting one another. It was night-time, all dark outside the building.

There were some loud noises — could have been chemical stock exploding, could have been those glass panels breaking, could have been gunshots. Those cowboys liked to carry six-shooters; some of the buildings still had bullet holes in them from the Essanay cowboys. There was black smoke from the chemicals and film stock. Must have been poison; we didn't know about toxic fires then, but people remembered the Great War, the gas in the trenches. People were clawing at each other, falling down and writhing around on the floor. I never want to see anything like that again.

You want to know the strangest thing about that night? Well I'll tell you. That band, a colored band all the way from San Francisco, they kept on playing. Oh, not through the whole disaster, the whole fire, but at first they did. Then somebody started yelling *Fire, Fire*, and then the smoke came pouring in and everybody started trying to run away. The band stopped playing then.

You know the last song they were playing when the fire started? They were playing 'The Man I Love' by that Gershwin man. My wife was dancing with Arturo Madrid, Whiskers Tennyson was giving them his hate look, Mammy Bess was staring at them. And Lola looked at me; Arturo Madrid whirled her around, and she looked right past him and looked at me, and I could see her mouth. She looked right at me and she said the words of that song, *Some day he'll come along, the man I love.*

And right then a big billow of black smoke came rolling into that room, and everybody knew the building was on fire. People started yelling; the band stopped playing.

I just ran. I just ran straight through that cloud of smoke. There were sparks and flames in it too, but I didn't care.

There was a terrible crash. A whole panel of glass exploded in the roof and came pouring down like raining spears. One piece caught Arturo Madrid. It was horrifying. It sliced down the side of his face; just opened a line from the top of his skull to the edge of his jaw and then stuck in his shoulder like a dagger. I don't know how he survived that, how he recovered and resumed his career. He must have had plastic surgery or something, or else worked with a pound of makeup on his face. He just stood there; he didn't look as if he was in pain. Just so startled he didn't know what was happening. Then he turned red, just bright red with his own blood.

I snatched my wife out of Arturo Madrid's arms. She was standing there, his blood spattering all over her, but the only glass on her was a few pieces that landed in her hair and didn't do any harm at all. I picked her up in my arms and I ran like a movie hero, like Alonzo Nash. I couldn't get to the door, I couldn't get anywhere near the door, but that glass wall was half broken down, big shards of glass falling in, and I just jumped through a big hole where a pane of glass had gone.

There were spikes of glass left. I went through. You want to see something, look at this scar. See it right here on my arm? I got that from a piece of glass as big as a spear. Now think of Arturo Madrid with a scar like this down the side of his face — practically cut his ear off. I was spraying blood all over the place. As if poor Lola didn't have enough blood on her already, I was spraying it on her too. They told me afterwards I would have bled to death if somebody didn't help me.

Who saved my life? I don't know. They stuck a tourniquet on me, somebody did, and somebody sewed me up. I guess it hurt. It must have hurt, but I don't remember. Lola was all right, but her mama was burned up in there. So was Whiskers Tennyson. So was Will Hargess.

Specs Lincoln escaped, Walter Davies escaped; Alonzo Nash, Johnson Locksley, Bonnie St. Paul. Specs worked for me at MacReedy Grand Films. He worked until 1948. Had a nice little place in Compton. Burglar got in there one night, killed him in his bed. Shot him. Specs was married. His wife was in the bathroom. She heard a shot, one shot; came out, and the murderer was gone. She looked at her husband. He seemed all right. She shook him, but he didn't answer. She pulled back the covers, and there was the bullet hole. Murderer shot him once, right in the heart, then pulled the covers back up and left. Specs' wife never saw him. Never a clue.

No, you're right, I don't know he was a burglar. Didn't take anything. Just Specs' life. Lawmen came and looked at Specs, thought maybe his poor wife did it. That didn't go anywhere. Door was jimmied. Never found the gun. Never solved the crime.

That was just a year after Philip Quince died. He never made it big; always worked in the Poverty Row studios. Worked for Monogram, Mascot, Republic, Allied Artists. But he stayed friends with Arturo Madrid. Madrid made some movies for Pinchpenny Quince before he hit the big time. Even then they stayed friends.

They used to go boating together. Went for a speedboat ride in 1947. Boat blew up. Terrible tragedy. Quince died; Arturo Madrid managed to cling to the wreckage till the Coast Guard came to the rescue.

Not a scratch on him. I suppose it evens out. Madrid got cut up so bad in that fire, but not a scratch on him when the boat blew up. Mr. Quince drowned, just a year before Specs Lincoln got murdered.

Walter Davies made more movies, but he was mainly a radio man. He got a job as a comedian. Course he still had to play a valet, a waiter, a shoeshine man. People couldn't see you on the radio, but they *knew* he was colored, see, so he had to play colored. He made a good living.

The whites? Pinchpenny Quince lived through that fire. I told you Bonnie St. Paul got out okay. Adolfo Gonzalez perished. Arturo Madrid and Sarita Morgan — he married her for a while, then he married somebody else. How many wives he's had — five, six? Never had any children. No children . . . He missed life's greatest pleasures.

That was the fire. What else can I tell you? How it started? Nobody ever knew. Those noises, those might have been gunshots. Who could find bullet holes in that rubble, in those ashes? If anybody got shot and then burned up, who knows;

246

they weren't looking for bullet holes then. Probably wouldn't have found them anyway.

That was the fire.

My, but I am tired.

Just one more, hey? All right, what is it? Funny thing, that. I had that camera in a carrying case; roll film was just coming in then and I had a roll film camera. Had a roll of exposed film in the case, and the film in the camera. When I picked up Lola and ran, that camera case was hanging 'round my neck, flopping and flapping, and when everything was all over I still had the film. Developed it, and these prints came from that film.

The Werewolf of Harlem? Lost. Flat lost. Not one frame survived. Just a couple production stills. Never tried to make it again. My heart just wasn't in it, and there were always plenty of other movies to make.

And *The Werewolf of Wall Street*? Philip Quince saved that. It was Arturo Madrid's first really big movie. Made his career. Quince was taking his dailies out of the studio building and hiding them over there in the Stoll Hotel. I guess he had the right — they were his dailies, it was his movie. That film saved Pan-Pacific and made Arturo Madrid. And nobody ever knew that it was Will Hargess in most of the shots. Will was a great mimic. He could imitate a voice as well as a walk. He had Madrid down pat. And Arturo Madrid was drunk most of the time we were making that picture. But I guess he learned a lesson. He was never a drunkard after that.

★   ★   ★

Kari Fielding greeted Lindsey with her usual sneer, and Elmer Mueller as usual was absent from the International Surety office.

Lindsey checked his paper and electronic mail, made a note to get a report off to Ducky Richelieu, then phoned Cletus Berry at SPUDS in the Bronx, New York.

Berry was surprised to hear from him. 'Thought you'd gone on to fame and fortune in the outside world, Lindsey. I've been hearing about your exploits, even saw you on CNN with that Duesenberg.'

'Right. That was my fifteen minutes of fame. Then back to the salt mine. How are things in the Bronx?'

'Oh, the sky's always blue here. I also feel like the little Dutch boy, except the dike keeps springing leaks and I never have enough fingers to go around. Maybe you'll fly out here and lend me a couple. For now, though, what do you want? You didn't call just to shoot the breeze, did you?'

Lindsey picked up a yellow pad. He'd transferred the notes from his pocket organizer. The top sheet was covered with names and jotted events. He'd drawn circles and arrows trying to make a pattern of them but it just hadn't worked. 'Look, Cletus, I need a little research. A fellow named Israel Mannheim.'

'What about him?'

'Well, he changed his name to Arturo Madrid and became a movie star. But I'm trying to get a line on his early life.'

'Looking for what?'

'I don't really know. I've got into a very messy situation here in Berkeley, but

Madrid seems to be involved. I can't figure out how.'

Berry whistled. 'Yeah. I saw something about Arturo Madrid on TV the other night. My wife loves those old pix. Is that geezer still alive? He must be a million years old.'

'Not quite. He was born in 1909 or thereabouts. Somewhere in New York City, probably in the Bronx. Could you check him out for me?'

Lindsey waited. He guessed that Berry was jotting notes on a yellow pad of his own. After a while Berry said, 'What do you want on him?'

'That's the tough part. You could verify that birth info. Then anything else you can find. Academic stuff, early career before he moved west and changed his name. Family. Police record if any. Just let me know what you can find.'

'Okay, roomie. I'll look into it. Roger Wilco. Over and Out.'

18

'A date? You have a date?'

'A very nice man at work asked me out for dinner. He's divorced, he has a married son living in Bakersfield and a married daughter living in Portland and grandchildren, he lives alone and he owns his own home. I don't know if you'd exactly call it a date, Hobart.'

Mother sat on the sofa, Lindsey in an easy chair. Dinner was over and the cups and saucers were on the table.

'His name is Gordon Sloane. He's in product development. He's a very nice man. What else can I tell you?'

'I just have to get used to this. You were, ah — ' How do you say this? *You were crazy?* He didn't want to hurt her.

She said, 'I know what you mean. All those years were like a long, terrible dream. You were all that kept me going for those years, Hobart, but it was only when you started moving away from me that I was able to stop dreaming. But I'm here now. I'm . . . awake.'

'Can you trust this man?'

'Do you mean, is he an ax murderer? I know that he's intelligent and has a sense of humor, and he treats me with courtesy. We've had lunch out a few times.'

'You didn't tell me.'

'I don't have to. We're going out for dinner. It doesn't have to mean anything more than that.'

'Just be careful, Mother. Please.'

She reached across the coffee table and patted his cheek. 'It's so nice that you care.'

*   *   *

'That's what it was like,' Lindsey told Marvia Plum. She had taken him to a jazz club and they were finishing their dinner, waiting for Stanley Turrentine to appear and play.

Marvia warmed him with her smile. 'So tell me about this Sloane individual.'

'I only met him for five minutes. He arrived to pick Mother up. He came in the house and we sat down and chatted. He looks presentable enough; dresses nicely. We spoke about the day's news, and off they went. That was all.'

'And afterwards?'

'You mean, did I wait up to make sure she was safe? Wouldn't that be a little too much like role reversal?'

'I guess.'

'Marvia, what about this firebug mess?'

She laughed ruefully. 'Haven't you seen the posters? Dylan Guevara's gang are really going to town. They're planning a funeral for Celia.'

'I don't believe that.'

She handed him a folded sheet. He spread it on the table. The flier was rimmed in black. The display type looked professional and the print job was first class. It reeked of the Corcorans and the Anti-Imperialist League. The jazz club's lighting was not designed to facilitate reading, but he was able to make it out.

COMUNITTY RALLY
A DAY OF SOLEMITY AND RAGE
Saturday Noon at Peoples' Park — come

and Join us to Celabrat the Life and Observe
the Foul Murder of Our Sister in Strugle
Celia Varela.

Murderred by Fascist Pigs.

Fearlass Fighter for Justice and Eqcuity.

Not Since the Brutal Slayying of Sister
Rosebud.

Rally . . . Bon Fire . . . Chantting to
Exercise Evil Demonds of Fascism . . . Free
Food . . . Music . . . March on City Haul...

Deman Returne of Peoples Property!

Deman Punishmet of Fascist Pig Mur-
derres!

Every One Welcome!

Assembl at Peoples' Park 11:00 AM March
at Noon!!!

A FUNERAL WILL BE HELD
People' Ad Hoc Commitee to Aveng Sister
Celia

Lindsey let out his breath in a whistle.
'You think this comes from Dylan
Guevara, don't you?'

'It reads like his handiwork. I don't
believe that spelling. He probably thinks
it makes him part of the underclass. We've
been checking up on him. He tried to get

254

a job with the CIA, tried to join the Marine Corps, and applied to NASA for astronaut training. Got turned down everyplace — emotional instability. We had a hell of a time getting his records.'

'I thought they had a freedom of information act.'

'Tell that to the feds.'

'Not that it matters, but that spelling business is as phony as a Swiss ruble . . . What are you going to do about the march?'

'What *can* we do?' Marvia sighed. 'If we try to stop it, every wacko radical and glory-seeking lawyer in a hundred miles start screaming at us and trying to get injunctions. We'll keep an eye on them, if they start throwing rocks and looting stores we can arrest them.'

'Will you be there?'

'I plan to. How about you? You want to sit in our little bird's nest? Keep an eye on the scene? Maybe you'll learn something useful.' She folded the paper and put it away.

The lights dimmed even more and an

emcee strode onstage to announce the musicians.

Lindsey whispered to Marvia, 'How can they have a funeral? I thought Celia's family claimed the body.'

'They did. I told you, these loonies make their own reality.'

★   ★   ★

Lindsey parked his new 1965 Volvo in the Sather Gate garage and walked south on Telegraph. He had dressed in the closest thing to Berkeley scruffy he could manage, and skipped his morning shave. He must have done a good job of it because most of the spare-change artists on the avenue bypassed him in favor of richer pickings.

Copies of the Day of Solemity and Rage handbill were posted everywhere. Light stanchions had been plastered with them. A vacant storefront had been completely covered in a variety of colors. Lindsey checked his watch. It was eleven o'clock. Half an hour to assembly time, an hour until the march was scheduled to begin.

A police cruiser rolled past, drawing stares from vendors and browsers. Lindsey saw a cluster of figures coming out of a nondescript building located between a bookstore and a bakery. Some of them were in police uniforms. Others wore casual civilian clothes. One of them was Marvia, in jeans and quilted vest. Lindsey approached her.

She asked, 'You want that free balcony seat? We keep a little field office here. Not exactly secret, just low profile.'

'No, I think I want to watch this up close.'

'Okay.' She moved away from him. 'Just keep your distance. Watch but don't mix.'

He moved through jostling pedestrians, walked up Haste, past Amoeba Records and the People's Park mural. The park itself was stirring. A few bleary faces peered from sleeping bags, bewildered individuals who had lost their way in the world and had little idea what was going on around them.

At least a dozen camcorders were going. A couple of them looked like professional equipment; the crews running them sported press credentials on bead-chain lavalieres. The rest were the property of the poor, the homeless, the oppressed of society.

The flier was accurate with regard to the free food. Tubs of scrambled eggs were being unloaded on a wooden stage, and ragged men and women stood in line to get their share. A free café had once been established in the park; Lindsey remembered the footage of that on the evening news. It provoked one of the many crises in the three-cornered tussle involving the city, the university, and the population who made the park their home. Finally the authorities had hitched a tow vehicle onto the café and dragged it away.

Some of the park people carried musical instruments. They all played at once, but no discernible tune emerged. There were signs with slogans on them, mostly lifted from the Solemity and Rage handbill, misspellings and all. A few bore crude portraits of Celia Varela. A trombonist and two drummers posted themselves in front of the wooden platform. The tubs of scrambled eggs, now empty, were carried away. Lindsey checked his watch. It was 11:30. A discordant fanfare sounded.

As if from nowhere, Dylan Guevara popped onto the stage. He wore tattered jeans, an army fatigue jacket and a black beret. Someone handed him a microphone. Its wire ran to an amplifier and a couple of huge loudspeakers that had also appeared on the stage. The local press had stationed themselves around the platform, camcorders whirring away, capturing events for the evening broadcasts and the morning papers.

Guevara started his speech, speaking so softly that it was difficult to hear him, even with the loudspeakers. A group of women in long dresses began chanting, 'Sister Celia, Sister Celia.' Guevara increased the volume and the pitch of his voice. He began pacing the wooden platform, holding the portable mike in one hand, gesturing with the other. He made a dramatic point and the bass drummer whacked his instrument a couple of times for emphasis.

Now Guevara was shouting. He pulled

off his beret and pointed at the audience, one finger extended. The oratorical style was one Lindsey had seen in historical compilations: Adolf Hitler. The speech wound up with Guevara weeping theatrically, beating himself on the breast, and falling to his knees on the platform.

Marshals appeared and formed up the crowd into a movable mass. They poured out of the park and started down Haste Street toward City Hall. At the corner of Telegraph and Haste the police had set up barricades to keep the marchers from fanning out and looting. A couple of trash containers had been overturned and a fire had been started in one. The flames had died down but acrid smoke still rose from it.

Lindsey felt a hand on his arm. Marvia asked, 'What did you think of it?'

'Dylan Guevara scares me.'

'Me too. Mostly these little tinpot dictators only make a nuisance of themselves, but this guy reminds me of Hitler.'

Lindsey nodded. 'I had the same thought.' He watched the moving crowd for a while, then said, 'There have already been two, maybe three murders. Three arson fires, if you include my car. If it's Dylan Guevara's work, we've got to pin him. If it isn't, we have to figure out whose it is.'

'You're talking like a cop, Bart.'

He nodded. 'I'm starting to think that we have to choose sides.'

They followed the march to City Hall. When the crowd got there, Dylan Guevara mounted the old Gothic steps and stood with his head bowed. The musicians stood to one side. A row of marshals wearing black arm bands held Guevara's followers back to maintain a clear area in front of him.

He stood with his head bowed solemnly. The snare drummer began a very soft roll. The trombonist played. The bass drummer began a low, pulsing beat. Guevara raised his head and extended his hand. A marshal handed him a battery-powered megaphone.

'Let us bow our heads in remembrance of our departed sister,' Guevara began. The speech was maudlin, then angry, then mournful. Then he urged his followers to return to the park and build there a shining city on a hill.

The crowd drifted away.

19

Lindsey's voice mail included a callback request from Cletus Berry. He punched Berry's number and caught him at his desk.

'Got a little stuff on your boy Mannheim,' Berry said. 'You got the straight poop on him. Who's your source?'

'Old Hollywood hand named Edward MacReedy. Worked with him back in the 1930s.'

'Speedy MacReedy? Is he still alive, too?'

'Why does everybody know about this guy except me?'

'You ain't black enough, man. Anyway, look, Mannheim. Attended Public School 107, High School of Performing Arts, City College of New York, class of 1930. Married Tillie Steinberg, also 1930. One child, Avner or Abner Mannheim, also born 1930.'

'Sounds like a shotgun wedding. What

about the wife and baby?'

'There must have been a divorce. Maybe Mannheim stopped in Reno on his way west. I haven't found any record of a New York divorce, but I did turn up school records for an Abner Steinberg starting in 1936, and there's no sign of an Abner Mannheim. If Israel and Tillie were divorced and Tillie took back her maiden name, she might have enrolled her son under her own last name. It all fits very neatly.'

Berry paused to consult his notes. 'Abner disappears around 1950,' he resumed. 'Tillie never remarried, as far as I can tell. She lived until 1986. Cause of death was heart failure complicated by pneumonia. Buried about fifteen minutes from here.'

Lindsey had covered a second sheet of yellow note paper. He said, 'Thanks, Cletus.'

'I do have one thing for you. Found a photo in the *Mosholu Parkway Jewish Community Center Bulletin*. Interesting Depression-era wedding party, all the men in old-fashioned tuxedos, bride dressed in white lace, beaming relatives. The women are all in their 1930 best. Stand by; I'm going to fax this over to you.'

Lindsey stood by the fax machine as a page from the July, 1930 publication rolled out. He flattened it on his desk and studied the photo. The festive Tillie Steinberg Mannheim could have passed for Florence Corcoran's younger sister. Or for her younger self. Of course, neither of those was possible. But Tillie had a son, who disappeared from Cletus Berry's story in 1950, at age 20.

How old was Florence Corcoran? Lindsey had met her only once, but he guessed that she was roughly between 30 and 35. So she would have been born somewhere around 1960. Abner would have been 30 at the time. Was Abner Florence's father? If so, where was he now? He'd be in his sixties, in all likelihood still active at whatever profession he'd chosen.

The pieces were starting to fit together. If all of the hints proved out, then Florence Corcoran could be Arturo Madrid's granddaughter. If the Corcorans were providing computer support for the big Arturo Madrid blowout, the connection was unlikely to be coincidental. And if Florence and her husband were the masterminds behind Dylan Guevara and the Anti-Imperialist Front, and Guevara was really the arsonist behind the Film Archive and Robeson Center fires, then a motive for the fires was beginning to make its faint, shadowy appearance.

Was Arturo Madrid's granddaughter trying to obliterate the link between Madrid and Edward 'Speedy' MacReedy? And if that was true . . . *Why?*

Lindsey headed for the Robeson Center. When he got there he found Mathilde Wilbur and MacReedy in the lobby. He phoned the Pacific Film Archive and located Walter Scoggins. Walter was working with Tony Roland. MacReedy's personal treasure trove had been moved to the Art Museum and Scoggins and Roland were deeply immersed in inventorying the contents of the filing cabinets.

Seated in the lobby, Lindsey asked MacReedy about contacts he'd had with Arturo Madrid after the Niles fire.

'None. After that fire, most everybody scattered. There was nothing left in Niles.

Folks had to make a living, you see? I got out of the hospital; I tried to talk to Arturo. I thought, Will Hargess saved Arturo's career, so maybe he would contribute something to a little memorial fund for Will's family, for the other folks died in that fire. Will Hargess left everything to his widow and his little ones, but there was hardly anything to leave. No.' He shook his head. 'No, not a red cent, not even a letter. Arturo Madrid must have been in terrible shape, the way he was cut up when that glass fell in. He went into retreat. Nobody saw hide nor hair of him for at least a year. I suppose he was healing, maybe getting that plastic surgery.'

'Did you ever talk with Madrid in Niles before the fire?'

'Only business. White and colored didn't mix back then. That was why the wrap party was so special, why Whiskers Tennyson was so mad. I can still see him giving that hate stare to white and colored dancing together. Fools.'

Lindsey looked up. Ms. Wilbur was stationed at the desk. The Berkeley police officers had been withdrawn once Mr.

MacReedy's files were moved to the Film Archive, and there had been no further visits from Dylan Guevara, or whoever the arsonist had been.

'You said that Arturo Madrid was married lots of times but he never had any children. Is that right, Mr. MacReedy?'

'As far as I know. But I never talked to him after 1934.'

'Did you ever hear that he was married before he left New York, when he was still Israel Mannheim? Did he ever say anything to you about a wife and baby? This would be back in 1930.'

'In 1930 I was still thinking about being a writer. My last book, *The Ghost on Lenox Avenue*, was never published. Pandolfo was close to a charity case by then. I was doing a little better, but my business was slowly sinking. I think I just kind of lost faith in the printed word. But I filmed that finally. Not at H-M-R. That was a MacReedy Grand Film Corporation project. I still had Johnson Locksley, he was the young man. Walter Davies played the ghost and the comedian, both. Alonzo Nash was between projects; I put him in a bed sheet to double for Walter when the ghost had to be on screen with him. And of course my Lola was in it. This was what, 1951. Near the end of MacReedy Grand Films. Lola was 33 years old, beautiful as ever. She could still play a young girl. Lola Mae Turner, the Sepia Siren. That was a good picture.'

'But about Madrid. I mean, Mannheim.'

MacReedy shook his head. 'No. I don't know anything about that. I never knew him before Niles, and I never knew him afterwards. We passed like two ships in the night.'

Lindsey thanked the old man. He borrowed Ms. Wilbur's telephone and punched in Marvia's office number. He was told that Marvia was at Herrick Hospital with her father.

Minutes later he was at the hospital. A receptionist gave him Marcus Plum's room number. 'But he's in very grave condition. Unless you're immediate family — '

Lindsey didn't stop to argue. He found Marvia at her father's bedside, her brother Tyrone standing behind her, kneading her shoulders. Marvia held one of one of her father's hands in both of hers. The old man looked skeletal. He had aged decades in the months since Lindsey had seen him last. Tears shone on Marvia's face. Tyrone turned and nodded silently to Lindsey. Marvia did not turn from her father. Marvia and Tyrone's mother sat farther from the bed, her face stony. She looked expressionlessly at Lindsey as he entered the room, then away. He stood behind Marvia's chair and placed his hand gently on the back of her neck.

The old man was connected to intravenous feeding tubes and breathed through an oxygen feed. His chest rose and fell in a barely perceptible rhythm. For a moment it stopped, then resumed, then stopped again. This time, it did not resume.

Marvia dropped her head onto the covers. Her shoulders shook. Her mother rose and left the room.

Lindsey asked no one in particular, 'Shall I stay?'

Tyrone Plum looked at his sister, then nodded.

Gloria Plum re-entered the room, followed by a doctor. The doctor looked at

Marcus Plum. He gestured to Lindsey, who drew Marvia away. She stood and leaned against him. The doctor gestured again, and Lindsey led Marvia from the room. As they reached the door, the doctor said, 'There's a chapel in the building. If you think it would help . . .'

★   ★   ★

Tony Roland said, 'This is Fabia Rabinowitz.' To the woman he said, 'Hobart Lindsey. He's been working with Edward MacReedy and Walter Scoggins on this investigation. Hobart, Dr. Rabinowitz is our resident computer whiz, on loan from the UC computer science department.'

Lindsey shook hands with Fabia Rabinowitz, then sat down. They were arranged around a battered conference table: Lindsey, Rabinowitz, Tony Roland, Walter Scoggins, Edward MacReedy, Mathilde Wilbur. Ms. Wilbur had ferried MacReedy to the Film Archive in her Toyota, then invited herself to stay for the meeting.

'First the hardware,' Rabinowitz began. She was tall and olive-skinned, with long black hair and dark eyes. She pointed to the electronic gear that sat in the middle of the table. 'I started with an ordinary computer work station. What it amounts to is a souped-up version of your garden-variety desktop computer. Twin Pentium chips, oversized RAM, heavy-duty turboed everything. Okay? Just think of it as a big, fast PC.' She leaned over the computer. 'I'm using this little Tracball — it's pretty much the same thing as a mouse. And instead of a dinky little monitor I've got the output hooked into a big screen.'

Her fingers danced across the keyboard and the screen sprang to life with an image of brightly-colored exotic fish swimming in an aquarium. The screen was big enough to belong in a sports bar. 'Mr. Roland has managed to locate videotapes of several of Arturo Madrid's films. These include his early works — that is, films made prior to his work with Philip Quince at Pan-Pacific in 1934 — as well as his later works. These also include *The Werewolf of Wall Street*, which was his last Pan-Pacific appearance.'

Tony Roland beamed. He took over

briefly. 'We also hope to get some of Will Hargess's films. Unfortunately, most of Mr. MacReedy's films are either totally lost, or are very hard to obtain. We've tracked down a warehouse in Saint Cloud, Minnesota that's rumored to have prints of several H-M-R and MacReedy Grand films. We're negotiating for copies, but nothing has arrived as yet. In any case, we have the wonderful outtakes that Mr. MacReedy had in the Robeson Center. Those are invaluable. Back to you, Fabia.'

'Now, we've made a lot of progress in image manipulation over the past few years. We've reached the point where we can take a set of blueprints, preferably with three-view drawings, and matrix them into a single mathematical model. The computer can turn that into a three-dimensional image and we can manipulate that, blow it up or down, rotate it, look at it from different angles, look at it from the outside in or the inside out. So far, we haven't done anything except to scan some frames from these films into memory and turn the software loose on them. We've got a nice model of Arturo Madrid. We can do all the things with it that I described to you. We can also age it. That is, we can start with the earliest Arturo Madrid image that we've got, that 1930 wedding photo. Next we have Madrid in his first known film, *Confessions of an Unfaithful Bride*. That was 1931. He appears in only two scenes, but we were able to match those images with the wedding photo. That was how we started building up our image file. Everybody okay so far?'

She walked to the wall and lowered the lights, then clicked at the keyboard until an image appeared on the oversized screen. A ghostly skull floated in blackness. Fabia Rabinowitz rolled the Tracball and the skull rotated — front, side, top, bottom, then back to full-face. 'This is the earliest version of Arturo Madrid that we have. Now, using the features from the 1930 wedding photo and from the 1931 *Confessions*, we add some flesh.' She rolled the Tracball, then clicked. Like a vampire preparing to rise from the dust when the stake has been pulled from between its ribs, the skull of Arturo Madrid developed ghostly flesh, then eyes, then hair. The head of the young matinee idol floated before them.

'Now we have four films that Arturo Madrid made between 1931 and 1934. We have quite a number of images of him, and they all matte very nicely onto the skull that we developed from his 1930/31 images. Take a look at this.' She manipulated the controls and the face on the screen went through a series of movements. The hair grew longer. A mustache appeared. The eyes closed, opened, winked, wept. 'Now watch this. This is 1934. This is *The Werewolf of Wall Street*. Here's where the real fun starts.'

Arturo Madrid's teeth drew back, his perfect teeth became elongated and pointed, his eyebrows grew bushy, whiskers appeared on his cheeks. He was a werewolf. It was like watching Henry Hull, Chaney Junior and Oliver Reed all rolled into one.

'But now look at this.' Fabia Rabinowitz froze the image of Madrid in his full werewolf makeup. She clicked away. The werewolf face on the screen shrank and moved to one side. A second face appeared beside it. Lindsey shifted his gaze from one to the other, unable to tell them apart.

'I can't see the difference,' he confessed.

'This way, they look identical. But look at this.' Rabinowitz manipulated the controls. The two images slid toward the center of the screen until they were superimposed. 'We got this technique from the astronomers. They would take two photos of the night sky and try to find something moving. Some clever bloke thought of superimposing the frames, then blinking them on and off alternately. Lo and behold, if anything moved, its image jumped back and forth while everything else stood still.' She ran her hand over the computer as if it were a favorite household pet. 'Here goes that blink technology.'

The images winked on and off, on and off. They were very much alike, but not identical after all. 'Look what happens when we go back to the underlying armatures.' Hair, flesh, eyes disappeared. The screen contained only the image of a skull. It blinked, blinked. 'You see? There are two skulls. This is really exciting — and puzzling. Is the only explanation that there are two Arturo Madrids? He must have used a double for most of *The Werewolf of Wall Street*.'

MacReedy stirred in his chair. 'I've told young Walter here all about that. Walter, didn't you tell the girl what I told you about Will Hargess and Arturo Madrid?'

Scoggins shook his head. 'I didn't want to influence Dr. Rabinowitz one way or another. I left her to draw her own conclusions.'

Sounding annoyed, Rabinowitz asked, 'What's the big joke that I'm not in on?'

'Well, I'm sorry.' Scoggins didn't sound sorry. 'You're exactly right. There were two werewolves in *The Werewolf of Wall Street*. One of them was Arturo Madrid. He got the billing, and *The Werewolf of Wall Street* was the making of his career. But Mr. MacReedy told me that most of the scenes were played by William Hargess, an H-M-R stock player, because Madrid was either drunk or hung over most of the time.'

20

'Bart, you're going to have to carry a beeper or get a cellular, one or the other.'

'Sorry. How many tries did it take?'

'Not so many. The office manager at International Surety in Walnut Creek said to try the Robeson Center. La Vonda Hendry said you'd be at the Film Archive with Ms. Wilbur and Mr. MacReedy. But, say, who is that lovely creature at I.S.?'

'Why ask that?' Lindsey was relieved that Marvia was handling the loss of her father as well as she was. He knew that she'd had time to prepare for it, and he knew that she dealt with death every day in her job. But still, he wondered at the odd blank space in his own emotional tapestry. It was the space where an image of his father should have been. But his father had been killed before Lindsey was born.

'She's Elmer Mueller's hand-picked replacement for Ms. Wilbur,' he said. 'Did you know that Mathilde is working at Robeson? At least the Hendrys get a little time to spend together now.'

'Aha. So that's why La Vonda sounded so happy. Listen, Bart, this isn't the time for small talk. I'm sitting on a report here that came in from one of Olaf Stromback's canvassers up on Oxford Street. Dorothy Yamura's about to go for an arrest warrant, but you're in this up to your eyeballs, and I want you to watch this go down.'

He laid down the telephone. The meeting had ended anyway. Fabia Rabinowitz had headed back for the university's main campus and her own lab. Ms. Wilbur had shepherded MacReedy out of the museum building and headed back to the Robeson Center. Walter Scoggins and Roland were huddling over film clips, videotapes and still photos.

Lindsey pulled the Volvo into a handy space and trotted up the steps at police headquarters. Marvia and Lt. Yamura were in the latter's office, along with Stromback and a uniformed woman Lindsey had never met.

Stromback introduced Lindsey and Officer Rossi. 'That was Mr. Lindsey's Hyundai that got cooked,' Stromback said. 'Would you tell him what you got?'

Rossi consulted her notebook. 'Sir, I was canvassing Oxford Street at Sgt. Stromback's direction. One individual reported seeing a white male dressed in an army fatigue jacket and black beret proceeding north on Oxford on foot just after the explosion. The citizen was more interested in the burning automobile than in a pedestrian, so she did not observe any further details, but she said that the white male ran to the corner, then turned east on Summer. Almost immediately a white BMW was reported proceeding southward on Oxford at a high rate of speed. The citizen isn't sure, but she believes she saw the man in the beret in the passenger seat, staring at the burning Hyundai as the BMW passed.'

'License number?' Stromback asked.

'My source says she was too distracted by the explosion and fire to notice the license. Or it may have been obscured, she wasn't sure.'

'Thanks, Rossi,' Yamura said. 'Thanks, Sgt. Stromback. Okay, we've got probable cause to pick up Dylan Guevara. If you feel okay with that, Sergeant Plum, let's go for it.'

'Nothing on the Beamer?'

'Dollars to donuts it's the Corcorans, but we don't have probable cause. Too many white Beamers around for that. We'll take it one step at a time. Che-baby first.'

'Let's go.'

Lindsey got to ride in the police cruiser from McKinley Avenue to Telegraph. Yamura had stayed at headquarters. Marvia, in her sergeant's uniform, was in charge of the arrest.

People's Park was quiet. A mock cemetery had been created. There was a new mock grave, with a wooden marker and a border of flowers. The marker bore the name of Celia Varela. Half a dozen officers fanned out, questioning park residents and passers-by. Lindsey wondered if any of the civilians being questioned, even the most ragged of park burnouts, were officers themselves, risking their lives as Celia

Varela had risked hers.

Marvia tapped Lindsey's arm. 'Come on.' She started toward the field office nearby. 'We're not getting anywhere,' she said.

Upstairs, overlooking Telegraph Avenue and People's Park, Lindsey sat facing Marvia. A fax machine burbled and a sheet of paper rolled slowly from it. When it had fallen into the tray, Marvia tossed it onto her desk. Lindsey leaned over the page. It had an elaborate border. The message had the look of professional lettering. The design smacked of an Anti-Imperialist League communiqué, but the text read more like a press release than a handbill.

PEOPLE'S PARK LEADER TO COMMIT SUICIDE

Berkeley, CA — People's Park, Berkeley's famed strip of land where the popular struggle against oppression has been fought for a quarter century, will be the site of a dramatic sacrifice, it was announced today. Within twenty-four hours, Dylan 'Che' Guevara, community activist and leader of Progressive forces, will give his life in protest against continuing oppression and persecution of the broad masses of people in Berkeley and throughout the world.

Guevara, a close relative of the martyred Ernesto 'Che' Guevara, is expected to make his final appearance in the cause of direct community action against the University of California, the City of Berkeley, the City Gestapo, and the Federal Bureau of Intimidation, all of which have tried repeatedly to silence his heroic voice and its uncompromising demand for justice for the People of Berkeley and the Park Community.

Guevara, a founding member of the Free Speech Movement, People's Park Community, Symbionese Liberation Army, and the Berkeley Anti-Imperialist Front for the Liberation of People's Park, will give his own life in the cause of the People. He warned authorities, 'Don't try to stop me, and don't come anywhere near me. Anyone who tries will get hurt. Don't say I didn't warn you.'

Comparisons to the Jonestown and Branch Davidian disasters are inevitable, but Guevara has asked his followers not *to follow his example, but to consider him a martyr in whose memory they will struggle to inevitable victory.*

Up with the People!

Down with the forces of Greed and Oppression!

Venceremos

'Wow.' Lindsey shook his head. 'What do you make of that?'

Marvia's phone rang. She picked it up. 'Yes. Here too. All of them, hey? What do you make of it? Me too. All right. No he doesn't. Even so, we'll get down there.' She laid the handset down. 'That was Dorothy Yamura. They must have sent those faxes to every police department, broadcast station and newspaper from San Jose to Sacramento. The phone is going nuts at McKinley Avenue.'

'What are you going to do?'

'He's threatened suicide before. Got hauled off to the hospital a couple of times for mental evaluations. They decided he was crazy but not insane, if you take my meaning. DA tried to prosecute him for it a couple of times, but Carl Shea — '

'Carl Shea!'

'The very one. Made a monkey out of us. So we stopped paying attention, so Guevara stopped threatening. But now he's up to it again.'

Lindsey looked at the fax again. 'What's this about being a close relative of Ernesto Guevara?'

'For some reason, a lot of these radicals identify with Fidel's revolution in Cuba. Maybe because he managed to thumb his nose at Uncle Sam and get away with it. And Che is their martyr. So our boy just wipes his background away and announces that he's the original Che's cousin or whatever.'

Lindsey stood and walked to the window. He could see men and women milling around in People's Park. He turned. 'What are you going to do?'

'We're going to arrest him. For arson.'

Berkeley and UC police had strung a cordon around People's Park. There were more TV camcorders in the park than Lindsey had seen in his life. The usual residents of the park had been forced out and onto the sidewalk. The streets bounding the park on three sides had been closed to traffic, but pedestrians milled around, craning for a view of the wooden platform where Dylan Guevara made his appearances. Lindsey stood on the sidewalk at Haste Street. He had a good view of the platform.

As if by magic, Dylan Guevara appeared. His personal musicians were there, and he held a battery-powered megaphone. Even if the police had Telegraph heavily patrolled, the constant stream of students, merchants, shoppers and itinerants could have given him cover to slip though. The trombone and drums sounded. Guevara lifted the megaphone. Two squads of police moved into the park, one from Guevara's left and one from his right.

He raised his hand above his head. The megaphone carried his amplified voice. 'Hold it!'

The police stopped. A couple of them reached for their guns.

Dylan Guevara moved his hand in a narrow circle, showing what he held. It was a hand grenade. 'I've already pulled the pin. Don't make me let go of this thing.' He looked pleased with himself. He'd stopped a platoon of pigs. 'You'd better back off. Let the cameras approach. You fellows better be careful, though. Don't come too close. When this goes, you don't want to go with it.'

The reporters stirred and edged away from the platform.

'I don't want to take my friends with me, either.' He smiled benevolently at the musicians. 'You stay close to me until the end, all right? I'll give you some warning before I let the handle go. But stay here so the pigs don't decide to get cute and play sniper with me.'

He lowered his hand and turned side to side. 'Won't make any difference, pigs. One shot, the grenade goes. Maybe I'll be able to toss it away so my friends don't get it.' He swung his arm back and forward, like a bowler going for a strike. A couple of TV reporters jumped sideways.

Dylan Guevara laughed. 'You never believed me, did you? You with the battery belt.' He pointed at a TV crewman. 'You, yes. I recognize your logo there. Your station would never give me airtime. Your network ignored me. The have time for dog shows and every damned politician as long as he bleats about saving the system, but you don't have room for the people's authentic spokesman, do you? *Do you? Answer me!*'

Lindsey heard the crewman's voice. 'The managing editor makes those decisions — I don't control it.'

'Right. Bunch of pettifogging bureaucrats. Try and call 'em up, they hand you to another department, put you on hold, cut you off. Try and go see 'em and you can't even get past the front door.'

He swung around. '*Back off!* I warned you cops, don't try that damned sneaking up business. If I let go of this handle, you're going to lose three good people. If I throw it into that camera pool, you won't have any TV news tonight. That would be tragic, wouldn't it?'

A cop raised a power megaphone of his own. 'Let those people go, Che. They haven't done anything. Look, we can get a containment device out to you in seconds. You can drop the grenade in, it will deflect the force upward. Nobody needs to get hurt.'

'And nobody will know about it. I'm not gonna settle for a tape bite on the local news. I want the nets. And I know how to get 'em!'

He signaled the musicians. They marched half a dozen paces, the drums rolling, the trombone sounding a sour fanfare.

Now only the snare drum sounded. Guevara said, 'In the name of the people, the people's struggle, the people's justice.' He dropped the megaphone and released the handle on the grenade. The flat crack of a sniper's rifle echoed across the park and was reflected off the nearby buildings. A red flash obliterated Guevara, then he lay on the dirt in front of the platform, writhing.

The TV cameras descended on him like ants on a struggling beetle.

★   ★   ★

Mother was out with her new friend, Gordon Sloane. Lindsey and Marvia had the house to themselves for the evening. It was like playing at being newlyweds.

Marvia cooked and Lindsey stayed out of her way. She told him, 'Don't get used to this. I expect you to do your share. But I know you don't know how to cook, and I am good at it. I am seriously good at it.'

After a delicious meal they drank coffee in front of the network news. 'He got what he wanted, poor fool,' Marvia said. 'Look at the network coverage.'

The network had picked up a local cameraman's tape. The camera pointed straight at Guevara. His last few words came from the TV set. *The people's struggle. The people's justice.* Then the crack of the sniper's rifle. The red flash hid Dylan Guevara for a fraction of a second and then he came tumbling straight at the camera, rolling on the ground, red splattering, his face half gone, the rest of it registering amazement.

'That shot was incredible. Guevara can thank Marty Bilson, our police marksman, if he pulls through.'

Lindsey put down his cup. 'I never want to see that again. Is he in the hospital now?'

'Took him straight down to Herrick. I hung around for a while, but he wasn't coming out of surgery for a long time. That Marty, though, he is really something. Can you imagine, hitting that grenade from the roof of a record store? Perfect aim, perfect timing. Hit it right in Guevara's hand. Drove it right into the ground as it was exploding. What Guevara got was mainly the primer charge and a face full of dirt and gravel. Even so, he'll never be the same. What a fool.'

The TV image had cut away from the anchor desk to an automobile commercial. Lindsey held the remote. He hit the mute button. 'What's the prognosis?' he asked.

'I talked to the emergency room chief. A Dr. Chandra.'

'I know him.'

'Small world. He says even the primer charge took off Guevara's hand and half his jaw. He'll be blind in one eye. What a mess. How do you feel about your Hyundai now?'

Lindsey looked at her. 'How do Annabella's parents feel about getting her back from America in a box?'

'Yeah. Well, Guevara's parents are

headed out here on the Red Eye. They'll be in tomorrow morning. I'm going to be there when they talk to him. And I suppose he'll have to have a lawyer present.'

'Dollars to donuts he'll have Carl Shea.'

'Lousy bet. Who else would he have?'

Lindsey put his arm around Marvia's shoulders and drew her to him.

*   *   *

Later, lying in bed, he asked about Jamie and about Marvia's mother and brother. How were they dealing with her father's death?

She pushed herself upright and sat with her back against the pillow. The streetlight and the moonlight combined to cast a pattern of shadows on her skin. 'Gloria's doing what she's been doing ever since Dad was diagnosed. She's throwing herself into her job. You know, she recovers overpayments for the Social Security Administration. She'll get a bonus if she keeps it up.'

A key grated in the downstairs lock and

the front door opened, then shut again softly. There were sounds from the kitchen — the refrigerator door shutting with its solid thump, the microwave beeping when its timer ran out. Then silence.

Lindsey watched the play of light and darkness. 'Don't you think you're being a little hard on her? How many years were they together?'

'Forty-three. And how many times did I ever see her touch him, hear her say a kind word to him? Never mind. He's gone. She won't suffer.'

'And Tyrone? And Jamie?'

'Tyrone is Tyrone. He's made his own life. He has his own friends. He's a terrific guy, but I don't see him very often. And Jamie's all right. He goes to his school friend Hakeem White's house, just down the street from Gloria's house. Then she picks him up on the way home from work.'

'But Jamie spent so much time with his granddad, this has to have an effect on him.'

'You're right, I know. I'll have to deal

with it. I'll have to help him.'

'Maybe I can help.'

She rubbed her forehead against his shoulder and made a noncommittal sound.

Lindsey said, 'Mother wants to sell the house and get into a condo. I think she's getting serious about this guy Sloane. I hope he isn't going to hurt her. I think it's about time for us, Marvia. For you and Jamie and me.'

Clouds had rolled in from the Pacific and swarmed across the face of the moon, lowering the light level like a dimmer switch. After a silence, Marvia said, 'Maybe you should find a nice white woman for yourself.'

He looked at her and she was crying. He said, 'I only want you, Marvia.'

21

Lindsey and Marvia Plum met his mother and her friend Gordon Sloane over the breakfast table. There was a momentary embarrassment, then everyone laughed. Lindsey introduced Sloane and Marvia. Sloane shook her hand.

The Guevara suicide attempt was front page news in the *West County Times*. The paper ran a color photo that must have been snapped a split-second after Marty Bilson's high-powered bullet struck the exploding grenade from Dylan Guevara's hand. The grenade was visible, a dark blob suspended in midair. One side of it was obscured by the beginning of its flash. Guevara was shown, a look of mingled triumph and shock on his face.

They shared muffins and juice and poached eggs. Marvia said, 'This is the best breakfast I've had since I was in the army.'

Sloane looked surprised. 'You were in the army?'

'Military police. That's how I got into police work when I left the army.'

'Signal Corps. Served in Korea. I was just a kid then. Got called back during 'Nam but I never got farther than Fort Ord. That's how I wound up in California when I got out.'

After breakfast, Sloane and Mother drove to work together.

Marvia had left her Mustang in Berkeley. Battling the freeway in the rain, Lindsey asked, 'What do you think of him?'

'Hey, we ex-GIs stick together.' Then, 'He seemed okay. Did you see that glow around your mom? You thinking what I am?'

Lindsey blushed and punched the radio into life. He hit the scan button and wound up with another dose of Ken-and-Barbie.

' — and then there's the whole issue of the militarization of society and the establishment of the urban police state,' Ken intoned in his nasal baritone. 'Since when did the people ever give their permission to have — '

' — snipers in Berkeley?' Barbie took over. 'The capitalist class won't stop at anything, will they? I don't think I can remember ever hearing anything about that policy, do you, Ken? I mean, aren't we supposed to have some kind of civilian control over the military, I mean the fascist police? Or am I mistaken?'

'No, Barbie, I think you're absolutely right, we have to — here's our guest. He must have been held up in traffic. You know, with the streets clogged and slippery this morning in that surprise Pacific storm . . . '

A chair scraped and something banged against a microphone. Barbie said, 'Welcome.'

'Nice to be here.'

Ken said, 'Well, our guest this morning is an old friend of ours, civil rights attorney Carl Shea. And I should mention, author of the new book, *What They're Doing to You and What You Can Do to Stop Them*. How you find time for all of this is a wonder. Carl — may I call you Carl?'

'Sure.'

'Carl, don't you think this incident yesterday in People's Park calls for serious attention from the community? It was tragic, of course. A man is hovering between life and death even as we speak. At least according to the last word our reporter at Herrick Hospital had . . . '

Carl Shea cleared his throat. 'Dylan is holding his own. His doctors say that his chance for survival is better than fifty-fifty.'

'Well, that's good news, isn't it? But don't you think that the presence of an official police sniper represents a threat to the safety of everyone in the community? We hear talk about too many weapons, violence and so forth, but who has the weapons? Who commits the acts of violence? Isn't it our own police force? What are we coming to in this town? Snipers sitting on top of buildings picking off citizens like sitting ducks, and they're police themselves?'

Shea's voice faded. 'Say, I'm sorry to chat and run, but I've got to get to the hospital.'

Ken took over again. 'Well, Barbie, we

have just a few minutes left. Let's get to that community calendar. The Peruvian Dance Troupe of Cuzco will be performing at — '

Marvia hit a preset. Some music replaced the irritating voices.

'You want me to drop you at Oxford Street or at HQ?'

'Neither. Drop me at Herrick Hospital. Dwight Way.'

'Keep me posted, will you?'

'I don't know how much more there will be. This case is getting too hot. Dorothy said she was going to get involved.'

Lindsey frowned. 'You know, he did burn up my Hyundai. I feel as if I have some connection here.'

After dropping Marvia off, Lindsey phoned the Robeson Center and learned that Ms. Wilbur had ferried Mr. MacReedy to the Film Archive.

Tony Roland met him at the doorway. 'Good timing; we were just about to get started. They FedEx-ed the tapes in from the midwest. Why in the world there's an Edward MacReedy stash in Saint Cloud, Minnesota is a mystery to me, but you never know where something wonderful is going to turn up.'

He led Lindsey to the room where Fabia Rabinowitz had her souped-up computer system. MacReedy sat at the table, dapper in his old-fashioned suit. Walter Scoggins, camcorder at the ready, hovered.

Rabinowitz looked up and gave Lindsey a smile of recognition. A notebook was spread on the table and she scratched away at it. In the age of super-micro computers, the pencil and the yellow pad were not yet outmoded.

Scoggins tossed Lindsey a casual salute. 'Tony, tell Lindsey what films we got from Saint Cloud. This is marvelous!'

'*Murder on the Bar-20* — both versions. *The Lucky Ghost, The Preacher and the Gambler* — Mr. MacReedy didn't even remember that one. We've got *Fate's Roulette Wheel.*' Roland pulled a huge bandanna from his pocket and used it to mop his face. 'And even five chapters of a serial, *Horror of Haunted Canyon.* Then there are a couple of fragments, I'm not sure what they are. Maybe parts of other serials.'

MacReedy nodded. 'We didn't make any serials at H-M-R, but I was always interested in 'em. Saw some chapters back in the silent days and I always thought they were a good idea. By the time MacReedy Grand Film company was a going concern, we decided to try one. Big success. Audiences had to come back next week and see how Johnson Locksley escaped from the flaming coal mine, or whether Alonzo Nash would get away with kidnapping Lola Mae. We made *Haunted Canyon*, *Spook Ship*, and *Cannibals of the Congo*. Shot that one in Griffith Park. Made a lot of money.'

Lindsey slid into a chair. 'These are actual films?'

Roland said, 'These are prints. Negatives would have been nicer, but we're happy with what we've got.'

Lindsey asked Fabia Rabinowitz if her computer could handle the films.

She shook her head. 'What we're doing now is transferring the images to CD-ROM. We can convert the images frame for frame, digitized, then we can read those into RAM and turn the software loose on 'em.'

She turned to MacReedy. 'I'm sorry, is this all Greek to you, sir?'

MacReedy smiled faintly. 'When I was a child we rode in mule-drawn wagons or we walked barefoot on dirt roads. Now we have these jet airplanes and spaceships. I made a movie about a spaceship in 1939. *Marauder from Mars*. Not successful. My audience was not interested in outer space; it had nothing to do with their lives. I learned to read by kerosene lamp, and the first recorded music I heard came from a wax cylinder. Everything changes. I don't understand your seedy romp or whatever it is, but don't let that stop you. You just go ahead.'

Rabinowitz smiled. 'Well, once we have the images on CD-ROM we can start analyzing them. I certainly want to develop armatures and progressive visualizations of the ongoing actors, especially William Hargess. Once I've got a good file of Hargess images I can compare it with all the images from *The Werewolf of Wall Street* and the ones we lifted from Mr. MacReedy's stills, both the shots from *The Werewolf of Harlem* and the pictures he took at the wrap party that last night in Niles. Then we'll see what we can put together.'

The phone sounded on Roland's desk in the next office. He bounded from the room, then came back with a cordless handset and handed it Lindsey.

Marvia said, 'You'd better get over here right now, Bart. Mr. Guevara wants to see you. Or Mr. Garfinkel the younger. Dorothy Yamura's here, Garfinkel's parents, Carl Shea — it's mob city.'

Lindsey blinked. 'Do I need Eric Coffman?'

Marvia hesitated. 'I don't think so. It couldn't hurt, but just don't sign anything or make any promises, and you should be okay without him.'

Guevara was in a private room. A uniformed officer was posted outside the door. It was a scene Lindsey had watched a hundred times in gangster films. Lindsey showed the officer his ID and the officer nodded him into the room.

Guevara was propped up, peering through mummy wrappings with his remaining eye. A stationary tray extended over his bed. A black laptop computer was opened on the tray, and Guevara was tapping at the keyboard with his remaining hand.

Dr. Apu Chandra stood beside the pillowed head, keeping close watch. He acknowledged Lindsey's arrival with a quick nod. The elderly couple seated at the bedside had to be the senior Garfinkels. Shea was there, in his lawyer suit and trademark bow tie. Dorothy Yamura was in civvies, Marvia in uniform.

Marvia pulled Lindsey back into the hallway. She closed the door behind them. 'This is a first, Bart. Daniel asked for you — '

'Daniel?'

'Daniel Garfinkel. He's had a near-death experience and it has changed him profoundly. He has decided that he's been on the wrong path for the past twenty years. He's taking back his true identity, returning to his roots, confessing his sins and seeking to make amends. He believes he's dying and he wants to clear his conscience before he goes.'

Lindsey made a face. 'You believe that?'

'I believe he's going to recover. A little doctor told me so. He's going to have a very tough time from here on out, and he's going to be in a lot of trouble with the law, but he is not dying.'

'That's why Carl Shea is here, eh?'

'I know that Daniel or Dylan has been through a terrible experience and I think that maybe he really is thinking things over. But he's going to have to stand up in front of a judge and jury, and I think his pal Shea is planning on a psychological approach. A sort of Patti Hearst defense only done right. You know, politically naive young man comes out to Cal in a vulnerable emotional state and at a time when the nation is in turmoil, falls in with bad companions, winds up brainwashed and in a weird persistent fugue state. They tell him lies about himself and he believes them, becomes a kind of living robot doing the will of others.'

'When did he snap?'

'The real Che Guevara died in '67. Could have been any time after that. I'm sure Mr. Shea will tell us all about it.'

Lindsey grunted. 'Where do I come in?'

'Well, torching your Hyundai is pretty small potatoes compared to some of the other charges he'll have to face. But I think he wants to start off on his new life by apologizing to you. Then I'm sure Shea will ask you to drop the charges against him. Without your cooperation, the DA will probably let the matter slide, and Shea hopes the others will follow. At least, that's what I think.'

'Huh. You think I should drop the charges?'

'That's entirely up to you, Bart. You might want to consult your attorney before deciding. Let the DA decide whether to prosecute, and if they prosecute, then let the court decide whether he's guilty or not.'

The heavy hospital door shushed behind them. Lindsey turned to see Carl Shea stride angrily from Guevara or Garfinkel's room. Lindsey said, 'Mr. Shea,' but the lawyer swept past him and disappeared down the corridor.

Marvia ran past Lindsey, back into Garfinkel's room. Lindsey followed. Garfinkel's father was clutching the bed sheets in his hands, leaning over his son. His mother was whispering fiercely to Dorothy Yamura.

Whisper or no, it was no problem to hear her words.

'I don't care what he wants and I don't care what he says. This boy is severely injured, and he's sky high on painkillers and utterly out of his mind. I want a lawyer for him.'

Yamura shook her head. 'He had his rights. He says he doesn't want a lawyer here. He had one and he fired him, you saw that.' She turned from the older woman. 'Dr. Chandra, is Mr. Garfinkel able to cooperate with us? Can he understand questions and answer them?'

Chandra bent over Garfinkel and peered into his face, as much of it as was visible. 'In my opinion, Lieutenant, he is competent to answer your questions.'

'Okay. Dr. Garfinkel, I'm going to have to ask you and your husband to leave the room for now. This is a police procedure.'

'I will not leave my patient.'

Yamura sighed. 'First, he's not your patient, he's Dr. Chandra's patient. Second, he's under arrest. Your son is accused of several Class A felonies. He has agreed to answer our questions, and that is exactly what's going to happen.'

'I refuse to leave my son.'

Yamura turned to Marvia. 'Sergeant, will you call in the officer there? Thank you. Mr. Garfinkel's parents are leaving now. If they refuse, I will personally place them under arrest and we'll have them removed forcibly.' She turned back to Dr. Garfinkel. 'Please, Doctor.'

The older woman leaned over her son. 'Not a word, Daniel, you understand? Not a word to these Cossacks. I'll get you a lawyer, or your father will. They're persecuting you and they're not going to get away with it.' She continued all the way to the door, followed by her silent husband.

Lindsey turned to look at Daniel Garfinkel. A tiny Star of David was pinned to the shoulder of his hospital gown. Lindsey asked, 'What happened to Shea? I thought he was representing Dylan. Ah, Daniel.'

'I don't think I can divulge that information, Mr. Lindsey. Mr. Garfinkel has certain protections.'

The injured man was waving his sole

hand, gesturing Lindsey and Yamura to him. He tapped a few keys on the computer keyboard and his message appeared on the screen. It read, *OK WANT HIM TO STAY*.

Yamura looked dubious. 'You want him to hear what went on in here? You waive confidentiality?'

YES. And after a pause, *YOU TELL*.

'All right. Mr. Garfinkel made several very serious accusations against Mr. and Mrs. Corcoran. Essentially, that they were his mentors for the past decade or longer. Prior to that, his guru was one Abner Steinberg. Steinberg died around 1985. He'd been a shadowy figure, living halfway underground, using a variety of names. Steinberg introduced Florence Corcoran to Garfinkel as his own daughter, Steinberg's daughter. Are you following this?'

Lindsey nodded.

'There may or may not have been some sexual connection between Daniel and Florence, and possibly a drug involvement. Mr. Garfinkel is not certain he wants to discuss that. But the Corcorans bankrolled him, gave him his instructions, provided him with safe houses and support when needed.'

'What about Shea?'

'Shea is the Corcorans' lawyer. They sent him over here to look after Garfinkel's interests. Soon as he heard that Daniel wants to tell the truth, Shea ordered him to shut up. When Daniel refused, Shea had to resign from the case. You can't represent both the accuser and the accused. Wouldn't work.'

Lindsey sank into a guest chair. 'He told you all that? On the laptop? Is that admissible?'

'Probably not.'

'What about the Corcorans?'

'We'll have to check out the accusations.' Turning, Yamura said, 'Dr. Chandra, I'll leave Mr. Garfinkel in your good care. Please don't leave him alone. If you do, see to it that a nurse or orderly is with him, or that our officer steps in here and keeps watch.'

22

'You want us to buy you a new car, too? I didn't think your employment agreement called for I.S. to buy you a new car, Lindsey.'

'It isn't a new car and I'm not looking for it as an employee benefit. I'm an I.S. customer, too. My car got torched. It's a total loss and I want fair market value for it.'

'Right, I've got the paperwork here. And the Blue Book valuation. Okay, I guess we can pay that. What are you going to replace that beauty with?'

'I've already replaced the car, sir.' Let Richelieu stew over that.

'Now look, Lindsey, that's petty cash. I'm more concerned with the Pacific Film Archive claim. We can't hold off much longer; we're going to have to shell out. In fact, if your pals at the University of Cockamamie pester you about it — '

'They haven't.'

'I see that wacko town of yours is in the news again. That lunatic with the hand grenade. Is he dead yet?'

'No, sir. He's in the hospital. And it isn't my town. I live in Walnut Creek. Our office is in Walnut Creek. The company wants to cover policyholders in Berkeley; we're going to get involved when there are claims.'

'Right. Okay. You wouldn't have anything to do with this Che Dylan individual, would you, Lindsey? You seem to have a way of getting tangled up with nut cases out there in Loonieland.'

'His name is Daniel Garfinkel, sir, and in fact I'm very tangled up with him. I wish I weren't.'

A pained sigh. 'Tell me.'

'Garfinkel, formerly Guevara, formerly Garfinkel, is the man who torched my Hyundai. More to the point, he very likely — I'd say almost certainly — set the Film Archive and Robeson Center fires. And he is also a prime suspect in the murder of an undercover police officer. She was strangled with a length of wire. She'd worked her way into Garfinkel's confidence. Then she slipped somehow. Maybe she was seen too often at a covert police rendezvous point. Anyway, Garfinkel has been arrested on a slew of charges.'

'And this darling is your new little playmate?'

'Hardly.'

'Does he have any assets we can go after with a civil action?'

'He doesn't have anything. But his defense, it looks like, will be that he was brainwashed and used by a couple of evil masterminds. And they have major assets: house, new cars, couple of businesses. Computer system consultants and real estate.'

'Hmm. And they were running this wacko rabble-rouser? What's their lifestyle?'

'Upper-upper middle class. Large private home, good neighborhood. Good dress-ers, high livers, associate with the movers and shakers. Have you been following the Arturo Madrid celebration?'

'I'm not much interested in Hollywood news.'

'Well, it's pretty big out here. They're providing computer support for the event.

I think they've been doing a lot of Hollywood-oriented computer jobs.'

'Then I still don't get it. If they're so successful in business, live such a pleasant lifestyle, why are they running a ninth-rate Fidel Castro wannabe?'

'If I or the police could figure that out, we'd have the case solved.'

'Cripes. If only John Edgar were still alive . . . Keep me posted, Lindsey. And try and save International Surety a few bucks, will you? Remember what we pay you to do? Don't even say yes, just go thou and do, all right?'

★　★　★

'Marvia, let's do it,' Lindsey said. 'We can register at City Hall as domestic partners today, and then we'll get married as fast as the law allows.'

She shook her head. 'Not yet. Not with my daddy — I mean, it's too soon.' She padded to the dresser and pulled on a Billie Holiday sweatshirt, then sat on the bed. 'I'm not ready.'

'I'm sorry. I was so worried about how

Jamie was taking it, I didn't think of you, Marvia.'

She put a CD on the player. 'All right.' She managed a smile. 'Let's talk about something else. Let's talk shop. What else can I tell you in violation of department policy and citizens' rights of confidentiality?'

'What about Daniel Garfinkel? And his parents?'

'Okay, parents first. Papa the rabbi is beside himself with happiness. He's sorry that his Danny is missing a hand and an eye and he's feeling second-hand remorse for his crimes. But mainly, it's the prodigal son returned to the fold. As long as Daniel has given up the crazy 'Che' business, Papa Garfinkel knows that God will provide.'

'Huh. Must be nice to have such faith.'

'Sometimes you need to believe things that you know aren't true.'

'And what about Mama?'

'Doctor Garfinkel is a different kind of cookie. She's a real go-getter. As far as she's concerned, Carl Shea is a case of good riddance to bad rubbish. She didn't like him to start with and she's pleased as punch to see the hind end of him. She went out and hired a legal hotshot to represent little Danny. I was right about Shea's original strategy, trying to show that Garfinkel was brainwashed and zombified by evil companions; that he wasn't responsible for anything he did.'

'But that failed in the Patti Hearst case. We've talked about this before. Hearst wound up in prison.'

'Country club prison, and not for very long.'

'Still.'

'They made two mistakes in that case. One was that Patti's zillionaire family weren't satisfied with a local lawyer for their little girl, so they dragged in Flee Bailey from the east coast. He didn't know the Bay area; he attacked some sacred local icons and he lost the jury. And then Patti herself really blew it. She went on the stand when she didn't have to, and then she changed her mind and refused to answer questions that she didn't like. Got the judge peeved, got the jury mad at her.'

'You think she could have got off, otherwise?'

'All she had to do was cry a little, say she was dreadfully sorry for what she'd done, play the poor-little-rich-girl card, punch up the horrible experiences she'd been through and ask for mercy. She'd never have seen the inside of a cell.'

'And you think Garfinkel is going to try that?'

'He's going to try everything that Hearst tried, plus he's going to throw in some contrition and beg for mercy. And he'll have a prosthetic hand and an eye patch.'

'Still, the way he killed Celia Varela . . .'

'But did he? Or did your wonderful friends up on Cedar Street do it? He was willing to use Celia while she was alive and to go on using her after she was dead, but that isn't at issue. Mr. and Mrs. Corcoran are Garfinkel's ace in the hole. Patti Hearst blamed everything on the Symbionese Liberation Army, and they were all either dead or in jail or in hiding by the time she came to trial. But Daniel Garfinkel can throw all his garbage in the laps of Martin and Florence.'

'I can understand Dylan Guevara turning back into Daniel Garfinkel. Sort of. After the experience he's had. But the way Daniel's turned on his closest friends, the Corcorans — that I don't understand.'

'But you haven't seen the full transcript of his statements. You don't know about the hand grenade.'

'Yes I do. I was there when it went off. He'd be dead if Marty Bilson hadn't been such a great sniper.'

'Nope. You think Guevara was trying to commit suicide. But remember, he had a long record of phony suicide attempts. According to the born-again Daniel Garfinkel, that was supposed to be a trick grenade. It was supposed to go off with a bang and a flash and release a charge of red dye. Phony grenade courtesy of the good offices of Florence and Martin Corcoran.'

'Holy God! They betrayed him. Is that it, Marvia? The poor sap thought he was getting the trick grenade. But they gave him a real one, and when it blew, it was supposed to kill him. The Corcorans must have felt that he'd outlived his usefulness and they were going to get rid of him that way.'

'Yep. Or that's his story, anyway.'

'You think he'll walk? Really?'

'He'll either walk or he'll get sent to the hospital. You mark my words.'

Lindsey looked out Marvia's turret window at Oxford Street. He could see the blackened pavement where Dylan Guevara had torched his Hyundai. He turned back. Marvia was fully dressed. 'What now?' he asked.

'I've got a strategy session planned with Dorothy this morning. We'll see if Danny Garfinkel is still in a singing mood. Once this story gets out, he'll have more camcorders pointed at him than he can count. That ought to make him happy. I don't think anybody ever confessed by computer before. This will be one for the books . . . What about you?'

'I want to follow up on the MacReedy angle.'

'Is that going anywhere?'

'I think so.'

Tony Roland surprised Lindsey by inviting him out for lunch. They wound up at the Public Market in Emeryville.

'Listen, Mr. Lindsey, I want to thank you for bringing Walter Scoggins to me. And Speedy MacReedy. They've been a double-barreled bonanza.'

'How so?'

'I mean, the fire was a terrible thing. And Annabella's death was a terrible tragedy. A lovely young woman, a fine scholar, dedicated, energetic. A tragic loss.'

'That doesn't sound like the best thing that could have happened.'

'No, of course not.' Lindsey waited while Roland chewed and swallowed. 'Scoggins is a gem. You know, when he came to us he had little interest in film history *per se*. Turns out he was a kind of closet student of cinema anyway, and he's in it up to his elbows now.'

Lindsey nodded. 'And when he heads back to Louisiana? You know, this is supposed to be a honeymoon. I hope his bride isn't too unhappy with you for taking her husband away.'

'I don't think so. She's been in a couple of times. She seems to like the region just fine, and so does he. That's what I wanted to talk to you about. You knew them both before Walter came to the Film Archive.'

'Barely.'

'Well, I mean, I'm going to offer Walter a job. Annabella Buonaventura was with us on a visiting fellowship. I can get that changed to a permanent position; I've been working on it and I want Walter in that job. With the MacReedy collection in house, I can get Walter a special curatorship. MacReedy alone has been a goldmine of information and history. Without him we wouldn't have got the Saint Cloud collection. Our relationship with the computer science people is the best it's ever been. Fabia Rabinowitz is doing wonderful work for us; we're going to be in the journals thanks to her. It's all coming together beautifully.'

'What about the Saint Cloud materials? Fabia said they were digitizing the images for her computer.'

'That and more. I mean, this *is* film we're talking about, so we're striking new negatives and putting the material onto safety stock. That's both to prevent a fire — '

'Thank you.'

' — and for preservation. Then Fabia needs her digitized images for her computer work. And then we're going to get copies onto videos so they'll be available to anyone who wants them. I mean, some scholars get so possessive, they don't want to share what they've got with anybody. But I want the world to see the Saint Cloud collection. It's like King Tut's tomb, that's what it's like. Artifacts and images from the past. A window into a lost world.'

'I wouldn't call the 1930s and '40s a lost world.'

'You'd be surprised . . . Anyway, I wanted you to know about this. We're trying to get in touch with Arturo Madrid's representatives. He's protected by layers of publicity people, personal managers. And now that the network is so involved, there are more layers. But we're working through the mayor's office in Oakland and when he's up here for his big bash we're going to get him to look at the Film Archive work.'

Another pause while they ate, then Roland added: 'And we're negotiating with the network to add MacReedy to the lineup for the Paramount show. Arturo Madrid and Speedy MacReedy together for the first time since *Werewolf of Wall Street*. Isn't it something? Young Walter Scoggins just wanted to complete his doctorate. He didn't know what he was starting!'

Lindsey sipped his drink, then asked, 'Have you talked this over with Mr. MacReedy?'

'I didn't make an issue of it. But I mentioned it.'

'And?'

'He didn't exactly say yes. But he smiled this funny little old man smile of his, and he nodded, and got this funny kind of faraway look. I think he's pleased. I think he'll do it, if Madrid's people and the network people all go for it. But you know how difficult they are.'

23

'There's no honor among thieves, is there?'

'I wouldn't exactly call Daniel Garfinkel a thief. A murderer, yes.'

Marvia had her back to Lindsey. It was raining on Oxford Street. She said, 'He killed Annabella Buonaventura, no question about that. And now he's admitted starting the Film Archive fire.'

'What does his new lawyer have to say about that?'

'Torrie Hazlett-Jones. She's still going with Mama's zombie defense. But she's trying to bargain the charges down at the same time. If she can't get him off completely, she wants to get him off light. It makes sense. Interesting strategy. Torrie wants to settle the whole thing without a trial, but just in case, she's pushing for involuntary manslaughter instead of felony murder in the Buonaventura death.'

Marvia was sitting on a chair, leaning

her elbows on the window sill. Lindsey stood behind her, his hands on her shoulders. He asked, 'Do you think he'll get away with it?'

'There's a chance. He's been spilling everything, and it's gorgeous. He just sits there with that laptop computer in front of him. We'll ask him a question, and he goes clicking one-handed around on that keyboard.' She turned to face Lindsey. 'How do you feel about wearing a flak vest and a helmet?'

'What?'

'Don't panic, Bart. Can you handle that?'

'Sure. Listen, over the past few years I've been beaten up, shot twice, thrown in the Bay and left to drown. And if you and Dorothy and your pals hadn't broken into the Corcoran house when you did, I think I was in line for the same treatment that Celia Varela got. Hey, why not wear a flak vest?'

She smiled at him. 'You're a changed man, Bart!'

'What's the party?'

'We're going into a big raid.'

'After the Cedar Street fiasco?'

'What kind of business are the Corcorans in?'

'What is this, a quiz show? They design computer systems. They're consultants and they make good dough.'

'They have another business. Mr. and Mrs. Yuppie can't survive on just one source of income. Remember the other?'

Lindsey frowned. 'Real estate.'

'Right. We didn't find any contraband in Cedar Street, but nobody thought to execute a warrant on any of the *other* properties they control. The way they work is, they'll take over a warehouse or a vacant factory building, usually at a distress price. Spend a few dollars to upgrade it, find the right client — usually somebody they got to know through their computer business — and unload the building at a big fat profit.'

'Holy cow. I think I can see where this is going.'

'According to Danny Garfinkel, Florrie and Marty are big-time fences. He claims that they store stolen property and contraband in their vacant buildings.

Then they sell it to customers who can't resist a bargain even if the goods are a little bit tainted.'

'What do they fence?'

'Computer components. A few little little chips smaller than your thumbnail can be worth thousands of bucks. A cigar box full is worth a million. And the companies need the things. Garfinkel claims that the Corcorans mastermind these burglaries. He's their strawboss, and the peons are a cadre out of People's Park.'

'That's a stunner. Park people? Street people? How can they do that work? I've seen them, you've seen them. They're just not functional.'

'*Most* of them aren't, but some of them have jobs, bank accounts . . . you'd be amazed.'

'After a couple of performances by Dylan Guevara and his three-piece band? Yes, I would.'

'Anyway,' Marvia continued, 'Daniel's statements look like probable cause, and we've gone for another search warrant and we've got it. The toughest part was tracking down a list of all the buildings the Corcorans control. There's a maze of dummy corporations and odd partnerships. And they keep buying and selling. But we put together what we think is a pretty complete list. If we break into something that they've legitimately sold and the new owners have an indoor petunia factory going, we'll have to apologize and pay for the damage. But I think it's a good list.'

'You go back to the same judge as last time?'

'No, we got enough of a chewing-out after that screw-up. No, we have some partners this time. With everything that Daniel had to say, we think there might be some smuggled components, too. Stuff brought in without proper clearance, chips and boards built by slave labor or close to it in China, Pakistan, wherever. Can you believe this? Slaves building computers?'

'Welcome to tomorrow, and isn't it strange?'

'So we have the customs folks with us, and that got us into federal court, so we have a federal warrant and we even have the FBI for backup.'

'Wow.'

'So put yourself on standby. I'll let you know when this raid is going down. We're going to have a press pool with us, and you'll be the only other civilian in the party.'

★ ★ ★

Lindsey rode in a van marked Honeypie Confections. The van had seen better days. One panel of the two-piece windshield was a cobweb of fracture lines.

The van jounced along East 14th Street toward San Leandro. Exhaust fumes rose through cracked floorboards. Lindsey shared the former freight compartment with a mixed detachment of police, customs and FBI agents. They were dressed in midnight blue or black, with dark knitted watch caps. Their helmets rested between their boots. Bulky flak vests and black face paint made them look like images out of a futuristic movie. Lindsey reached up with one finger and touched his own cheek, feeling the greasy consistency of the paint.

The cops in all their variety were armed with rapid-fire small arms. Heavier equipment lay on the floor between the parallel benches. Lindsey's opposite number hefted not a weapon but a portable video camera. Right, this was one of the survivors of Dylan Guevara's hand grenade stunt. Dylan Guevara's stunt or Marty and Florrie Corcoran's betrayal.

The van clanked to a halt. Its side panels were of solid metal, but the rear doors as well as the driver's cab had windows in them. Lindsey looked out. There were few street lights on this part of East 14th. Small businesses lined the street, English and Spanish alternating in the window signs. He could hear the squad commander in the passenger seat talking on the radio. A green-flecked Camaro cruised past, music blasting from giant speakers. A couple of motorcycles roared by in the opposite direction. An empty AC Transit bus rolled past.

The squad commander, face blackened like everyone else's, twisted in his seat and leaned back into the van body. He kept his voice low. 'Okay, folks, we're going in. Ram team and shears ready. You two civilians keep down, keep out of the way, and remember — you're on your own. You get in trouble, I'm not risking my people's lives to get you back out. Understood?'

Lindsey managed a nervous nod. He could see the TV reporter grin widely. With a jolt he realized that the black face paint covered a woman's face, and he recognized her from a hundred TV newscasts. The most recent was one in which she led another camera operator on a tour of the Oakland Paramount theater, puffing up the coming gala for Arturo Madrid. Geraldine Gonzalez, that was her name. He grinned at her. Nobody to point a camera at her this time; she was on her own.

The radio crackled again. The commander muttered a few syllables and signed off. He hissed to the raiders, 'Okay. Hand signals from here on, sound discipline.' He gestured toward the van doors. The two dark-suited raiders twisted handles and dropped to the pavement. One of them had POLICE in bright yellow on his back. The other had CUSTOMS. The

FBI contingent must be preparing to follow.

After the last cops had slipped from the van, Lindsey and the camerawoman followed. At least parking was no problem here. A couple of vehicles stood at the curb. One was a sprung Ford station wagon. Another was the stripped remnants of what once had been an AMC Pacer.

At some signal unseen by Lindsey, floodlights sprang to life. *Hercules and Western Moving & Storage* stood out in all its grimy neglect. An officer pounded on the door. 'Police, search warrant, open up.'

Question: Who would be in a warehouse at this hour of the night?

Answer: A night watchman.

A heavy chain and oversized padlock held the warehouse doors in place. Police officers used a pair of giant bolt-cutters to open the chain and ran to swing the heavy doors back. Armed police charged inside the warehouse, Lindsey and the TV camerawoman Gerry Gonzalez close behind.

Police floodlights cast spotty illumination inside the warehouse. Crates and pillars threw ghostly shadows. The ceiling rose two stories overhead, with a catwalk halfway to the opaque panes of a one-time skylight. A low railing surrounded the catwalk. Something moved on the catwalk.

Muzzle flash stroboscoped from the catwalk, left and right. Explosions like strings of giant firecrackers echoed through the warehouse. Lindsey dived for the floor. He could see Gerry Gonzalez, silhouetted against a police floodlight, pointing her video camera at the catwalk.

The police returned fire. The commander's sound discipline regime was as meaningful as King Canute's command to the tide. Figures ran, dived, pointed weapons upward and fired. One of the gunmen on the catwalk somersaulted over the railing, bounced off the upper edge of a massive crate and crashed to the concrete floor. His weapon clattered across the concrete. He twitched, moaned, raised a hand like a child requesting permission to leave the room, then collapsed.

The surviving gunman stopped firing. A few more rounds flashed from the police weapons, the sound frighteningly loud. Then they stopped.

The gunman on the catwalk yelled at them, 'Don't kill me.'

The police commander answered, 'Toss your weapon over the railing and stand up. Hands raised.'

'Don't kill me, don't kill me.'

Floodlights glared. The man stood up. He wore a dark watch cap and a black sweatshirt and blue jeans. He tossed a matte black weapon over the railing. It hit a packing crate and bounced to the floor with a clatter of plastic and metal.

'Hands up.'

The gunman resumed, 'I didn't hurt nobody. You can just let me out of here. You don't need me for nothing. I only shot at the walls. I never wanted to hurt nobody. I just needed the money. I don't hurt people. You can leave me go.' He was crying, shaking visibly, wracked with sobs.

Geraldine Gonzalez was on her feet, her camera whirring away.

'Don't move a muscle. How the hell do we get up there?'

The gunman jerked his head, pointed with one hand without lowering his arms. 'It's right over there. Come on up them

334

stairs. Watch out you don't trip.'

'You men.' A couple of cops moved in the direction the gunman indicated. 'Put him in cuffs and bring him down here. Watch your step. He might have some helpers.'

The cops' combat boots crashed on metal stairs like iron hammers pounding on anvils.

The lower level turned into a strange diorama: floodlights, crates, police, Gerry Gonzalez with her video camera, Hobart Lindsey with his eyes open and his oddly icy hands.

Hammers pounded on anvils. Returning cops emerged from the metal staircase, their prisoner between them. He must have been six and a half feet tall and weighed 300 pounds. A one-time football or basketball star, Lindsey guessed. A would-be pro, a nearly-made-it millionaire. If he'd been two inches taller, been a little faster on his feet, a little tougher when the lines collided, he'd be asleep in his Mediterranean Revival home in Danville right now. But he was handcuffed in a warehouse in Oakland.

One of the cops said, 'Nobody else up there. Just a brown paper bag with a container of egg salad and a plastic fork. And half a pickle. And a stack of girlie magazines. And what looks like a baggie of dope and a couple roaches.'

'You want to finish your meal, sir?'

'I lost my appetite.'

Gerry Gonzalez looked happy. She might get a bonus for this.

24

Lindsey rarely got up and watched the early morning TV news, but today he clicked it on. They played the footage that Geraldine Gonzalez had shot during last night's raid. There was the dead gunman and there was the survivor. Gonzalez even caught part of his dialog. And there in one pan was Hobart Lindsey, flak-vested and face-painted and looking pretty exotic at that.

And there was Gonzalez live, holding a microphone for a sleek individual in a three-piece suit. Behind them stood a display table covered with electronic gear. Gonzalez introduced the sleek man as the agent-in-charge of the local FBI office.

'In a series of raids last night we found not only a major cache of 486 and Pentium computer chips, but monitors, circuit boards, scanners, CD-ROM multimedia units, printers, keyboards, and mice. Many of these have serial numbers that will permit us to trace their source and match them to recent burglaries.'

Gerry Gonzalez asked, 'How many arrests were made, and were there any casualties?'

The agent-in-charge said, 'Raids were carried out at some dozen locations in the East Bay. Nearly 200 law enforcement officers, FBI agents assisted by other federal and local agencies, participated. Law enforcement officers suffered two officers killed, five wounded. Some thirty suspects are now in custody, including six wounded and one dead.'

'Aside from the stolen components, was anything else seized?'

'We seized weapons caches in three of the twelve locations raided. Also small amounts of illegal drugs and pornographic materials. There is also reason to believe that several of the warehouses were used as holding areas for incoming illegal immigrants from the Far East, but we have yet to develop those leads.'

'This is Geraldine Gonzalez at FBI field headquarters.'

And back in the studio, one of the slicked-up boy and girl anchors read a sidebar off a monitor. 'While last night's raids were in progress, Berkeley police and FBI agents waited outside the well-kept North Berkeley home of Martin and Florence Corcoran, operators of a prosperous computer consulting business and sometime real estate speculators. Every location raided last night was controlled by the Corcorans, and someone at one of the raided buildings must have got off a warning to the Corcorans, because they jumped into their brand-new BMW and headed down their driveway at top acceleration and with their headlights turned off.'

The anchor paused and smiled as if about to share a private joke with just one viewer.

'The BMW barreled into the side of a Berkeley police cruiser parked across the mouth of the Corcorans' driveway. Fortunately, the automobile was equipped with dual airbags. The Corcorans are uninjured, in police custody this morning. The police cruiser was unoccupied at the time.'

★   ★   ★

Lindsey left his new car in a commercial garage near the county courthouse at Lake Merritt. He found Angelique Tesla's office fifteen minutes before he was due there and sorted papers in his briefcase while he waited for his appointment. The MacReedy case was the most complicated he had ever worked on. And all for a $25 death claim.

Tesla was tall and fair-skinned, with strawberry-blonde hair. She made a fascinating contrast to Fabia Rabinowitz. Where Fabia was dark and sensuous, Angelique was pale and thin-bodied and sharp-featured. She thanked Lindsey for coming in. She seemed to be waiting for him to offer a comment. Finally she yielded, but only to ask a question. 'Why are you so concerned with this Berkeley situation?'

'It's my job.' Lindsey laid one of his business cards on her desk. At the rate he was using them, he'd have to order a new box soon.

Tesla picked up the card, looked at it and nodded. 'You also have a gripe against Daniel Garfinkel, I understand.'

'He torched my car.'

'So I've heard. Are you unwheeled now?'

Lindsey smiled. 'I work for an insurance company. I was covered for vandalism. I've replaced the Hyundai.'

Tesla nodded. 'So your personal interest is satisfied. Unless you're angry with Garfinkel and you have a punitive interest in following his case. And your professional interest is what? I understand from the Berkeley police that your company covers the University Art Museum and the Pacific Film Archive. You had a loss there caused by the fire.'

'That is correct.'

'Well, you know, Mr. Lindsey, we're trying to put this thing together and it's very complex. Do you agree?'

'I was thinking the very thing a few minutes ago.'

'All right.' Tesla had stood when Lindsey entered her office and had extended her hand. Now she was seated behind her desk. 'Suppose you run down the facts for me. As much as you know.'

'Don't you have the information from

Dorothy Yamura and Marvia Plum? Have you read Garfinkel's statement?'

'Just tell me what you know.'

'Wait a minute! Am I a suspect?'

Tesla smiled. 'No, you're not. I haven't even Mirandized you. I just want information. We might need you as a witness later, but right now this is just for me. Okay?'

'Okay.' He shuffled papers in and out of his briefcase, collecting his thoughts. 'I think this goes back to the East Coast. To New York. Have you seen the 1930 wedding photo?'

'Got a copy. Thanks to your friends in Berkeley.'

'Yeah. Look, this is a kind of family saga. Young man named Israel Mannheim marries one Tillie Steinberg around July, 1930. This is in the Bronx. Before year-end, Tillie gives birth to a son. She was probably pregnant at the time of the wedding. By the next year, poor Tillie's husband is disenchanted with married life. Chances are he never wanted to get married to start with. He leaves wife and child and sets out to make a name for himself in California. The name he makes is Arturo Madrid.'

'Madrid? He's been all over the *Oakland Trib* and the *Chron* and Channel 2. He's due in town for his big bash at the Paramount this week.'

'Yes.'

'Wait a minute. The Bronx, New York? I thought he was a local boy. Pride of Oakland, the All-American City.'

'Hollywood press wizards can make you a native of the Planetoid Punkus if they want to.'

'Point taken. Proceed.'

'While Madrid is making his way in the talkies, his little boy Avner or Abner, who has taken his mother's maiden name, is growing up back east with Mama. But Abner moves to California too, in due course, and becomes the father of a little girl, one Florence Steinberg. In time she marries Martin Corcoran, and we have the charming squire and squiress of Cedar Street.'

'Can you prove this?'

'I haven't checked birth and death and marriage and divorce records. Maybe they'll be there and maybe they won't. But I have the fact that Florence and Tillie could pass for twins.'

'Don't prove nothing, my friend. But go on, I want to hear your theory anyhow.' She offered Lindsey a glass of water.

'Okay. As our movie friends would say, cut to Niles, California. It's 1934. Two film companies are co-producing were-wolf movies. Lots of makeup is required. One film cast is all-white, the other is all-black. Our boy Arturo Madrid, a.k.a. Israel Mannheim, is starring as the werewolf in the white version. A fellow named William Hargess is the black werewolf. Hargess is a very light-skinned Negro, as was the custom in black-oriented cinema at the time. Hargess is also a master of makeup and disguise. 'The Charcoal Chaney,' they called him.'

He paused and took a drink of water. 'Now, we know that Arturo Madrid had become a heavy-duty booze hound by this time. For this, I have the testimony of Edward MacReedy. He was the producer and director of the black werewolf film.

He was also the real director of the white film, although they pretended that the white producer was the director, to avoid offending white cast members. He's still alive, he lives in Berkeley, and he told me that Madrid was sick in quarters half the time and non-functional on the set for the other half. He's only in a couple of scenes, even though he's billed as star of the film.'

'And you're telling me that this Hargess doubled for Madrid for almost a whole movie.'

'I am telling you exactly that.'

'Okay. That's an interesting piece of ancient Hollywood history. What does it have to do with recent events?'

'Bear with me. When the film shoots were completed, they held a party for the cast and crew of both movies. Everybody mixed, black and white. There was a lot of drunkenness, there may have been some drugs used, there may have been some shooting, and there was a deadly fire. I don't know the full number killed, but Arturo Madrid was badly cut by flying glass, just slashed to ribbons. And William

Hargess was killed outright. He *may* have been shot by an unreconstructed southern black-hater. In any case, he was burned almost beyond recognition. End of Hargess's career, of course. Madrid recovered and went on to fame and fortune.'

Tesla had been jotting notes as Lindsey talked. She pointed the pencil at him. 'End of story? Waste of time, yes?'

'No, and no. Edward MacReedy is at the party. Snatches his teenage bride from the arms of the bleeding and seemingly dying Arturo Madrid. They'd been dancing. Following his recovery, Madrid proceeds to marry his own fiancée, one Sarita Morgan, who had been rumored as having a chocolate-and-vanilla affair with William Hargess.'

'Spare me the Depression-era gossip column, please. Where is all this heading, Mr. Lindsey?'

'It's heading to Saint Cloud, Minnesota. And then it's heading to the Pacific Film Archive and a computer wizard named Fabia Rabinowitz. That's where it's heading.'

Lindsey explained the work Rabinowitz had done with *The Werewolf of Wall Street*. While Lindsey spoke, Tesla nodded and jotted a few words. Finally she said, 'So this wizard and her magic computer have proved that the actor who plays the werewolf and the actor in all these later Arturo Madrid films are the same man.'

'In most scenes. Both actors appeared in the movie. The werewolf was always Arturo Madrid, of course, but there were two Arturo Madrids.'

'I'm very slow today. So what?'

'But don't you see? The Arturo Madrid in most of *The Werewolf of Wall Street* wasn't Arturo Madrid. That is, the Arturo Madrid who used to be Israel Mannheim. He was William Hargess. Mannheim-Madrid was too drunk to work, so Hargess doubled for him.'

'What does that get us?'

'That man has been Arturo Madrid to this day. Not Israel Mannheim — *Will Hargess*!'

'And where is Israel Mannheim?'

'Dead. Hargess didn't die in 1934. Mannheim did. Hargess then took his place. As Will Hargess, his career was seriously limited. There was no room for a Denzel Washington in 1934. Hargess could either work in all-black films where the budget was nickels and dimes, or he could work in white films and play porters and chauffeurs and cooks for the rest of his life. But by becoming *Arturo Madrid* he could go anywhere, do anything. He could even marry Sarita Morgan — which he did.'

Tesla sighed and laid the pencil on her pad. 'All right. Let's accept this computer wizardry at face value. Which I don't think a court would do, by the way. It doesn't prove anything unless old Mr. MacReedy is telling the truth about Niles. If this Fabia person has proved that two actors played the Arturo Madrid role in that picture, it could just as easily be that the real Madrid — your Mannheim-Madrid — was in most of the scenes, and Hargess only doubled in a few.'

'There's still the Moshulu Parkway photo. That matches to the Arturo Madrid, who is only in a couple of scenes.'

'Flimsy. Very flimsy.'

'Let me make a telephone call. I'll use your phone, Ms. Tesla. I want to call Tony Roland or Fabia Rabinowitz at the Film Archive. You can talk to them.'

'What could they add?'

'The Saint Cloud cache. Dozens of early H-M-R films, black cast films made by Edward MacReedy before 1934, and right up to the Niles fire. They're at the archive now. If Rabinowitz can scan them into her computer and do the same kind of analysis she did on the Madrid retrospective films . . . '

'Then what?'

'Will Hargess was in most of MacReedy's H-M-R films. All Rabinowitz has to do is compare her images of the early Hargess with the two Arturo Madrids of *The Werewolf of Wall Street*, and with the later images of Arturo Madrid. Hargess is bound to match one of the werewolf Madrids. Let's see which one. And let's see if he matches the Arturo Madrid of the later films.'

'Make the call.'

Lindsey got Rabinowitz. He explained his idea to her. Could she do it? Would it work? After she answered his questions he handed the phone to Tesla and listened while the DA and the computer scientist conversed. Finally Tesla laid the handset on its cradle. 'Sounds kind of crazy, but your friend says she's already started work, and she thinks you're going to be right . . . Trouble is, the work is going to take months. It's a big project, and the Film Archive won't give her much money to work with.'

'Don't you have a budget?'

'For some kind of science-fiction project because somebody guesses that we've had a case of mistaken identity or willful impersonation in 1934? In 1934? Not a chance.'

Lindsey had to play all his cards. 'There's more to it, Ms. Tesla. There were the deaths of Philip Quince in 1947 and Specs Lincoln in 1948.'

'No sale. Mr. Lindsey, even if you're right, these things are for historians, not law enforcement.'

'I thought the police never closed an unsolved murder case.'

'Right. And the search for Amelia

Earhart goes on. Come back to the real world, Mr. Lindsey.'

'Daniel Garfinkel confessed to starting the Film Archive and Robeson Center fires, both on orders from Martin and Florence Corcoran.'

'I really shouldn't comment on that case at all. And I don't see what this has to do with your movie research.'

'Did Garfinkel confess to attacking Nola MacReedy, a.k.a. Lola Mae Turner?'

'I can't say more about Garfinkel.'

'Why do you think he set those fires? Why did he attack Nola MacReedy? I'll tell you why. Annabella Buonaventura was getting too close to the truth about Arturo Madrid. Nola MacReedy *was* too close; she was dancing with Israel Mannheim the night he died. Nobody would believe Edward MacReedy. The man is ninety years old, and he was practically a recluse until Mathilde Wilbur and Walter Scoggins started drawing him out. Gerry Gonzalez' TV feature on the MacReedys was the beginning of the end for Nola, and it might have destroyed Edward as well, in time. But one way or another the story had to come out.'

'You lost me. Why would the Corcorans want to cover up Arturo Madrid's secret — assuming that he had one?'

'Because Florence Corcoran, née Florence Steinberg, is the granddaughter of Israel Mannheim. When Arturo Madrid dies — and at his age, he can't have many years left — his heirs will inherit an estate worth millions. Remember, as Madrid he had lots of wives but never any children. He has no current wife. It isn't public knowledge but it must be common Hollywood gossip that Arturo Madrid isn't really a California-born descendent of Spanish grandees; that he's a Jewish boy from the Bronx.'

Tesla was listening attentively now. 'So Florence Corcoran is waiting for Madrid to cash in his chips so she can inherit his millions. Knowing Florence, I can believe that. But why would she send Daniel Garfinkel after those people? If it's going to come out anyway, that Madrid is really Mannheim. In fact, she needs that to come out, doesn't she?'

'Bull's-eye! She needs it to come out

that Madrid is really Mannheim — but not that Mannheim died in the Niles fire and Hargess took his place. MacReedy told me that Hargess had a wife and children. Lord knows where they are today, but under Hargess's will — MacReedy told me this, too — everything goes to them. To Hargess's descendants, not Mannheim's. Florence Corcoran is not Will Hargess's granddaughter, she's Israel Mannheim's. Florence Corcoran is no relative of Hargess's at all. Florence Corcoran loses millions if Arturo Madrid is identified as Hargess instead of Mannheim.'

A grin unlike any Lindsey had seen in his life illuminated Angelique Tesla's face. 'What a wonderful scheme! And you think your friend Fabia Rabinowitz is going to prove this.'

'I think she is.'

Tesla stood and walked around her desk. She held out her hand to Lindsey and said, 'I'm going to ask you to keep quiet about this. I'll work with your computer friend and as soon as she's done her work on those films, we'll shift into high gear. Looks like Civil Division work, actually, but we'll take care of it one way or another. In the meanwhile, of course, both Corcorans are going to be up to their ears in boiling pigshit over the warehouse caper and the electronic component robberies. More to the point, if it looks as we can make Danny Garfinkel's testimony stand up, I'm going to push hard for murder one on Celia Varela.'

'I thought Che — Danny — killed Varela at the Lafayette Escadrille.'

Tesla nodded. 'Danny and the wonderful laptop are still filling in details. According to him, the Corcorans killed Varela, then drove her body to the Lafayette Escadrille. Danny was waiting for them in his Che persona. He's a big, strong kid. Celia was a small, light woman. He took her from the Corcorans, got an arm around her as if she was drunk and semi-conscious, and got her through the bar to the back room. She had a key in her clothes. He used it to get the room open, dumped Varela's body, and left. Corcorans never had to set foot inside a dump like Laffy's place.'

Lindsey rubbed his forehead and

waited for Tesla to go on.

'Every cop in the county is pissed about that one, and so am I. What a break they used the same wire on you up at Cedar Street. That wire is going to hang those two bastards, if I get my way.'

So the icy Angelique Tesla was actually pissed off about the murder of Officer Celia Varela. Everybody had an ignition point.

'And one more if,' Tesla wound up. 'If you don't mind, I just might call on you to explain this to me a few more times before I get it all sorted out.'

Lindsey picked up his attaché case and started for the door, but Tesla stopped him just once more. 'I really do want to thank you, Mr. Lindsey. It's cases like this that make my life a pleasure.'

He couldn't help asking, 'How many cases like this do you see?'

'Well now, I've been working in this office for almost seventeen years. This is the first.'

★　★　★

Lindsey drove to the I.S. office and got off a memo to Desmond Richelieu, with a copy to another department. It was brief and to the point. He'd thought of phoning Richelieu but decided that this was one that belonged in the archives. Not that Ducky would ever deny that the conversation had taken place; but still, Lindsey wanted an official record.

'Mr. Richelieu,' the memo read, 'please note that International Surety has paid out major claims in the Varela/Corcoran/Guevara situation. I'm certain that you have full data on this case. In view of recent developments, I am confident that we are in a strong position to recover all benefits that have been disbursed. As for whom to recover from, I will cite our standing policy, *Who has the deepest pockets?* The answer is, our good friends Martin and Florence Corcoran. I'm sure that Legal will be more than willing to pursue this matter, and I will copy them on this memo.

'If in doubt, feel free to query me.'

25

Lindsey held one of Jamie Plum's hands while Marvia, seated just beyond him, held the other. Jamie's dress-up outfit was a compromise between his grandmother's choice of bow tie and blazer and his own preference of superhero tee shirt and baseball cap. Marvia had laid down a ruling, and Gloria and Jamie had acceded.

They had assembled at Gloria Plum's house on Bonita Street. Lindsey met Marvia on the sidewalk. Inside the house, they found Jamie lying face down on his grandfather's bed. Marvia had told him of Marcus's death, and had told Lindsey later that Jamie had cried, but had acted with remarkable calm. At Marvia's request Lindsey had attended the funeral. Jamie had not. During the ceremony Lindsey had sat behind the family, surrounded by Marcus Plum's friends, all of them old, most of them black.

The preacher wore a clergy suit and a bright African scarf and cap. He referred to Marcus Plum by his Ashanti name. Lindsey hadn't known about that. At the end of the ceremony the preacher announced that each member of the immediate family would place a handful of earth imported from Ghana on the coffin.

After the burial, family and friends gathered at Bonita Street, where tables of food had been laid. Lindsey saw that Tyrone was caring for his sister; their mother was accepting the condolences of the visitors with quiet dignity.

Lindsey felt a pressure on his back and turned. Marvia leaned against him. He put down his sandwich and held her. 'Are you all right?'

'I guess I'll have some ups and downs.'

The preacher who had conducted the service appeared. He took Marvia's hands in his. Marvia introduced Lindsey. The preacher shook his hand. 'You can give strength to your mother now, my dear,' he told Marvia. 'You will get strength by doing that.'

Marvia nodded. The preacher embraced her and drifted away.

'I've never buried anyone,' Lindsey said.

Marvia looked up at him. 'We didn't bury my dad in that box. Maybe he's noplace. I don't know. Most of the time I think religion is all a lot of nonsense. Once in a while . . . I just don't know. But I know that my Dad isn't in that box.'

The next day Marvia found Jamie's favorite toy, a scale model, World War II vintage, B-17 bomber, smashed and buried in the household garbage. The bomber had come from Lawton Crump, also deceased. When Marvia asked why Jamie had smashed the bomber the boy had run at her, screaming and kicking.

Marvia had taken bereavement leave from the police department and Lindsey had come to Bonita Street to be with her. 'Jamie says everybody who loves him dies, and everybody he loves dies.'

'Maybe he needs a real home,' Lindsey said. 'A real mom and dad.'

Marvia looked stricken.

'You're a real mom, of course. But if he could live with both of us, I think it would be good for him.'

They sat on Marcus Plum's bed, the two adults with their arms around the child. Jamie pressed his face against Marvia's torso, but one small hand held Lindsey's. Lindsey held his lower lip between his teeth. He could hear Gloria Plum's radio from another room. Tonight was the big Arthur Madrid salute at the Oakland Paramount. Marvia decided that it would be best for them to go, if only because this was a once-in-a lifetime opportunity for Jamie.

Occupying a box seat was new experience for Lindsey, as was the limousine ride and the VIP treatment that all of Edward MacReedy's party received *en route* to the Paramount. The other occupants of the box were Walter and Martha Scoggins. Walter had settled into his job at the Pacific Film Archive, his doctoral dissertation nearly completed. Martha was busy furnishing their apartment. Once that task was completed, she would need a job, and Lindsey was angling with Desmond Richelieu for the budget to hire her.

At the Robeson Center, waiting for the limos to arrive, Lindsey watched Mathilde Wilbur flitting around MacReedy, brushing imaginary dust from his rented tuxedo. Walter Scoggins stood by, his omnipresent camcorder whirring softly.

The old man started one of his reminiscences.

'I visited the Paramount once before, you know. It was opening night. December 16, 1931. We were established in Niles by then. H-M-R was getting rolling. We read about it in the old Oakland *Post-Enquirer*. It was to be a gala. The governor, the mayor, marching bands, and a stage show. And of course the opening feature. I'll never forget. *The False Madonna*, with Kay Francis.'

Scoggins pointed the camcorder up at MacReedy's wizened face.

* * *

Will Hargess said, 'Let's go.' I just laughed. This was a week before the opening. It rained all week and we were idle and depressed. I told him they'd never let colored into something like that. He said, 'I'm going, Ed, and I'm going to get in.' I never believed him, but on the big day we all went together.

We dressed in our finest. Raided the wardrobe department for fancy wear. There must have been a dozen of us. Will's wife. My Nola and her mother. Alonzo Nash, Walter Davies, Johnson Locksley, Specs Lincoln. We climbed on a Southern Pacific train. They made us all sit at the back end of the last car of the train. When we got to Oakland, some friends of Will's picked us up and took us to the theater.

We got to the theater and marched into the lobby in all our finery. Some usher caught sight of us and scampered away to find the chief usher. He came running. He took one look at us and said, 'Why didn't you go to the stage entrance? Don't you know we can't have the talent mingling with the public?' And he took us around to the stage entrance and shoved us inside and disappeared. We saw the whole show from the wings. It was a grand evening. When it was all over we made our way back to the depot and rode back to Niles. It was a wonderful night. And now I'm going back to the Paramount.

Just inside the door of the Robeson Center, MacReedy stopped short. 'There was one more thing that night. When we were standing there in the wings, looking out over that auditorium, waiting for the show to start . . . Will Hargess said something I'll never forget. He said, 'Ed, I'm going to be on that screen someday. And I'm going to stand on that stage.' And I said, 'Will, you just dream on.' And after that we went back to Niles and made movies.'

★ ★ ★

Edward MacReedy and Mathilde Wilbur had arrived at the Paramount and been escorted from the limousine, to spend the evening backstage. MacReedy visited privately with Arturo Madrid while the full house enjoyed the hours of entertainment.

The house lights brightened and the

full pit orchestra began to play a medley of themes from Madrid films. The curtain had fallen on the final scene of *Fade-Out*, Arturo Madrid's semi-autobiographical and, by his own statement, final film.

Fade-Out had included a sequence on Arturo Madrid's days with Pan-Pacific, and even a segment dealing with the Niles fire. But how accurate had that been?

In the Robeson Center, waiting for the limos to arrive, Lindsey had found a quiet moment with only MacReedy and Scoggins, and MacReedy had talked about Arturo Madrid and the tragic party. According to his version, Madrid had rescued half a dozen of his colleagues from the flames before succumbing to smoke. Madrid's heroism, at least on that occasion, had been real enough.

And now at age 85, filled with years and with honors, and with plenty of gold in his vaults, Arturo Madrid had announced his retirement. The auditorium filled with the applause of 3000 guests, most of whom had paid premium prices to be present at the final public appearance of the immortal Arturo Madrid.

And now the dual masters of ceremonies took the stage. A spotlight splashed onto his midnight-blue tuxedo and her sparkling, sequined, sea-green gown. They called Arturo Madrid onto the stage to receive a personal ovation from 3000 loving fans. He strode from the wings, tall and straight and perfect despite his 85 years, wading in a movable pool of light as a second spot hit the stage and tracked him to the microphone. His pompadour was thick and snowy white. His smiling teeth glittered in the spotlight. He took an ever-so-slight bow.

The audience rose to its feet, applauding and cheering. Madrid bowed again, this time more deeply. Lindsey reached for Marvia's hand. He felt a lump in his throat and tears in his eyes.

The male emcee said, 'We do have a special announcement, ladies and gentlemen. Tonight you all saw a clip from *The Werewolf of Wall Street*. For sixty years the direction of that film has been credited to the late Philip Quince. But in fact, one of Hollywood's best-kept secrets was that Phil Quince was producer of that film, while the *director* was none other than the great Edward Joseph MacReedy.'

Now the female emcee, turning so the spotlight flared like an emerald flame on her sequined gown, took over. 'And with us tonight, joining in tribute to the great Arturo Madrid, is none other than that same man, Mr. Edward Joseph MacReedy.'

The orchestra switched to the theme music of *The Werewolf of Wall Street*. Another spotlight hit the proscenium. Lindsey caught just a glimpse of Mathilde Wilbur in the wings as MacReedy, tiny and bent but with head high, walked slowly to the center of the stage.

The two old men, one tall and robust, the other thin and fragile, first shook hands, then embraced like brothers in the spotlight.

★   ★   ★

Later there was a champagne reception, and in an odd moment Hobart Lindsey found himself singled out by Edward MacReedy. The old man laid his dry hand on Lindsey's sleeve. He said, 'This all started with you, Mr. Lindsey. With you and Ms. Wilbur. I want to thank you both.'

Lindsey was speechless.

'I only wish my Nola could have seen this. But I'll be with her soon and I'll tell her about it. You know, one of these young people told me they're talking about remaking *The Werewolf of Harlem*. Some young director named Townsend, I think. Said he'd already done some nice work. I guess I'll get some royalties for once if they do. That would be a nice change. Maybe Nola can watch it with me. She'll enjoy that, I know she will.'

Lindsey leaned toward the old man. This might be the wrong time to tell this to MacReedy, but Lindsey had carried it around inside him, and he could hold it no longer.

'You know, Mr. MacReedy, after studying those films from the Saint Cloud warehouse, I think the computer is going to prove that Arturo Madrid is really Will Hargess. The original Arturo Madrid, Israel Mannheim, was the man who died in Niles. Hargess took his place.'

MacReedy looked up at Hobart Lindsey.

'I knew that. That's why I enjoyed my chat with Will tonight. We had a wonderful time. We talked about my Nola.'

Lindsey had to grab his glass to keep from spilling the champagne. 'You already knew? How long did you know?'

'Since 1934.'

*　*　*

Later, Lindsey, Marvia and Mathilde Wilbur sat in a saloon on Claremont Avenue near the Oakland-Berkeley city line. A pitcher of beer stood in the middle of their table. Lindsey finished repeating the story he'd given to Angelique Tesla at the District Attorney's office near Lake Merritt.

Marvia said, 'There are some good investigators in the DA's office, but I don't envy them trying to find all the pieces of this mess and put them together.'

'You don't think the Corcorans will get off, do you?' Mathilde Wilbur took a long pull at her glass.

'No way. Even with that rascal Carl Shea fronting for them, there's a good chance they'll never see daylight again. We're going to get them for killing Celia Varela, and for a dozen lesser charges — everything from criminal conspiracy to smuggling. As for the Buonaventura murder, if they put Dylan Guevara up to the Film Archive arson, they're equally guilty of both the arson and the felony murder of Buonaventura. I've told Ducky and Legal to sue 'em to get their fire insurance payment back.'

'What about Garfinkel?'

Marvia shrugged. 'Maybe he'll make the brainwashing defense work. Hell, maybe he even deserves to get off. He was responsible for Buonaventura's death, probably for Nola MacReedy's, and for Celia's, directly or indirectly. Not to mention his lesser crimes. But why did he act that way? The Corcorans had the simplest of motives, and one of the oldest. Simple greed. They were crooks from start to finish. But Daniel Garfinkel — I'm glad it isn't for me to decide.'

Lindsey looked at his watch. 'It's getting pretty late. Can I offer anybody a ride home? Marvia? Mathilde?'

Mathilde Wilbur said, 'That's very kind of you. My car is up at the Robeson Center. If you wouldn't mind.'

The three of them rose and headed for the door. On the way, Lindsey said, 'You know, I still don't understand how somebody like Edward MacReedy can be so calm about his wife's death.'

'I can answer that,' Mathhilde Wilbur said quietly, 'after working at the Robeson Center. When they're that old, they live with death all the time. Somebody dies when you're young, you can be devastated with grief. I'm sorry about your dad, Marvia. I know what happened. I'm sorry.' She drew a deep breath. 'But these old folks, well — death is just a part of their life.'

Outside the saloon they stood beneath a street lamp, waiting for the pedestrian signal to change. Marvia shook her head. 'Bart, you said that MacReedy told you about a couple of deaths back in the 1940s.'

'Right. Phil Quince was killed in a boating accident in 1947. And Specs Lincoln was shot by a burglar in '48.'

'Doesn't that bother you? Don't you

remember Yamura's law of coincidences? Don't you think it's a funny coincidence, those two survivors of the Niles fire dying violently thirteen or fourteen years after the fire? And one of them was in a boating accident with Arturo Madrid, and the other one's killer never identified?'

'You think Madrid was responsible? That would be Will Hargess, the man Mr. MacReedy embraced onstage tonight?'

'Arthur Madrid, a murderer?' Mathilde Wilbur was scandalized.

The pedestrian signal changed and they crossed the broad intersection and climbed into Lindsey's new blue 1965 Volvo.

'I don't know,' Lindsey conceded. 'And I don't think we'll ever know.'

We do hope that you have enjoyed reading this large print book.

Did you know that all of our titles are available for purchase?

We publish a wide range of high quality large print books including:
Romances, Mysteries, Classics
General Fiction
Non Fiction and Westerns

Special interest titles available in large print are:
The Little Oxford Dictionary
Music Book, Song Book
Hymn Book, Service Book

Also available from us courtesy of Oxford University Press:
Young Readers' Dictionary
(large print edition)
Young Readers' Thesaurus
(large print edition)

For further information or a free brochure, please contact us at:
Ulverscroft Large Print Books Ltd.,
The Green, Bradgate Road, Anstey,
Leicester, LE7 7FU, England.
Tel: (00 44) **0116 236 4325**
Fax: (00 44) **0116 234 0205**

Reunited with his English war bride, Sybil, after two years, Tim takes her back to the USA with him — but where to live, in the middle of the post-World War II housing crisis? They meet a friend of Sybil's deceased father, who promises to help. Next thing they know, the New Jersey chapter of the British-American War Brides Improvement Association arranges accommodation for them in the isolated coastal community of Merry Point. Here they meet their curmudgeonly landlord and an inept handyman. Then Sybil finds a body on the pier . . .

FIRE IN THE VALLEY

Catriona McCuaig

Spring is just around the corner in Llandyfan, and the first crocuses are beginning to bloom. Then the beautiful morning is shattered by the discovery of a corpse in the glebe — the victim of a grisly murder. Who could have wanted poor Fred Woolton, the mild-mannered milkman, dead? Midwife Maudie once again turns sleuth! Despite expecting a baby of her own, she is not about to take it easy while a case needs to be solved . . .

THE SHADOW

Donald Stuart

When Emma Mason inherits a house on Orkney from her Great-aunt Freda, she is mystified — she knows nothing about Freda, and her parents are of little help. The only thing for it is to visit Orkney herself. On the ferry, she meets Gregor McEwan, a wildlife photographer and passionate Orcadian. Together they begin to piece together Freda's story, whilst becoming increasingly attracted to each other — though there are serious obstacles in their way: Gregor is struggling with a past tragedy, and Emma's life is firmly rooted in Tyneside . . .

THE BODY IN THE SWAMP

Ardath Mayhar

When several bodies are washed up in the swamplands of east Texas, the local police suspect drug-runners, and the Feds are called in to investigate — but can discover little. Possum Choa lives off the fat of the land, but his way of life is now threatened by the criminals infesting the area. With the help of his old friend Lena McCarver, possessed of mysterious powers of her own, and Police Chief Washington Shipp, Choa and the residents of the swamplands join forces to stop the evildoers once and for all.

A QUESTION OF GUILT

Tony Gleeson

Dane Spilwell, a brilliant surgeon, stands accused of the brutal murder of his wife. The evidence against him is damning, his guilt almost a foregone conclusion. Two red-haired women will determine his ultimate fate. One, a mysterious lady in emeralds, may be the key to clearing him of the crime — if only she can be located. The other, Detective Jilly Garvey, began by doggedly working to convict him — but now finds herself doubting his culpability . . .

TWEAK THE DEVIL'S NOSE

Richard Deming

Driving to the El Patio club to see his girlfriend Fausta Moreni, the establishment's proprietor, private investigator Manville Moon does not expect to be witness to a murder. As he steps from his car outside the club, he hears a gun suddenly roar from the bushes close behind him. Walter Lancaster, the lieutenant governor of the neighbouring state of Illinois, has been shot! The assassination will not only make headlines all over the country, but also place the lives of Moon and Fausta in deadly danger . . .